"BRIAN WIPRUD WRITES SOME OF THE FUNNIEST, MOST MADCAP CRIME FICTION OUT THERE TODAY."
—*Mystery News*

PRAISE FOR

TAILED

"Garth breezes through one catastrophe after another with such ease that I am always anxious to see what is in store for him in the future.... The most coolest of dudes. Highly recommended series. A–."
—*Deadly Pleasures*

PIPSQUEAK

*Winner of the Lefty Award
for Most Humorous Crime Novel
A Barry Award Nominee*

"Demented and fun! This book is a hoot!"
—Harlan Coben

"The flat-out coolest mystery I've read in years, not to mention the funniest. Brian Wiprud is either a genius or a lunatic. Or maybe both." —Steve Hamilton

"The Nick and Nora of taxidermy meet the Maltese Falcon...er...Squirrel in another crazy, funny mystery from Brian M. Wiprud." —Sparkle Hayter

"The wildest mystery to come down the pike in a stuffed squirrel's age." —*Publishers Weekly*

"No *Pipsqueak*—this is a muscular adventure! Admirers of Donald Westlake and Elmore Leonard, especially, will find much here to enjoy."
—*Mystery Ink*

"Part caper, part comedy and part mystery... Any wordsmith who can make you laugh out loud one minute and shiver the next is well worth exploring."
—*January Magazine*

SLEEP WITH THE FISHES

"A laugh-out-loud triumph... This suspenseful black comedy [is] a page-turning, one-sitting read."
—*Publishers Weekly* (starred review)

"If Carl Hiaasen wrote for *The Sopranos*, it might be half as good as this.... A page-turner that's part wicked humor and part just plain wicked." —Lee Child

"*The Godfather* meets Carl Hiaasen in this darkly humorous meeting of the Mob and fishing.... A good, quick, amusing read." —*Mystery Ink*

"A black-humored crime novel that can sit comfortably on the same shelf with the works of Carl Hiaasen, Elmore Leonard, and other politically-incorrect genre icons. *Sleep with the Fishes* is a fast, fun dip into the Crime-Fiction-With-An-Attitude sub-sub-genre." —*Mystery News*

CROOKED

"Wiprud writes with a flair for dialogue that is unique and thoroughly enjoyable.... This should be on everyone's to buy list." —*Crimespree*

"Wiprud's engaging, hard-boiled style draws readers into both the art world and the underworld of New York, and his colorful cast keeps things moving with wit to spare.... The journey is a thrilling one, with an ending even the most astute readers won't see coming." —*Publishers Weekly*

Tailed

BRIAN M. WIPRUD

A Dell Book

TAILED

A Dell Book / June 2007

Published by Bantam Dell
A Division of Random House, Inc.
New York, New York

This is a work of fiction. Names, characters, places, and incidents
either are the product of the author's imagination or are used
fictitiously. Any resemblance to actual persons, living or dead, events,
or locales is entirely coincidental.

Dell is a registered trademark of Random House, Inc.,
and the colophon is a trademark of Random House, Inc.

ISBN 978-0-440-24314-4

Printed in the United States of America
Published simultaneously in Canada

www.bantamdell.com

OPM   10 9 8 7 6 5 4 3 2 1

For two stalwarts of my everyday life who deserve recognition:

Jim Quinn: A friend who has turned me a lot of favors over the years that I never seem able to repay, everything from lending me his house to his car to making sure my books are face out at his local bookstore.

Bob Martinez: Supportive of my work, and of me personally, Bob has also been a fount of wit and wisdom that from time to time grace these humble pages.

Gentlemen, *okole maluna*.

Acknowledgments

As always, thanks go to my editor, Caitlin Alexander, who must suffer through less-than-perfect versions of my stories and then make me make them better.

I am thankful to my mother, Helen Hills, for being a terrific, loving mom and for in no way imaginable being anything remotely like Garth's mother, Gabby.

I'd also like to thank Chris Van Brunt, owner of an M3 Half Track, who kindly gave me a tutorial on the workings of that versatile war machine.

When one dog barks at a shadow, a hundred bark at the sound.

—*Fortune Cookie,*
Woo Ho Fat Szechuan

Tailed

permits, top guides at top lodges, prep and export fees, and a whole gamut of red tape that only the rich can untangle with a few snips from cash's giant green scissors. But the expenses don't stop there—it's also none too cheap to have an elephant's head mounted. And, of course, you have to have the kind of palatial abode with space enough to hang one of those suckers and not make it look like it's crashing through the wall.

But the inventory of Mr. Fulmore's trophies that I carried in my briefcase included a lot more than those five animals. He had an appallingly large collection of dead stuff for a man in his early thirties.

Yes, Garth Carson carrying a briefcase. My taxidermy rental days weren't entirely behind me, but I'd more or less handed over the day-to-day reins of the operation to my Russian assistant, Otto. To anybody who knows the little goofball, that may have seemed a rash move on my part, but despite his goofiness Otto's not dumb and he knows my stock of taxidermy intimately. He took the promotion quite solemnly, too, and started wearing one of his boxy, belted Soviet-era suits to the apartment every day.

So Carson's Critters had become a sideline for me. My new job involved appraising taxidermy collections for Wilberforce/Peete, a large specialty insurance company that caters to everything from the rich and famous's taste for collecting dead animals to aerospace company missile projects. How did I land this peachy gig? For once, my brother, Nicholas, had brought sunshine to my life rather than forbidding black clouds. He's an insurance investigator and had used his connections to hook me up. Before the insurance work, with my taxidermy rental business, I'd been more or less just holding my own, my nose pressed against the glass ceiling. I'd no idea insurance companies needed people with my expertise. Or how well they paid. Because of this surge in profits, Angie and I now owned our apartment. At forty-six, my midlife-crisis days were well behind me. Every time I looked at that briefcase, a big smile spread across my face.

My Danger Days were behind me, too. There had been a period when I just couldn't seem to stay out of trouble—with the criminal element or with the law. It had been two blissful years since anybody had tried to kill me. And by the looks of things, I was free and clear.

Okay, so maybe not so free and clear, since I was now fighting my way across six lanes of the Indy 500 trying to make the Wacker Drive exit. But I'm a New Yorker. I simply bullied my way across the interstate, leaned on my horn, and cut everybody off. Tires screeched and legions of irate Chicagoans flipped me the bird, their lips pantomiming expletives. The scariest part was that a disproportionate number of them actually looked like their patron saint, Mike Ditka.

I'd never been to Chicago before. Downtown seemed much like parts of midtown Manhattan but with more named instead of numbered streets. It's just that there was a river cutting through part of the city, and I had a little trouble getting across it to my hotel. Soon enough, though, I was in the semicircular driveway of the glass monolith, a posse of valet parking guys eyeing my car with the thinly disguised trepidation of cowpokes approaching a fiery bull. I was used to this. To these twenty-five-year-old kids, my black '66 Lincoln convertible, with its giant steering wheel, knobs, and tranny hump, was an alien, unpredictable thing. Other than some SUVs, cars haven't been made this heavy or this long since way before these hombres were born.

As the bellhops unloaded my gear from the trunk, I eyed the oldest valet. "You ever drive a vintage ride like this?"

He paused, and did so too long.

The youngest of the bunch piped up.

"My gramps has a '72 El Dorado. Drove it to Vegas last summer. She made wide turns, you know?"

"Circle gets the square." I tossed him the keys.

"Dope!" He smiled. "Circle gets the what?"

"Forget it." I tucked a twenty in his shirt pocket as he moved toward the driver's seat. "Car has a new paint job, so be nice to her."

I followed the bellhops into the shiny building, did all that check-in stuff, and by 7:00 P.M. I was lying on the bed in my shiny room. Then the phone rang.

"This Carson?" a man's voice asked.

"Who's this?"

"Wilberforce/Peete, right?"

"Yes. Is this Mr. Fulmore?"

"Yeah, that's me. Car'll pick you up in an hour. Howzat?"

"Sounds fine."

"That's cool. I'll leave the front door open. See you in a few."

"Sure."

I'll be the first to admit that I have a prejudiced perspective on big-game hunters because my work seems to bring me eyeball to eyeball with the worst of them. But a lot has changed since midcentury, back when trophy hunting was done without conscience or forethought. True sportsmen today are equal part conservationist, promoting sustainable-use programs and contributing to international efforts to keep the populations of game animals healthy enough so that they can continue to kill them. I know, it sounds counterproductive, but I guess it's the Omelet Theory in action, and they're breaking a few eggs. Argue that it would be better to hatch the eggs if you must, but there's no denying that these big-game hunters channel a lot of money, effort, and influence toward conservation efforts that otherwise wouldn't be there. For example, the biggest, oldest, and most venerable award in trophy hunting used to be called the Oglevy Cup and was awarded to the hunter with the most spectacular kill. Today, that same award is called the Oglevy Conservation Award and is given to the hunter who has contributed the most toward improving the sport—i.e., keeping the animals around. Hats off to the nature lovers who do their bit, but the luminaries of big-game hunting do their bit and then some.

For obvious reasons, most of the big-game hunters I visited were eager to try to grease my wheels. They wanted the highest appraisal possible, if not for insurance reasons, then for bragging rights. If they ever got into a pissing contest with other hunters, even if they didn't have a saber-toothed wombat or hoary tree kangaroo among their trophies, they could always pull the trump card by announcing how much their collection was worth. Sad, really. True collectors such as myself tend not to be competitive on that scale—we're more apt to be kindred spirits, appreciating the sensibilities evidenced in someone else's collection. Taxidermy is art. But with hunters, their "trophies" were exactly that: a show of prowess.

My motto? Don't let other people make their problems yours. If these guys wanted to smoke cigars, drink sixty-year-old scotch, and lock horns over whose dead animals were bigger, better, or more valuable, let them have at it. Besides, it benefited me. Whenever I visited these big-game hunters, they wined and dined me, sent cars, and lavished me with Cuban cigars I didn't smoke—it was only the gold watches and home entertainment systems that Wilberforce/Peete forbade me to accept. And of course, these erstwhile Hemingways, knowing I was exposed to some of the finest trophy collections in the country, wanted me to be their magic mirror and tell them theirs was the finest in all the land.

An hour after Fulmore's call, I was in a limo headed for an upper-crust Chicago suburb. And I couldn't help but reflect, once again, how dramatically my life had changed in a year. Nothing highlights the notion that you're no longer treading water more than having the captain send out his launch for you. Pipe me aboard! I was liking this new life. A lot.

Once off the highway, we cruised through a Tudor-style retail strip and into a lane canopied by the thick branches of towering sycamores. Portico lights twinkled through the hedgerows.

It was trash night in Upper Crust, Illinois. You know you're in a schmancy neighborhood when all the houses have matching trash cans—the clean, green PVC kind with rubber wheels, whisper-quiet hinged lids, and no house numbers spray-painted on the sides. I'd bet the garbage trucks were electric and the sanitation workers wore matching white jumpsuits and ballet slippers so as not to wake anybody. Like the tooth fairy, the rubbish fairies fluttered in and out without so much as causing a head to lift from its pillow.

The chauffeur slowed as we approached a drive with a white lawn jockey next to it. For the uninitiated, a drive is distinguished from a driveway by the semicircular, dual-entrance design that obviates having to use reverse gear. When you think about it, the less you have to use reverse gear, the richer that means you are. Anyplace you shop has valet parking. You just pull straight up to the entrance and somebody else parks and retrieves your car. You don't have to park in the regular parking spaces at the Foodco because you no longer food shop—your staff does. If you have a garage, somebody brings the car "around for you." And eventually, you just stop driving all together—why even risk having to use reverse in an emergency? All that bothersome neck and head twisting. That's what you pay a personal trainer for, after all.

Passing a sea of green stuff—it was way too neatly trimmed and uniform to be grass—the limo approached a Georgian façade: red brick, white-pillared portico, ivy, dormers. I had to remind myself I wasn't dropping in on a bank president, but a running back named Sprunty who probably favored wild pool parties awash in cheerleaders and controlled substances. I could only imagine the fuss his neighbors had made when he'd signed the deed to this mansion. But that was their problem. Not mine.

The limo rolled to a stop and the driver killed the engine. This wasn't like calling a town car in New York. Here, a limo would wait, no matter how long. And instead of some surly Balkan malcontent sharing his highly original views on impromptu capital punishment to the accompaniment of a radio blaring balalaika disco, my driver hadn't said a word the whole trip. If he was Bosnian or Croatian, I had no idea. He could have been Hutu or Tutsi. I didn't notice.

My briefcase and I stepped out of the limo, and from the portico's vantage I surveyed the sea of green. Fireflies looped and blinked their way through the vapor looking for their mates. Toads chirped. Crickets cheeped. As somnolent a June evening as ever there was.

I turned to the door, which was about six feet wide. When Sprunty had said on the phone that he'd leave the door open, I'd thought he meant unlocked. But it was open open.

"Mr. Fulmore?" My voice bounced up and around the soaring entryway like a SuperBall. An Escheresque staircase stood directly ahead, so long it should have been an escalator. "Hello?"

No butler or housekeeper in evidence. I stepped into the foyer. "Hello?"

On my right was a living room, all in white, with lots of plants and nothing on the walls. To my left was an open door that led to an oak-paneled library, the kind you'd think more appropriate for *Masterpiece Theater* than Fulmore. Ahead, to the right of the stairs, was a white door held partially open by a black bear's paw.

Bear's paw? The right front paw, to be exact.

"Mr. Fulmore?" I strode over to the paw, which was lying on the floor. It was nearly the size of a baseball mitt, with claws like golf tees. Had to be from a huge black bear. And old. I instantly recognized that the stuffing was excelsior—a straw-like material made from aspen—wrapped with wire. Taxidermists once "stuffed" animal skins by forming manikins from these materials. That method was replaced in the 1970s by off-the-shelf foam urethane forms that were much lighter and rendered more realistic mounts.

I pulled the door open. It was one of those spring-loaded jobs that swung both ways, and it led into a pantry. Attached to the paw was the bear's forearm, and I picked it up with both hands. By the looks of the stump, it had been hastily cut from its mount. A few feet ahead was a large red puddle. I froze. Then I looked closer.

A woman's slip. And beyond that? A large brassiere, also red. I'm no expert, but I'd guess it was a 38D. Okay, so what man at forty-five doesn't have some knowledge of bra sizes?

I didn't like the looks of this. The trail led to a door on the far side of the pantry. Beyond? The red panties, no doubt. I grimly surmised Sprunty was in rut, and I didn't want to be the one to turn the hose *au deux d'amour*.

So the bear arm and I beat a retreat to the living room, where I sat upon a couch that looked like it had never been sat on, neatening up the contents of my briefcase: a calculator, some lined legal pads, twenty-five-cent pens, a date book, some bottled water, and a box of Milk Duds. Not exactly the contents of Donald Trump's attaché, but I'm told he does like the occasional Milk Dud.

Also contained within was a stack of papers Angie

had handed me before I left—a dossier of dog breeds. I'd been avoiding reading through it because I wasn't sure I really wanted a dog. But Angie seemed dead set on acquiring a canine to share our digs. We already had Otto, our jack-of-all-trades, and he was like a dog, wasn't he? Better still, I didn't have to chase him down the street with a Baggie on my hand, picking up his warm, moist loaves from the pavement.

On the other hand, I felt a wee bit guilty. Angie and I had opted not to have kids, and if she felt the urge at this late stage for a third party, how could I refuse her a fur-bearin' critter? One that wasn't stuffed, that is.

On the third hand, assuming I had one, I had never owned a dog. Not that my brother, Nicholas, and I hadn't begged our mother for one. But my mother wouldn't have it. "Animals," Gabby would say, "are meant to be free." There was a goose and a duck that lived out back, but they were hardly pets.

Well, there was one pet, once. At the tender age of seven I found a puppy—of sorts—by the railroad tracks and hid it in my tree house for a week or two. Let's just say it ended badly.

With a sigh, I began to flip through the info on mid-sized to small terriers. Jack Russell, wire fox, miniature schnauzer...but it was hard to stay focused.

I couldn't imagine Sprunty hadn't heard me enter. Surely when he was finished slipping the wood to that cheerleader he'd come looking for me. He wouldn't want to keep his appraiser waiting long. I might get testy.

After half an hour of looking for the least objectionable mutt, I was getting impatient. If I had a cell phone, I would have called somebody. The bear arm was beginning to worry me, too. Why would Sprunty cut the arm off his own bear mount, and right before an appraisal? Was it possible he'd cut it off somebody else's trophy on a wager or something?

Weary of the delay, I determined to barge in on the couple. Half an hour was long enough for Sprunty to have done what he needed to do. Now they were probably just in there having cosmos and cheese curls or something.

I pushed through the door at the far end of the pantry. When the door swung closed behind me, I was submerged in darkness, awash in ripples of aquamarine, in the depths of the hushed silence of wall-to-wall carpeting. Across a sizable room and beyond a gargantuan sectional sofa was a large array of sliding glass doors leading to a patio and lighted pool. Ah—they must be out by the pool.

But moments later I was standing next to the turquoise glow and somnolent hum of the pool. No Sprunty. No cheerleader. No panties. Just the frogs and crickets chirping away.

I walked back through the sliding doors and felt along the wall for a light switch. Suddenly, Sprunty's trophy room blazed all around me. I could see that it extended almost the full width of the house, with dark paneled walls, white cathedral ceilings, white wall-to-wall shag, and white upholstered furniture.

Fulmore certainly had bragging rights. The pieces on the wall were mostly exotic, many full-bodied, and few of them small. A brooding black Cape buffalo the size of a Mini Cooper was parked in one corner, a gnu at full gallop charged out from another. Along one wall, three rows of gazelle heads were arranged by size like some taxonomic display. There were mountain goats standing on fake rocks in the room's center, a lion jumping a Grant's gazelle beyond that. Elk, moose, and rhino heads up there, a five-hundred-pound black marlin up over there. A snarling polar bear clawed the air to the left of the stone fireplace, a cougar jumped a pronghorn by the bar, and a wolf gnashed its teeth over the door. It was like one of those sporting goods megastores. Taxidermy overkill. Or just plain overkill.

My eyes finally locked onto the black bear, which was standing in the corner to my right, his elbows stirring the air. Both forearms were missing, and I held only one of them in my hand. What kind of nut mutilates one of his trophies?

Even from across the room I could see the bear was out of place. All the other animals here were modern taxidermy. It's not unusual for collections to include a number of older pieces, but it's less common to contain only one. Big-game hunting is a passion often passed from one generation to the next, right along with the old money, and many of the collections I appraised contained older pieces passed down from father to son. Whether that was the case with Sprunty I had no idea. It was certainly true for me: my love of "wildlife art" began at a tender age in a home filled with my grandfather's trophies, even though my father didn't hunt, and neither do I.

The black bear was helping the polar bear flank the fireplace on the far side of the large sectional couch, and to get there I sauntered behind the sectional, around the mountain goats, and in front of the bar. Ahead I saw something red.

The panties. I reached down to pick them up.

But what I encountered was wet. It was two dimensional. It was a stain.

My eyes swam—it must be red paint, cranberry juice, grenadine, Campari, raspberry syrup . . . but then the metallic bite of blood stung my nose.

I found my back pressed against the front of the bar, my hand reaching for the phone next to the beer taps. Fumble: Carson knocks the phone off the bar and onto the floor behind it.

"Nine one one, nine one one..." I was afraid I might forget the number as I stumbled behind the bar in search of the phone.

I stumbled, all right.

Onto Sprunty.

He'd been mauled by a bear. How'd I know? Sure, those gashes in his chest could have been made by a knife. But Fulmore's intestines were wrapped around the bear's missing arm and paw.

There was blood everywhere, and I almost slipped in it as I reached next to his head for the phone. I was averting my eyes from the gore, my breath coming fast, grunting with disgust, when I grabbed Sprunty by the nose by accident. His eyes, thankfully, were mostly closed. But his mouth was open. Something white was sticking out of it. A lizard? No, a gecko, probably a common house gecko. Dead, too? I didn't know, I didn't care.

I grasped the phone and wheeled back around to the other side of the bar, falling to my knees on the clean white carpet. I misdialed three times before I got it right.

That was the day Sprunty's problems became mine.

chapter 2

I didn't like my new job much in the days after Sprunty's death. Being interviewed by the police was one thing, but being hounded by the press was another. At first they camped in the hallway outside my hotel room. When the hotel kicked them out, they hid in vans outside the hotel. When I tried to make my getaway toward New York, they followed and jumped me at a gas station. Meanwhile, back at my New York homestead, they'd beset Angie looking for details. I even saw Otto on the evening news, microphones shoved toward his smiling steel dental work as he tried to flirt with one of the lady reporters. They kept asking what he meant by "not lookink."

Media frenzy? I'd call it media ape shit. They were desperate for details, and the police weren't letting them have any. I was keeping my lip buttoned, too. Stella Lombardo, my handler at Wilberforce/

Peete, had reminded me of their policy against discussing any matter pertaining to policyholders with third parties outside the firm. I got so used to saying "no comment," that I reflexively said it to a Bob Evans waitress trying to take my order. Let's be honest: a waitress holding a pen and pad does look kind of like a reporter.

Thankfully, someone in the police department finally cracked and leaked a dribble of details that splashed across the headlines coast to coast.

FULMORE HACKED

SPORTS STAR SLASHED

BEAR MAULS BEAR

Mind you, I was avoiding newspapers. Having had the fun of discovering the body and living with the image of Fulmore's intestines wrapped around a bear paw, I had no interest in following the case. But what little I absorbed by the time I got to Cleveland five days after the murder suggested that the police were being ridiculed. No leads, no suspects. The case was getting cold.

Safely ensconced in the basement of Griswold's Funeral Home, I felt more at ease than I had in days.

Griswold's had nothing to do with Sprunty's end run through the mortal veil of tears. His funeral had played out the day before in Florida, his home state.

But Griswold's had everything to do with white squirrels. Lots and lots of them.

Don't ask me why, but there are a number of collectors who are fascinated by animal albinism. There's a historical society in Lima, Ohio, that displays perhaps the world's most extensive collection of albino taxidermy: porcupines, flying squirrels, hawks, owls, badgers, and any other domestic critter you might care to imagine. Or not.

Mr. Griswold, the funeral director, was one such fellow, and he flooded the basement of his mortuary with white *Sciurus caroliniensis*. I've seen my share of black squirrels among New York's legions of nut eaters, but never a white one. Though I understand there are towns across the land that stake their claim to fame as "Home of the White Squirrel."

But what made this collection unique was that the squirrels were all anthropomorphically arranged. That is, Griswold had seen fit to pose the white squirrels in the pursuit of human activities. Driving pink convertibles. Playing cards. Riding a Ferris wheel that actually turned to the hum of a motor. Drinking at a bar. Fishing. Golfing. Surfing. Each elaborate diorama was in a lighted display case built into the wall, like fish tanks at an aquarium.

A lot of white squirrels? I'd counted ninety-seven in all. It was a darn sight easier estimating the value of garden-variety trophies. Unless you count the stuffed-frog mariachi bands up for sale on eBay, you don't see a slew of anthropomorphic taxidermy for sale. Then again, Griswold's collection wasn't in the running for the big-game hunter sweepstakes, so I didn't anticipate that a lower-than-expected valuation would elicit the kind of thunderous, scotch-soaked indignation I'd get from some Lord Blastaway.

"Mr. Carson?" Devon, a pretty blond employee in funerary garb, was halfway down the basement steps. "There's someone here for you. From Wilberforce/Peete."

"Here?" I put down my pad and pen. Hmm. Had I screwed up somehow?

Descending past the blonde on the stairs was another blonde. Or should I say white. White shoulder-length hair, dark sunglasses, skin the color of pizza dough.

Stella Lombardo. My boss.

She was in a peach-colored pantsuit, aqua scarf around her neck, aqua pumps. Unlike most people entering a basement in sunglasses, the low light hadn't fazed her as she scanned her surroundings. She put a hand on her slender hip.

"Disgusting."

I looked around behind me at the squirrels, then back at her. This was kind of awkward. Someone with oculocutaneous albinism confronted by a room full of white, pink-eyed squirrels. An albino in a room full of albinos collected as oddities.

"Pretty unusual, I'll say that." I displayed a frown that I thought would please my boss. But I stopped short of asking her why she was there. No need. I was sure she'd tell me when she was ready.

Like a captain inspecting fresh recruits, Stella

slowly scanned the display cases, eventually coming back to me. I couldn't see her eyes, only their motion behind the dark glass. Nystagmus, a common side symptom of albinism, meant her eyes quivered uncontrollably, and her head wobbled slightly to counteract the effect so she could see straight.

"I'd say low estimate, wouldn't you, Garth?"

I glanced at my pad reflexively. "Not much resale value."

"Resale value? This stuff should be burned. Griswold is a freak, and this...gruesome display is a sick vendetta against albinism. Christ. What's the matter with people?"

I was beginning to feel implicated. "I've never understood the fascination with albino mounts myself."

"What's to understand? You don't see people collecting only yellow animals, do you? Or only red?"

I was tempted to point out that those weren't color variegations of any species I'd seen taxidermied. But I didn't. I'd learned a long time ago, in the trenches at Dairy Twist one summer, not to comment to the boss on the quality of the food.

"Are you almost done down here, Garth?"

"Yes." I almost said *Yes, sir.*

"I'll be in the lobby."

"Roger. Fifteen minutes." Wasn't I just the model staff sergeant?

After finishing my appraisal, I went upstairs and found Stella in the potpourri- and nicotine-laden "Comfort Lounge." An ultra-slim brown cigarette wisped between two fingers, like a smoldering pretzel stick held high and to the side. She sat uneasily in a wing chair as though the cushions were lumpy. But I knew it was just nervous energy. Stella never looked comfortable.

"Sit." She puffed, her head jiggling slightly. "We've got a situation."

This didn't sound good. I sat down in an overstuffed chair opposite her, and almost sank to the floor in its soft cushions.

"By 'situation,' I mean"—she puffed again—"I mean Sprunty isn't the first."

"First?" I squinted with confusion. "First what?"

"First victim."

"Ah…" What was she on about? First rule of being a toady is to pretend to understand your boss's most obtuse musings.

She nodded, waving her burning pretzel. "The police have determined there's a pattern developing."

I lapsed into the sycophant's patented cerebral pose, hand to my chin, head nodding gently, eyes skyward—like I understood. But I didn't.

"Titan, remember him?"

"Titan Harris? Sure. I appraised his trophy collection, in Texas, about a month ago, I guess." The clouds of obfuscation suddenly parted. I tried to sit forward with alarm, but sank deeper into the quicksand of my chair's cushions instead. "You don't mean…"

She stabbed her cigarette in my direction. "Dead.

At first, it appeared that his ram's head just fell off the wall onto his head. That the wall anchor gave way."

I knit my brow. Gads. A ram's head was hefty enough to put quite a dent in one's noggin. "I hadn't heard. So now..."

"Now..." She took a deep drag, then loosed a long, thin stream of smoke. "Now it appears that someone dropped it on Titan's head intentionally."

"How do they know?"

Stella stood, looking around suspiciously as she dropped her pretzel in the ashtray. "Outside."

My briefcase and I struggled from the grasp of the armchair and followed.

Out in the sun, Stella's white hair and skin fairly glowed, and she ducked her head against the glare as she climbed into the driver's side of her rental car. I got in the passenger side.

"This is strictly confidential. Nobody must know this detail. The police are already struggling with a media frenzy, and only the real killer will know this detail. Say 'hush-hush.'"

Making me repeat things was Stella's way of sub-jugating me. All bosses have some sort of dominance routine. If they only knew it made their employees suspect them of being nuttier than Mr. Peanut.

"Hush-hush."

"Good. It's hush-hush, so don't even tell your wife. The FBI didn't even want to tell me."

Angie wasn't my wife, but my urge to correct her was subordinate to my growing curiosity.

"I tell nobody. Hush-hush. So, how do they know Titan was murdered with the ram's head? And why do they think it was the same person who killed Fulmore?"

"A gecko."

I shuddered. My mental TV buzzed with the image of Sprunty's half-closed eyes and the lizard in his mouth. "There was a lizard in Texas, too?"

"Not just any lizard, Garth. A gecko. A white gecko."

White squirrels, white boss, white geckos? They say bad things come in threes. But this was creeping me out a little, making me feel like I was being sucked into the dank realm of the Morlocks, a dominion devoid of melatonin. I had a sudden itch to lather up with cocoa butter, crawl out from under my rock, and work up a golden brown tan.

"Didn't the cops, you know, think that was unusual?"

"They tell me geckos are relatively common in Texas. The local police just thought it had wandered into his house and somehow died in his hand. God, what I wouldn't do for an overcast day."

Stella surveyed the sunshine outside with contempt. Given how much I enjoy driving with the top down, soaking up the rays, I couldn't help feeling sorry for her. Albinism had rendered her eyes and skin at odds with glorious solar radiation. I was actually surprised she was able to drive, as many albinos'

vision is too poor. But I'd sensed from our first meeting that Stella was the type who'd insist on doing
jumping jacks if she had palsy. Sure, she was thin,
pink and blue and white, but under the surface you
could see she was constantly fighting, simmering. I'd
never had a dustup with her. And I hoped to keep it
that way.

"So, what's this have to do with Wilberforce/
Peete?"

Stella looked at me incredulously, and I caught a
glint of blue and pink from behind the shades. Albino
humans don't have pink eyes, usually just pale blue
ones. But sometimes in just the right light there was a
flash of pink from the retina.

"Two of our clients have cashed in their life insurance policies. Big ones. We don't want a third."

"So they think there's a killer targeting big game
hunters?"

"Not just a killer, Garth. Because of the commonality of the victims as big-game hunters, the mutilation of Sprunty, and the ritualism of placing a white
gecko on the victim, the FBI thinks there's a serial
killer at work. You have to help catch him."

If there had been an ejection seat in that car, I
would have thrown the lever.

"Me? Why me?"

"I will not whine. Say it."

"I'm not whining! I'm just surprised."

"Say it."

I groaned. "I will not whine."

"Better. But no groaning, either. I'd think you'd be a little more resilient, like your brother, Nicholas."

I closed my eyes, composing myself. Nobody likes to be chastised, much less to have their cut-rate Simon Templar of a brother held up as some sort of paradigm.

I opened my eyes and spoke with the calm, interstellar decorum of Spock addressing Vulcan high priestess T'Lar. "Stella, my brother is a professional investigator who, through the benefit of experience, is resilient in the face of things like murder. I, on the other hand, am not a professional investigator. I am an appraiser. I have no professional experience with murderers. Why have I been chosen to help find this serial killer?"

"Not to help *find*, just to help. You were one of the last people to see Titan Harris alive, and you had an appointment with Sprunty Fulmore right around the time he was murdered. Do you think you might have some idea who would want to kill these big-game hunters?"

I bowed my head, trying to remain calm. "Anybody at U.S. Fish and Wildlife would have the same guesses as mine. First suspect would probably be animal rightists."

"The FBI has discounted that. Doesn't fit the profile. They would have claimed responsibility, and they wouldn't have killed two geckos."

"OK, fine. That's all I've got. Unless you're willing

to entertain the notion that the trophies themselves are taking revenge on the hunters."

"Why don't you want this assignment, Garth? All you have to do is sit around and play expert, be our eyes and ears with the FBI and see if there's anything we can do to keep our other clients from collecting their life insurance prematurely."

"Stella, why not just put armed guards at all our clients' homes until this is solved?"

"Do you realize how many trophy-hunter clients we have? Besides, the FBI wants this kept under wraps."

"At the expense of Wilberforce/Peete's clients? Essentially, the FBI wants to use them as bait, am I right?"

"And we're none too happy about it."

"So I'm supposed to go in there and try to keep our clients from getting killed even as the FBI is hoping they *will* get killed."

Stella handed me a white folder.

"What's this?"

"Plane tickets. You fly to Seattle. Tonight."

chapter 3

In as much as airport security forbids anybody to meet a passenger at the gate anymore, I knew the man in the trench coat, short hair, and sideburns standing there must be a cop of some sort. He smiled politely as I exited the gangway.

"Carson, yes?"

"That's me."

"Special Agent John Bricazzi." He gave me the once-over, jerked his head to the side, and started walking. I followed, consciously stretching the wooden muscles in my legs.

I'm convinced airline travel is some kind of endurance test of the human mind and body. Isn't this the kind of thing they used to do to chimps in preparation for space flight? You're strapped into a confined space, fed low-protein food units, dosed with stimulants in the form of the planet's most profoundly bad coffee (if it even is coffee), gassed with recirculated oxygen, and forced to endure "air shopper" magazines filled with implausible merchandise like nose massagers and walkie-talkie barbecue spatulas. And to top it off, you're often forced to watch painfully unoriginal reruns of couch comedies. Somewhere in the belly of the plane there must be a control room full of behavioral scientists watching their monitors and oscilloscopes. These stern, bald men in lab coats shake their heads and in thick Austrian accents wonder aloud: "Zese humans are astounding! I zink dat one is going to buy the edible golf bag from der *Skyshopper* magazine."

Which is why I'd driven to Chicago in the first place, thank you very much.

A black sedan was waiting curbside when Bricazzi and I exited the terminal. We both climbed in back, me shoving my luggage in ahead of me.

The driver was a thick-necked Hispanic. He glumly locked eyes with me in the rearview mirror. "Agent Luis Stucco."

"Do I call you guys by your last names, like on TV, or do I have to use the 'agent' title?"

Bricazzi chuckled mechanically, like he'd heard that one before and was worse for it. Sliding an emery board out of his pocket, he began touching up his nails.

"Last names work," replied Stucco.

"Uh huh." Bricazzi and Stucco: all I could think of

were those commercials on WPIX for New Jersey Brickface and Stucco. "You can call me Garth."

Brickface inspected his nails for a few beats before he broke the silence.

"Luis? Let's stop for ice cream."

"You got it, John."

"You like ice cream, Carson?"

I sucked on my cheek a moment, then looked him in the eye. If the Feds thought they could give me the business, they had another think coming.

"There's this penguin driving across the desert on his way to Vegas," I began, "when all of a sudden, there's a loud bang from the engine, steam pouring out from under the hood. Luckily, he's able to make it to the next town, where he pulls into a garage. The mechanic tells him he can't look at the engine until it cools down."

"A penguin in the desert?" Stucco eyed his partner in the mirror uncertainly.

"So the mechanic tells the penguin he might as well go get some ice cream at the stand across the road while he waits. The penguin waddles across the road, hops up on a stool, and has a dish of vanilla ice cream."

It's a lewd joke, one told to me by my friend Rodney, and it ends up with the penguin saying: "I did not! That's ice cream!"

There was a pause, then Brickface pointed his emery board at me. "If the penguin could hold the steering wheel, why couldn't he hold a spoon?"

"And what's a penguin doing in the desert?" Stucco insisted.

"A mechanic would say 'gasket,' not 'seal,'" Brickface growled.

I couldn't tell if they were busting my chops or what. But I felt I'd better stay the course, see how far I could push it. "This penguin was part of a Department of Agriculture experiment to raise penguins at lower latitudes for cheap labor, in order to replace migrant workers at shrimp farms. And as for the spoon, well, it wasn't so much that he couldn't hold the spoon as that he'd been traumatized as a chick by a Norwegian seal hunter who'd bludgeoned his friends with a spoon."

There was a pause, but they couldn't hold it in this time. Stucco started first, his laugh deep and guttural like a rusty tuba, then Brickface joined in silently, his chest jumping.

"Good one, Garth."

"Anytime, John."

Brickface's laughter stopped abruptly, and he jabbed his emery board in my face.

"It's Special Agent Bricazzi."

arth, your mother called again." Angie, my soul mate, sounded annoyed. "You really have to call her."

"I can't call Gabby right now." I was whispering into the phone, huddled in the corner of a boardroom in a federal building in downtown Seattle. The long table next to me was filled with law enforcement types. My seat was between Brickface and Stucco, my brief-case holding my spot. "The meeting is about to start."

"Oh, and some people from that fraternal order called, the ones you rented the pronghorn to last week for their meeting."

"The Mystical Order of the Tupelca?"

"I guess. They want to rent something else, so they're coming by to look at what you have."

"Have Otto give them the tour. How are things shaping up for your trip to Chicago this weekend for the *Couture Magazine* show?"

"All packed and ready. Gee, Garth, I sure wish you were still coming, that this Sprunty thing hadn't happened."

"You and me both."

"I was looking forward to spending some time with you away. Now your airline ticket is wasted."

"Take Otto."

"Very funny."

"He could be your chauffeur."

Fortune had shined on Angie's aspirations to ascend from doing jewelry piecework for name designers to creating her own line of baubles. She'd made enough of a name for herself in certain lofty fashion circles to be invited to submit some of her work to the magazine's annual show. While she was thrilled, some of her customers weren't—the last thing they wanted was more competition, and from someone they saw as labor, someone beneath them. Well, that was my take on why some of the designers had stopped giving her work. But this show was the big time. If she was favorably reviewed—maybe even had her pieces shown in the magazine's accessories issue—she could start to hang her shingle as a true designer in her own right. So we'd booked tickets to Chicago to attend the show—time for her to do some serious schmoozing and for me to be arm candy. I know, it meant that I would have driven all the way to New York and then hopped on a plane back to Chicago. Life is frequently a lousy travel agent.

"So did you look at the doggie literature?"

"Uh huh."

"Well?"

"Golly, the miniature Great Dane looks good." I sensed an annoyed pause on the other end. "Look, let's discuss it when I get home. Right after Nicholas's wedding we can go dog shopping, how's that?"

The words came out of my mouth, but they surprised me. And scared me. With a dog came responsibility. What if I screwed up and it died? What if I didn't like it, or worse, didn't love it? Yet this was really important to Angie, and I couldn't stall forever, could I?

I heard her peevishness deflate with an audible sigh.

"Good. When are you coming home, loverboy? I miss you."

"Believe me, I'll come home just as soon as I can."

"Well, you'd better be here by next week, anyway. The wedding is just around the corner. By the way, I took your tux to the cleaners. It hasn't been cleaned since that night at the Savoy."

The night at the Savoy: that was the last time I'd attended one of Angie's jewelry do's, and the memory rendered me relieved I wouldn't be around to screw up this event for her.

"Did you really go over the information about dogs?" Her voice was bristling with glee. "I found a listing of breeders in the New York area." There was the muffled sound of someone talking in the background. "Oh, and Otto says he misses you, too."

I was about to say something characteristically mordant—but didn't get the chance.

"Garv! My friend!" Angie, that minx, had put Otto on the line. Prior to becoming a captain of industry in the taxidermy rental world, Otto had been our Ensign Fixit. He did a little bit of everything, from repairing broken taxidermy to helping Angie solder jewelry. An Old World craftsman, so to speak. Angie had discovered him setting up shop in the subway a while back. He was repairing watches and sewing buttons for money right there on the platform at Chambers Street. Ever since Angie bailed him out of the hoosegow for peddling without a license he'd been a devoted employee.

"Garv, I make to answer phone for beezness: 'Alo, Garv Carson Critters, please, tell to me if help.' Eh? Eh? Very nice, I thinkink. Please, tell to me, Garv, when home you to come? Otto very much not see you. We get doggie, yes?"

"Otto, you nincompoop, put Angie back on the line, I only have a second." Brickface and Stucco were glancing in my direction. I cupped my hand over the receiver and whispered, "I need to talk to Angie."

"I miss Garv very much, is to cry. Very sad my heart."

"That's nice, Otto." Sentimental maniac. "Put Angie on the phone."

At that juncture, a silver-haired man with a commanding stride entered the conference room. Those assembled sat a little straighter and adjusted the folders before them, like ball players watching their p's and q's. I didn't need anybody to tell me this was the Head Coach, the Special Agent-in-Charge.

On the phone, Otto broke into song, a high, wavering tune that, if I'm not mistaken, was the old Mary Hopkins version of the gypsy folk ditty "Those Were the Days."

"Те были днями мой друг!"

"Otto..." A screen was pulled down at the front of the room.

"Мы думали, что они никогда не будут заканчивать!"

"Otto..." A few other suits straggled into the boardroom and took their seats.

"Мы пели бы и танцевали бы навсегда и день!"

"Otto, if you don't shut up and put Angie on the line, I'm going to strangle you right through the phone!"

I turned.

All eyes were on me, including Head Coach's steely gaze and furrowed brow.

"Nice to sing, yes? Very old gypsy song to say—"

My voice dropped to a whisper again. "Tell Angie I'll call back later."

"Garv, please to call your mommie, eetz not lookink. We get doggie, yes?"

I gently returned the phone to its base and claimed my seat next to Bricazzi, who was working on his manicure. My face must have been red, because it felt like I'd left it on the radiator for an hour.

"Let's begin," Head Coach intoned wearily. Time for the game films. The lights went out and the screen lit up with an image of Sprunty sprawled behind the bar in his trophy room, his guts like spaghetti around a bear paw fork.

I put my hand to my forehead like I had an itch. My sudden interest in palm reading had to do with not reliving the horrific surprise of discovering Sprunty's mutilated body. That and the realization that my two-year hiatus from trouble was at an end. Well, at least this was just a *brush* with trouble. I was merely there to consult and then go home.

"Six days ago, Sprunty G. Fulmore, running back for the Chicago Bears, was found murdered in his suburban Chicago home by an insurance appraiser. Cause of death? Mauled by the arm of a stuffed black bear, one of his trophies. He had no live-in house staff, and we've spoken with everybody from the pool boy to the housekeeper. No witnesses. That we know of." Head Coach hit a button on the laptop, and another picture popped on the screen.

I peeked. This image was far less gruesome. It was Titan Harris III, his toupee askew, looking passed out drunk, slumped next to a wall. Not too far different from when I'd seen him. He drank almost a whole bottle of Johnnie Walker Blue while regaling me with the tale of his hunt for a Gobi yak. He fell asleep on the couch just as he was about to pull the trigger.

Next to him was a big white ram's head, leaning forward, its nose to the floor like it was staring at a passing ant. These sheep are monsters, very grumpy creatures, all white, with curled, stalwart horns like twenty-pound fists on the sides of their heads. And Titan's trophy would have been very heavy. I remembered it as being one of those older mounts, in which the excelsior manikin inside would have been smoothed over with plaster.

"Three weeks earlier, in Houston, Texas, Titan Harris III, oil rig manufacturer, was found dead. It appeared that he had been killed accidentally when a bighorn sheep head fell from the wall. Blunt trauma."

I felt someone's gaze on me, and I glanced across the table at a woman with short sandy hair, sun-flecked skin, and penetrating black eyes that were staring a hole through me. She looked to be the oldest person in the room, in her mid sixties, and though seated, perhaps also the shortest person in the room. In stature and demeanor she was what I'd call compact. A taut jaw and nervous fumbling with her pen made her seem highly caffeinated.

But something about her was different from the rest of the team. Could it have been her blue U.S. Air Force uniform? And if I wasn't mistaken, the little silver cluster of leaves on her jacket was that of a lieutenant colonel. On the opposite lapel was a medical caduceus pin. Well, it was nice to know they were pulling out all the stops to find the killer by enlisting the help of our armed forces—if all else failed, maybe a little selective carpet bombing would do the trick. But an Air Force *doctor*?

Everybody else was gawking at the gore on the screen, but she seemed to find me worthier of study. No doubt I cut quite the dashing figure, as always, but her interest seemed purely clinical, like she wanted a sample of me in a petri dish. So as with people who stare at me in the subway, I launched a defensive maneuver meant to break her gaze. I locked eyes with her and turned my head sideways, as if hearing my master's voice. My patented "Nipper the RCA dog" look.

She tore her eyes away, reluctantly, and I focused back on the screen.

The next slide was a close-up of Titan's half opened hand, the pale tail of a gecko curled around his diamond pinky ring.

Head Coach continued his game analysis.

"It was noted that Titan had a dead lizard in his hand. While somewhat curious, this was not deemed significant during the initial investigation. The lizard in question was misidentified as a Mediterranean gecko, which is common in Texas. In addition, the hook that held the ram's head on the wall was bent, leading local police to classify Titan's death as accidental. But our forensics team later determined that the blow to Harris's head occurred in the center of the room, away from the wall. So the ram's head must have been removed from the wall before being dropped on his head."

Next slide: a close-up of Sprunty's mouth, the front

half of a waxy-looking gecko in one side. I studied my palm again.

"Fulmore's body was discovered with a dead lizard in his mouth. The same variety of lizard found in Titan's hand. The killings appear to be without a sexual dimension. But the mutilation of Fulmore, the commonality of weapon and victim, and the calling-card ritual lead us to believe there's a serial killer at work. Those present in this room are specialists in disciplines that can contribute to the agency's efforts to compile information that could be instrumental in profiling the perpetrator. No party has taken responsibility for these murders, which suggests that the deaths are not the handiwork of an ideologue or domestic terrorist group. As of now, we know of no threats to these men from animal rights groups. Obviously, our agents have been interviewing friends, family, and associates of these two men to find a commonality. Let's establish a timeline of the murders. I'll start with Agent Stucco."

Agent Stucco stood, hiking up his pants and poking at the laptop on the table in front of him.

A split-screen slide of the red bra and red slip lit up the front of the room. Beat the hell outta seeing Sprunty's guts.

"Other evidence at the Fulmore crime scene included these red female undergarments: a bra and a slip. No panties." Stucco's delivery was flat and emotionless, but he paused to eye his audience. "We interviewed a female acquaintance of Mr. Fulmore's, one

Honey Espanoza, and determined that she had been at the Fulmore residence earlier in the evening, at approximately 5:30 P.M., and had left in a hurry to make a flight. The undergarments belonged to Miss Espanoza. We have confirmed her location at the time of the murder as in transit to Miami. She saw nothing unusual before she left, and only knew that Mr. Fulmore was expecting someone from the insurance company of Wilberforce/Peete later that evening for an appraisal. Mr. Fulmore was poolside, alone, when she last saw him."

Stucco sat and Bricazzi stood to take his place by the laptop. "Here's what we know about the lizard, *Hemidactylus vuka*, commonly known as a vuka night gecko, native to the extreme southwestern United States and northern Mexico. Often mistaken for *Hemidactylus turcicus*, or Mediterranean house gecko, which has a similar appearance. I'll spare you the complete taxonomic description, which is in your folders. These geckos are brown, with darker chevrons along their back. Could we have the next image?"

A close-up of a gecko popped onto the screen. It appeared to be sitting on the wall of a thatched hut, and was facing down. It sort of looked to me like a miniature alligator, its eye golden with a slit down the center. There's something about that seemingly mechanical reptilian eye, combined with the secretive curl to their lips, that affixes geckos with a decidedly sinister agenda.

"But by night," Bricazzi continued, "many gecko

species turn pale; like anoles and many small lizards, they have specialized pigment cells in their skin called melanophores that allow them to change color, presumably as camouflage. But in death they turn dark again. We considered the possibility that these were albino geckos, but technically they aren't. Peculiar to the vuka night gecko is a rather unusual recessive gene that renders whole populations of them white every hundred years or so. We have no independent pictures of these white-phase geckos as this hasn't happened since just after the turn of the twentieth century. But herpetologists have confirmed that this white phase is occurring now. Native Americans of the Southwest felt that the white geckos held special spiritual significance. We're looking into the possible religious or symbolic nature of these geckos as a possible factor in the motive for the killings."

Coach boomed: "Mr. Carson is here as a representative of Wilberforce/Peete, and had recently met Harris and Fulmore to appraise their taxidermy. What can you tell us about the trophy collections of these two men?"

I stood, in the process kicking my briefcase under the table.

"Ah, yes, well..." I tried to ignore the loud *whump* of my briefcase falling over. "Both men were big-game hunters and had large collections of exotics."

"Dr. Lanston." That was the lieutenant colonel's idea of self-introduction, followed by her question: "Exotics?"

Doc Lanston stopped twirling her pen, leveling her black eyes on me again. I couldn't tell whether she was acutely interested in what my answer would be or scrutinizing me. Perhaps both.

"Species nonnative to North America. Mostly African, like the 'big five,' but also—"

"Big five?" Head Coach asked.

"Lion, leopard, elephant, cape buffalo, and rhinoceros. Many big-game hunters want to bag the big five."

Lanston raised her pen. "Carson, did either man mention to you threats of any kind regarding their collections?"

"Titan spent the entire time bragging about his trophies and telling me where and how he got them. He got drunk and fell asleep. I never actually met Sprunty while he was alive, only spoke to him briefly over the phone when he called to tell me he was sending a limo to pick me up."

"What time was that?" Stucco asked.

I shrugged. "About ninety minutes before I discovered the body."

Everybody began flipping through their folders.

"Most of these big-game hunters are very competitive with each other over who has the larger collection of trophies and how much they're worth," I added.

"Hmm." Stucco looked up at me. "The medical examiner places Fulmore's death at about six that evening."

I shrugged again, but an awkward pause developed in which those assembled just stared at me. That's when I realized: Sprunty had called at 7:00 P.M. He was dead when he called. That is, it must have been someone else who called.

Head Coach threw up his hands. "Nobody noticed this until this juncture?" He pointed at Bricazzi. "Get the phone records for that call. Mr. Carson, I think we can assume that whoever called you was not Mr. Fulmore. Tell us about this call."

I felt sweat start to well in my armpits. "Damn it all. If someone else called me . . . it could have been the killer. He knows who I am!"

"Remain calm, Mr. Carson."

"Remain calm? A serial killer called me. He wanted me to find the body, he knows who I am. And I'm supposed to remain calm? I have a collection of taxidermy. He could be after me, for Pete's sake!"

I looked around. The import of this was not lost on the audience. They all had giddy lights in their eyes, like this was good news. Especially Dr. Lieutenant Staresalot across the table from me.

Bricazzi stood, tucking away his nail file. "What hotel were you staying at?"

"The Grand Carlita."

He ducked out of the room and I dropped into my chair.

"Mr. Carson, your help could be invaluable, so please, remain calm. What did this person say when he called?"

"Very little. When I picked up, I think he just asked if I was Carson. I asked who was calling. He said it was

Sprunty calling, asked if I was from Wilberforce/ Peete, I said yes, and he said he'd send a car for me in an hour."

"What did he sound like?"

"Jeez, I dunno, he sounded like a football player."

Dr. Lanston stopped twirling her pen again. "You mean he sounded black?"

I fidgeted. I couldn't be sure, but it seemed like she was intentionally putting me on the spot. "Well, he sounded a little hip-hoppy, a little gangsta, you know?"

Doc Lanston leaned in, eyes lowered as she opened another folder. "Mr. Carson, your grandfather was a notable big-game hunter, wasn't he?"

"I...I don't really know," I stammered. The Air Force had a dossier on me? "I never met my grand- parents, my parents never..."

"Some of your personal taxidermy specimens are from your grandfather's trophy collection, aren't they?"

She turned those black bull's eyes on me, scrutiniz- ing my reaction.

I very carefully said, "Yes."

Her eyes returned to her folder.

"Julius 'Kit' Carson. Born 1878, Minneapolis, Minnesota. Died 1949 in a shipwreck. He hunted with many celebrities of the thirties and forties, all across Asia and Africa. You're telling us you didn't know this?"

I spoke as carefully and calmly as I could. "No, I did not know this. My father was estranged from his par- ents, and he never spoke of them."

I met her eyes. Her pen was twirling rapidly. While tempted, I resisted giving her my Nipper again.

"Do you think it's possible, Mr. Carson, that your grandfather's legacy has anything to do with why the killer chose you to discover the body?"

"Oh, come on." I couldn't resist loosing a snort of derision. "The killer somehow knew I had an appointment to visit Sprunty that night. Where does my grandfather come into this? I have some of his trophies, and many more from other big-game hunters, not just my grandfather. If the killer was just after people with big-game trophies, why did he get me there and not kill me, too? Two birds, one stone."

Her jaw shifted as she suppressed a reptilian smile.

"Exactly. This isn't about trophies."

"Exactly," I agreed.

"But didn't kill you."

"For which I'm grateful."

"He wanted you involved, not dead."

"Unfortunately."

"Which means?"

"Means? I don't know what . . ."

I scanned the table, and the team was all giving me that giddy eye again.

"It means," she said, grinning like a croc in the shallows, "this is about *you*."

chapter 5

Gabby is not your typical mom, if there is such a thing. Let's start with the fact that she married a rather, shall we say, eclectic man. Dad was an entrepreneurial butterfly collector, to be exact. Although I was reared in an upstate New York town called Scuntakus Junction, Mom and Dad met as city people. City people? OK, I won't gloss it, they were early beatniks who met in some Greenwich Village coffeehouse called Monkey Shadow, where Dad earned a living by strumming a guitar.

At some juncture, Gabby and Stuart found themselves in a commune in Michigan. Commune? I'm glossing again. Just hard to admit your parents were nudists who lived at a ranch called The Sunny Gourde. Which may or may not have been where I was conceived. And as for how and why they left the nudist colony... well, all I know is that they inherited the upstate New York homestead from my father's uncle Leonard, who if you believed the prattle of women over the clotheslines in Skunk Junction (the nonobscene pet name for our fair town) was a regular Baby Face Nelson bank robber during the Depression. I'm murky on the details of all this— Stuart and Gabby weren't the kind of parents who reminisced about Little Orphan Annie on the radio, the time Uncle Bob ran over the neighbor's chicken, or Grandad's rattletrap Studebaker. In fact, Nicholas and I never met our grandparents, much less the noted big-game hunter "Kit," and the topic of family history was generally taboo. Over the years I managed to glean that Gabby and Stuart had each been disowned by their parents, and vice versa.

It was an odd childhood in that respect, having no extended family. And odd living in a run-down colonial loaded with taxidermy. With Uncle Leonard's house came my grandad's hunting trophy collection.

Childhood was odd but by no means dull. Instead of waiting on Christmas for Santa to bring us a new Hot Wheels set or Rock 'Em Sock 'Em Robots, we waited on Beltane for Danu to bring us a pine tree to plant. Schoolyard singsong taunts like "Your mom is a witch, your mom is a witch..." kind of gave away what the adults were saying. We were the local *Addams Family*.

Suffice it to say, Nicholas and I were never won over by the maypole, bonfires, and solstices. What Stuart and Gabby Carson had on their hands were a couple of regulation squares. Nicholas and I demanded the dreaded status quo: stockings on the hearth, trick or treat, and dyed eggs.

I admit that I feel a little sorry for what my parents went through. For sons, they'd have preferred Ginsberg and Hoffman. Instead, they got Orville and Wilbur. With so little structure in our family life, you'd probably suppose the Carson boys were ragamuffins, dirty-faced urchins with twigs in our hair. Quite the opposite. Nicholas and I did our own laundry, took our own baths, cleaned up after ourselves. I buy into the theory that an overly structured childhood is in want of free form, and vice versa. My brother and I needed a structured home life. By necessity, we embraced self-reliance, which demands a certain level of pragmatism, perhaps even conservatism. That's how we turned out, anyway.

At least I was into collecting, like Dad, and was generally pretty mellow. As Nicholas grew ever more avaricious, one couldn't help but wonder if the stork hadn't got the wrong address.

When Dad died, after Nicholas lost the meager family nest egg in a credit card scheme, Mom refused to stay in Skunk Junction. I was off at college in North Carolina, and Nicholas sought penance in the Peace Corps, so there was nothing tying her there. She sold the land our house was on, packed a suitcase, and blew that pop stand. I rushed back with a van to claim my grandfather's tuxedos and taxidermy collection just before the bulldozers knocked our condemned house over. In a few hours the dozers scraped it off the ground and hauled it off in giant Dumpsters.

Pretty devastating to watch your boyhood home wiped from the face of the earth. The room Nicholas and I had shared, the portico where I used to collect beetles by porch light, the backyard where the geese Steinbeck and Ginsberg shat all over the lawn—as heartlessly vanquished as though a horde of Visigoths had appeared out of the night with torches. The only thing that remained in the distance were the remnants of our clubhouse, a few rotting boards in a tree. Just like Stuart and Gabby's history, mine had been erased. And I was pretty bitter about Gabby's indifference. I knew personal history meant very little to her.

My own mother hadn't told me she was moving from my boyhood home. My eviction notice from my childhood was a few lines she jotted on a postcard from Michigan. I didn't talk to her for five years after that. I was on my own anyway, working my way through college as a projectionist at the college town triplex. I'd already written off Nicholas, and now her. I guess I was wrapping myself in the family legacy: don't look back, don't get attached to your past.

But why had Mom gone to Michigan? To rejoin the nudist colony, of course. And she's been there ever since, twenty-five years or so.

Before stopping in on Sprunty's corpse in Chicago, I'd been visiting Gabby in Ann Arbor. My mission? To give her the news flash about Nicholas's upcoming wedding.

Ah, the homecoming. The Norman Rockwell version: Ma in her apron shucking peas, Pa reading the paper and smoking a pipe. The reality: Ma naked as a jaybird, playing badminton with some leathery old dude covered head to toe in curly gray fuzz.

I had never been to The Sunny Gourde before. I guess most people think that nudist colonies are a thing of the past, that nudism dissolved like an Alka-Seltzer in the warm, licentious waters of the 1970s. I only wish. Of course, like everything else these days, the word "nudist" has been replaced with a euphemism: "naturist."

I had tried to goad Gabby into meeting me in town, at a diner or something, but she wouldn't budge. Fine. But I wasn't going to give her the satisfaction of watching me squirm, of bestowing her patronizing grin of derision or her cool flutter of her eyelids that shouted "Squaresville."

There's a Peter Sellers movie called *A Shot in the Dark*, in which buff young people frolic amid limpid swimmin' holes while a naked twangy combo riffs sleazy jazz. I didn't really think The Sunny Gourde would be that way, though I hoped it would be. Elke Sommer in her birthday suit? Bring it on.

One thing that was true to the movie was that I would not be admitted as a guest unless I, too, disrobed. At least Peter Sellers had a guitar to hide behind—I only got a towel, and the stated purpose was that it was for sitting upon. But I'd only be drawing more attention to myself if I wore the towel, or made any obvious effort to walk with it in front of me. No, I was going to do this chin up. I reminded myself of all the horrible situations I'd survived over the last five or six years: hand grenades, gunplay, kidnapping, homicidal freaks, and even poison arrows. Once you've sampled that black pie, airing out your birthday suit in front of a few strangers was only so much meringue. Or so I tried to remind myself.

The premise that the nude human form is beautiful is such a fallacy to me that I don't even know where to begin. Without sexual ardor, real-life buff is devoid of the airbrush's sympathies and the camera's naughty wink, despite what Hef would have you dream.

Adonis and I, alas, are cut from different stone. I had your standard issue love handles, perhaps a slight spare tire, but no belly, and I do have a fair upper body. Girls used to tell me I had a nice butt, and I was convinced I still did, though I hadn't made a point of checking the caboose recently. As soon as I stepped out into the open air of the grounds, though, I was quickly reassured—and more than a little mortified. There wasn't anybody within eyeshot who was under sixty-five, so I became Adonis by default.

Unlike walking around on the beach in trunks, or the bedroom *jaked as a naybird*, there is something decidedly odd about having the Travelin' Man and his luggage exposed to the afternoon breeze. I felt vulnerable to the elements. I mean, what if a bee or a fly went for my Travelin' Man? My wayfarer was used to being ensconced in the ship's better quarters, not out on deck like a vagabond. Although, to my surprise, he didn't seem alarmed enough to run for cover. In fact, he seemed downright curious of his surroundings. Not excited, just curious.

I spotted Gabby right away, the silhouette of that proud jaw and slightly Roman nose undaunted by age. Her long, yellowing white hair hung in twin braids down the hunch of her back. She was shrinking, the way old people do, slowly curling up like a fiddlehead. I tried to stay focused on her basic form, her face and motion, rather than the particulars. Rubenesque is one thing, but rumpled is another. And besides, isn't it written somewhere that after the age of five a son isn't obliged to see his mom naked—ever, ever again?

I kept my eyes straight ahead, acting casual, resisting a peek down to make sure bees hadn't beset my Ricky Nelson. In my peripheral vision, I could see people by the pool glancing my way: my farmer's tan and fish-belly shorts gave me away as a guest. *Hand grenades, gunplay, kidnapping, homicidal freaks . . .*

The furry dude playing opposite my mom glanced in my direction, and Gabby took that opportunity to spike the birdie.

"Point, game, and match, Chester! You owe me five bucks."

He made a sour face at her, then looked back to me, indignant that I had distracted him. I could see him checking out my tan lines, and I managed not to make a self-conscious inspection of Ricky. I just gripped my towel a little harder.

Gabby turned toward me as if she'd known I was there the whole time. Chester stalked off in disgust.

"Garth! You're next. I'll play you for five bucks."

"How are you, Gabby?" I tried to smile. Damn, this was like one of those dreams. A very unhealthy one. If only I'd wake up in my pajamas, if only.

"Tell you what, I'll spot you three points."

As I drew near, my mother stepped up and pulled me down for a kiss. Then a hug.

I didn't think it could get more awkward. But it had. Out of respect for Gabby, I won't elaborate, except to say that Ricky fled the deck for his cabin.

I held her at arm's length, where I could make eye contact. "Can we sit somewhere and talk?"

Her gray eyes scanned mine. Was she looking for embarrassment? Shock? Or was she taking stock of my resolve? I remember thinking how incredibly unsentimental she was. Had always been.

She held her ground. "You look good, Garth. Angie taking care of you?"

"We take care of each other and ourselves." I cursed myself, but the line was reflexive. It was what she used to say about our family. A mother is a powerful subliminal force, nudist or not.

She smiled at my response, the twinkle of appreciation in her eye. Those teeth that used to be so white and straight now looked overly large and ochre. I noticed then that she wasn't altogether steady, that there was a slight tremble in her body. Not a shiver but tired bones.

She turned and ambled toward the pool. I followed, taking an interest in the blue skies and indigenous trees.

We finally reached poolside—seemed like an eternity—put our towels down, and sat at a green plastic patio table.

"It is good to see you again, Garth." Some warmth came into Gabby's eyes. "You know, your father would have liked to see the man you've become. Strong, healthy..."

"Nicholas is back. And in New York."

Her eyes gained new warmth.

"How marvelous!"

I hadn't been sure how she'd take that news as she'd been more or less happy to see Nicholas go after what happened with Dad.

"How is he? What does he do? Still working on becoming a Rockefeller?"

"Insurance investigator."

"A what?"

"Private insurance investigator."

She frowned, confused by this ambiguous job description.

"Is he happy?"

"Getting that way, I think. He comes to dinner at our place on Sundays. Mostly."

"Sunday dinner?" Gabby looked exasperated. "Good God, Garth. Hard to believe two boys of mine could turn out to be so bourgeois."

"Gabby, we were always like that, remember?"

She looked off toward the pool. I could actively see her trying not to remember. Nostaglia wasn't her bag.

"You know, I could just as well say, Gabby, that it's hard to believe I'm talking to my mother in a nudist camp."

"*Naturist retreat.* The body is not something to hide, Garth, but something to celebrate. It's unhealthy to consider the naked body just as an instrument for sex. If not for your father, I would have raised both you boys the naturist way."

"Your pagan festivals didn't take, so what makes you think we'd have stayed naked when you were working at the library?"

She raised her chin and closed her eyes, and I could see her dismissing the memories again. Slowly opening her eyes, she said, "So, what brings you to Michigan?"

"I was in Cleveland, and I'm on my way to Chicago."

"Why?"

"I'm appraising collections of taxidermy."

She nodded, clearly uninterested in the answer— she was trying to segue into her next question. "And why after all these years have you braved exposing your body to come see Gabby? Hmm?"

Taking a deep breath, I said, "I came to invite you to a wedding."

Gabby opened her mouth to speak but then rolled her eyes instead.

"Nicholas's wedding."

Like a dog intent on a squirrel, Gabby cocked her head and looked intently into my eyes.

"A handfasting? To whom?"

"Does it matter?" I knew I shouldn't say what came out of my mouth next, but I was frustrated by her imperiousness and wanted to take her down a peg: "She's not a nudist, if that's what you're wondering."

Color came into her cheeks. "Don't you dare insult me, Garth."

I looked away, and saw that the people lounging on the other side of the pool had turned to see what was brewing on our side. "I'm sorry."

"No, you're not." She struggled up out of her chair. I could see by her crooked fingers that her hands were wracked by arthritis. "You don't approve of being skyclad? Well, it's not for you to approve. This is my life. You and Nicholas go off and lead yours, how's that?"

"Gabby, I said I'm sorry."

"Yes, you are sorry. Insurance! You boys are both pathetic." She waved a hand at me, turned, and started for the pool cabana.

OK, I did feel guilty, but only a little bit. Nobody

likes to disappoint a mother. But when you grow up a constant disappointment, you eventually become desensitized. Well, some people never do—but I had. I'd warned Nicholas that this wasn't going to work.

"Nicholas asked me to come." I made a last plea to my mother's retreating back. "He wanted me to invite you. He wants you there."

All I got was another dismissive wave.

What was a son to do?

chapter 6

So despite Angie's and Otto's entreaties, I wasn't what you'd call predisposed to return Gabby's call. The hell with her. What I couldn't quite figure out was why Nicholas wanted her at the handfasting...I mean, wedding. I'd tried to get it out of him, but he kept saying that it was the bride-to-be's idea. I suspected, somehow, there was some other motive behind this invitation.

After Colonel Dr. Lanston's brief grilling, I was excused from the FBI's meeting somewhat summarily. Here I thought I'd been brought to Seattle just to offer expert opinion about trophy collections. But no dice. I turned out to be as much a part of the problem as the solution. Head Coach apologized for taking me out of the game, but he hoped I'd understand that they had things to discuss that were confidential.

Needless to say my mood was uneasy. Like an ant in a room full of aardvarks.

I didn't like the way Lanston was focusing on me. She was playing I Have a Secret.

I didn't like the killer killing my clients. Somehow it made it seem like my fault.

I didn't like the killer calling me, having me discover the body. Unless he meant to kill me, there was no apparent reason to whisk me to Upper Crust, Illinois. He could have just not called and I would have sat in my hotel room until the next day and found out Sprunty was dead the way the rest of America did.

Something was going on. I didn't know what it was and I didn't want to know what it was. But something told me I was going to find out sooner or later, whether I liked it or not.

It was in that mood that I checked into my Seattle hotel room, which wasn't too far from the Space Needle. My room was clean but more or less a concrete cell dressed up to look like a hotel room. The headboard, the desk, and the TV were bolted to the walls. Last-minute travel arrangements had resulted in the subpar lodging. No feather bed. No minibar. No fresh flowers, fruit baskets, or home-baked cookies. None of the accoutrements I'd become accustomed to.

Just the sound of the highway outside my window. I was homesick, and called Stella.

"Can I go home?"

"Stay put. We want you to follow this investigation. The meeting: what happened?"

My heart sank, and my stomach cramped. "Look, Stella, I've been on the road for almost two weeks. I want to go home."

I heard her take a deep drag on a cigarette. "I will not whine. Say it."

"I'm not whining! Can't I miss my home? My girl?"

"Say it."

I groaned. "I will not whine."

"Better." I heard Stella exhale. "But no groaning, either."

"So, how long does it look like I'll have to stay in Seattle? I'm best man at Nicholas's wedding next week—I have to be back in New York by then."

"The meeting?"

I recapped.

When I finished, there was a pause on the other end, and I could hear Stella's cigarette tapping nervously at an ashtray. "Let me call the Feds and see if I can find out what's going on. I'll call you back."

"How about I call you back? I want to go for a walk and clear my head. This room is like a cell."

"One hour." She hung up.

I took off my tie, grabbed my key card, and headed for the elevators.

I set about the futile task of reassuring myself. What was there to worry about? I hadn't done anything. The FBI was all over this. So what if this serial killer knew who I was? I knew he knew, the FBI knew he knew, he probably knew I knew. It wouldn't make sense for him to make any kind of contact with me again. And if he did, he'd surely be caught.

And yet, I always had a sense for when things were about to get worse before they got better. It was sort of like lower back pain. It starts small, just warning twinges. So you stretch, you pop over-the-counter drugs, but you stop short of using a heating pad, or getting a massage, or taking the extra measures to avoid a major spasm. Instead, you try to ignore it, hoping it'll just go away. Then you sit up in bed one morning and it goes *sproing*. Next thing you know you're in a world of pain, a chiropractor is feeling up your back and saying, "You should do yoga." And as often as this may happen, as often as you see it coming, you seem incapable of heading off the *sproing*.

So how was I going to get out of this situation? I could see trouble coming from a mile away, and I was determined to avoid yoga.

Along the way to the elevators, I toured the room service trays lying on the floor next to various rooms. You could divine a great deal about a room's occupant by the remnants of their meals.

One had lipstick on the coffee cup, an uneaten grapefruit, and an empty pastry basket with the napkin carefully tucked in it: a woman who ordered the grapefruit as part of her diet, but with nobody around gulped down the sticky buns instead.

One had a bare greasy plate, numerous empty jelly containers, an empty aspirin pouch, and spilled coffee. The napkin had shave cream on it. Clearly,

Watson, here was an overweight businessman who'd drunk his fill last night.

The last one had scrambled eggs with only one corner missing, a sausage with one end gone, two empty boxes of Fruit Loops, and an empty glass of milk: Elementary: your basic sugar-hooked tike.

Would that my situation were as easy to fathom as the mysterious leftovers.

Was it too soon to get a lawyer? I watched the elevator numbers tick by toward the ground floor. I mean, the FBI couldn't keep me in Seattle. They had a branch in New York, for Pete's sake, and they could always reach me if they wanted to interrogate me further. And Stella? I just had to get tough with her. My temerity was mainly the result of not being used to being an employee of anyone other than myself.

At the lobby I snagged a map of Seattle from a display next to the front desk and went out the front doors. A herd of German tourists were milling about a tour van out front, whispering excitedly in their native tongue. There's something about the German language that sounds decidedly conspiratorial when whispered. Or perhaps I've just been subjected to a few too many WWII flicks. They were looking in the direction of an older man in a dark beret, tribal print shirt, and round sunglasses. He was reading the paper on a bench next to the hotel entrance. I guess they were scrutinizing the local fauna, *Americanus funkinae*. I'd seen foreign tourists do the same thing in New York, ogling a homeboy with the crotch of his pants hemmed an inch from the sidewalk and his boxer shorts up to his nipples. Made me homesick, believe it or not.

But there I was, a tourist in Seattle. I didn't have to consult the map to see where the Space Needle was—I just turned the corner and looked uphill.

'Twas yet another fine, sunny, warm day, completely counter to the rain and gloom we Easterners have come to expect from the Northwest. And it was just the kind of weather that's really annoying when the monkey of impending doom is on your back. First person who said "What a marvelous day!" was asking for a punch in the nose.

But I did feel better now that I was outside. After making my way steadily uphill through a patchwork of commercial and residential neighborhoods, the Space Needle towered just ahead, beyond a park. Somehow the massive sixties spire (or was it really a UFO launchpad?) didn't look as big as it had at the bottom of the hill. It was no different than approaching the Empire State Building or Statue of Liberty, I guess. In the park ahead I could see four sculptures that looked like jetsam from the "UFO," black and orange painted metal space junk, no doubt: warped warp drives, discarded dilithium crystal containment chambers, phase modulators stripped for parts. I crossed Broad Street and treaded the footpath leading through the debris toward the base of the Needle.

I wondered whether I should call Nicholas. He might have a useful perspective on my dilemma.

Whether I would take his advice was another matter. Some small part of me wanted to blame him for my predicament. Yet I knew that in the long run he'd done me a good turn by getting me into this line of work. How could he have predicted that a serial killer targeting taxidermy collectors would surface? Another part of me—like any older brother—was reluctant to turn to my little brother for help. He was, after all, my little brother, even if he was vastly more experienced in matters of crime. That aside, I was kind of keen to take another crack at cajoling him about why he wanted Gabby at the wedding.

Of course I still hadn't called Angie back, and was reluctant to do so until I had some idea of when I was coming home. And as usual, I didn't want her to worry. But maybe there was nothing to worry about. Maybe.

What was really irking me the most was the possibility that the killer knew who I was and had wanted me to find Sprunty. Could it have been that I wasn't killed because I wasn't a big-game hunter? Kit Carson, yes—but not me. But then why get me involved at all? Was he intentionally using my client list to line up his victims? If so, then the killer was privy to Wilberforce/Peete's files, or somehow knew my itinerary. But why even use my client list? If this psycho wanted to find trophy hunters for victims, he could just search the Web or thumb through a few hunting magazines.

Near the end of the curving path, I stopped in front of one of the sculptures, a large bronze square with a round portal flanked by a bronze cylinder and oblong, also with portals in them. A plaque informed me that this was something called MOON GATES. Hey, warp drives, wormholes, moon gates—I wasn't far off the mark.

That's when, like an alien empath, my sixth sense went off.

New Yorkers, while singularly directed in their movements on home turf, are also keenly aware of any suspicious characters: loafers in doorways, riffraff leaning on cars avoiding eye contact, feckless amblers in one's wake. In my peripheral vision I got a gander of *Americanus funkinae* in his beret and sunglasses, dawdling his way up the path behind me.

I was being followed by an aging beatnik. All the way from the hotel. Maybe not so unusual in New York to have someone walk the dozen or so blocks, but in West Coast terms that was like a trek up Kilimanjaro.

Was he FBI? Police? Or...

I resumed my march toward the base of the Needle close at hand, my eyes scanning for recourse. Ahead, in a plaza area around the base of the Space Needle, a bunch of folks in shorts, T-shirts, and windbreakers were gathered. They stared openmouthed up at the UFO. East or west, tourists look the same.

If Funky had wanted to catch up to me, he could

have, but he would have had to pick up his pace at least to a trot. My walking pace is more of a stride, and when I walk with Angie I have to shift from third to second gear. I was pretty confident that our surroundings were too public for the beatnik to try anything nefarious, but just the same I felt more comfy swimming in a school with those tourists at the visitors' center.

By the time I reached the base of the Space Needle, my fellow fishies had already gone inside and were buying tickets for the ride to the top. There were a few rent-a-cops inside, too, but their presence was only marginally reassuring. I'd seen a few too many Hitchcock films to feel comfortable ascending to the Mother Ship with Funky in tow. Next thing you know, I'd be up there dangling from the edge of the saucer, Funky playing Little Piggy Went to Market with my fingers.

With a quick glance over my shoulder I saw Funky approaching in a casual slouch, a poorly disguised grin on his face.

So, I did what I'd do in New York. Confront them before they confront you. Puts them off balance. There was a rack of tourista pamphlets nearby. I took one and wheeled toward Funky.

"Here, take one."

He chuckled as he came to a stop in front of me. I guessed him to be in his sixties. His face was all rubbery with deep folds bracketing a grin full of the tiniest, whitest teeth I'd ever seen. He turned his sunglasses from side to side, checking our perimeter. A veiny hand with exceptionally long fingers gingerly took the pamphlet from my hand.

"*Namaste!*" he hissed, and then waved the pamphlet like he was painting a question mark in the air.

I was this far from kicking him in the shin and taking off across the plaza. Hey, not exactly kung fu, but my method takes a lot less practice than spending all my off hours with a Shaolin priest, trying to snatch pebbles from his hand.

But the beatnik had said "*namaste,*" which, from random encounters with New York hipsters, I recognized as some sort of Hindu greeting. Something akin to saying "peace."

"What do you want, anyway?"

He dropped his jaw in mock surprise.

"What do I want?" He chortled mirthlessly. "I want what you want, Mr. Carson."

"Cute." I flashed him a smile that was mostly grimace. "Just tell me who you are and what you want and then leave me alone."

A family of forty or so rounded the base of the Needle at that moment, the kids surging ahead and attacking the rack of pamphlets like piranhas on a roast beef. They were swarming all around us. But Funky kept his round black sunglasses trained on me, unfazed by the sudden commotion.

"You don't know who I am?"

I sighed. "If I did, would I ask?"

His lower lip pouted a second, then with an air of conspiracy, he leaned in and intoned: "J. C. Fowler."

I squinted at him. All at once, he seemed somehow familiar. It wasn't so much his looks as his manner, at once casual and caustic, sweet and sour, kung pao chicken with extra nuts.

Fowler: now why did that ring a bell?

"Nothing?" He frowned.

"Look, J. C. Fowler, whatever it is that's bothering you..." Saying the name out loud connected a circuit in my brain. "Hey! You're the archeology guy, from that public television show..." I snapped my fingers. *"Ancient Times."*

A smile bounced onto his face and he clapped his hands. His head rolled back and he loosed a coyote howl that sent the family of forty scrambling.

For the uninitiated, J. C. Fowler was a TV personality from the sixties and seventies whose previously straightlaced image was tarnished when he took a "spiritual bent." I couldn't recall the details, but he'd been on a dig somewhere when he more or less lost his mind and went the way of Timothy Leary. Respected front man for science one moment, wild spiritualist who used "all his senses" (and probably no little amount of LSD) the next. In some circles, it had earned him a place as a countercultural hero, and he kept making low-budget documentaries on his own about things like spiritual liftoffs at the pyramids and awakenings at Machu Picchu. The IRS had swooped in on him, taken all his assets, and tossed him in jail for a while for tax evasion. As I recalled, his last documentary, after he got out of prison, had been an apocalyptic ramble about some ancient Native American archeological site that, according to Fowler, the government was preventing him from further investigating. So Fowler was an erstwhile Erich von Däniken with crazy rants about ancient civilizations and UFOs. He was a kook and a has-been. I'd assumed he was long dead.

Hardly. I had to wait about a dozen toe taps for him to stop his Count Floyd impression. When he ceased howling, he was flush from the exertion, and he broke into a coughing fit that I thought might just turn the old dude inside out.

"Look, it's nice to meet you, Fowler, really . . . You need a drink of water or something?"

He waved me off as he sank down to his knees, hacking. I turned away and pushed through the glass doors into the Space Needle visitors' center. The guards had already noticed Fowler, and one of them was pointing.

"Your friend need an ambulance?"

"More like a psychiatrist. He's not my friend, just some nut."

Fowler burst through the doors, his face gaunt and sweaty, and grabbed my arm.

"Don't talk to them, Garth! They're the enemy! Let's go!"

I allowed myself to be dragged back outside, but once there, I dug my heels in.

"Fowler, what could you possibly want with me?"

His rubbery cheeks vibrated with anticipation, and he started making grunting sounds. The Porkie imitation seemed involuntary, like he had Tourette's or something.

"I'm a javelina"—grunt grunt grunt—"I'm here to help you turn away the coyotes"—grunt grunt grunt—"and *El Viajero* of the Tupelca."

I started back toward the glass doors. There's an aggressive pig-like critter native to the Southwest and Mexico called a javelina. If Fowler was a javelina, it was only in his mind. "I think you need a doctor, Fowler. Just calm down…"

"How can I calm down when the killer of the white geckos is out there?" Grunt grunt grunt. "We need to put your vuka back in its rightful place."

I turned back around to face him. "How the…" Sprunty's death—and my involvement—had been splashed all over the tabloids. But to my knowledge the press hadn't picked up on the white geckos. Yet.

"Look, Fowler. I don't know what you're talking about. I am not the police, or the FBI. I don't look for bad guys, I avoid them. I'm sure you're a nice person, but I don't want anything to do with you, either. Do you understand?"

"But I have the key to set the vuka free!" From around his neck, Fowler held forth a leather cord, at the end of which hung a very old metal disc about two inches in diameter. Engraved on the disc were the outlines of five geckos, nose to tail in a circle. Two of the forms seemed to be filled in with white glass.

I recoiled from it.

"I was on a dig, before the government stopped me, and I found this." His grunting had ceased, but now he was hissing. "I had a dream about five white geckos, and this is the key! We're in the time of the white gecko, we have to act now!" He suddenly crouched, like some kind of snake ready to strike, and began waving a hand in the air.

First a coyote, then a pig, and now a snake. How many whoopie pills he'd recently ingested I could only imagine. The guards inside were scowling, probably wondering if they needed to intervene. I did nothing to dissuade them.

One of the rent-a-cops sauntered outside with his thumb in his gun belt.

"You OK, mister?" He said this to me while scrutinizing Fowler.

"I'll be OK as long as this nut stays away from me." I didn't like Fowler's metal disc, and I didn't like him.

Fowler suddenly straightened out of his snake pose and, with a flourish of his hand, painted a question mark in the air. *"Namaste!"* Then he turned on his heel and marched off toward the space junk, pretty as you please.

"We sure do get 'em." The cop scratched the back of his neck, but pointed with his elbow. "The bonko boys like him, that is. Think maybe I should call this guy in. Can't be too careful these days."

Watching Fowler's retreat, I suddenly felt sorry for him. I don't know why. Perhaps it's always sad to see someone, anyone, fall from grace. Or lose his mind.

"Nah." I scrunched my nose at the cop—I was tempted to say it was a West Coast thing. Then again, we were a long way from Venice Beach or Oakland. "He's probably just some Canadian."

Just when I didn't think it could get any weirder, it had.

chapter 7

 found a pay phone.

"Brickface?"

There was silence at the other end, and I corrected myself. "Bricazzi?"

"Carson?"

"Yup. Hey, something weird just happened that I thought you should know about." I briefly filled him in on my encounter with J. C. Fowler.

"Hang on, Carson, let me put this on speaker." The sound quality changed from clear to slightly fuzzy. I heard Bricazzi murmur to whoever else was in the room, "Someone named Fowler made contact with Carson, about the murders."

"Carson? This is Lanston. Fill me in."

I told my story again. When I was done, Colonel Lanston said: "So you first saw him at your hotel?"

"Yup. I didn't recognize him until he told me who he was."

"You didn't recognize him?"

"I just said I didn't."

"Even though he knew your parents?"

"I told you I . . ." My brain did a backflip. "My parents?"

This was like playing poker with my back to a mirror: she could see my cards but I couldn't see hers. It took me a second to collect my thoughts.

"Colonel Lanston, you've obviously done your homework on me and my extended family, which is commendable under the circumstances. But you have me at a continued disadvantage, which is maybe where you want me. I knew nothing of my grandfather, and still don't, and now I know nothing about Fowler having known my parents, which, to tell you the truth, doesn't surprise me, necessarily."

"What's your point, Carson?"

"I think it might be more constructive, Lanston, if what you have on me and my family were made available to me so I could flag any connections to a possible killer. I mean, we can go on like this, with you trumping me with what I don't know at every turn, but I don't see where that gets us."

"You might have filled us in on Fowler, Colonel," Bricazzi said, not quite far enough under his breath. He sounded a mite miffed.

"Us, Carson?" Lanston sounded almost sarcastic. "Or you?"

Surrounded by hostile Sioux, Tonto says to the Lone Ranger: *What you mean "we," white man?*

"Are you trying to tell me I'm not part of the investigation? Or are you saying that I'm now a *target* of the investigation?"

After a pause, Bricazzi cut in. "The FBI is investigating this matter, and you're not FBI, so we can't share all of our intelligence with you. It's against policy."

"That's not an answer to my question."

"We appreciate your continuing cooperation, Carson." Lanston couldn't have made the comment sound more perfunctory.

"Am I a *suspect*?"

There was another silence on the other end, and through the hiss on the line I could almost see Bricazzi and Lanston exchange uncomfortable glances. I don't like being toyed with—it makes me feel foolish, and when someone makes me feel foolish, I get royally PO'd. I didn't wait for a reply.

"I'll take that as a yes. Which means you can direct all future inquiries to my attorney, Nico Benevito. He's in the book."

Never mind that Nico Benevito was my barber—I was hot under the collar and fanning my gun. I hung up, not just once, but several times, so hard that I almost broke the receiver.

To hell with being the FBI's ball of string, to hell with Stella, to hell with Fowler, to hell with Seattle.

At least I now knew why the killer had arranged to have me find Sprunty, and possibly why he was using my client list. To make me into a suspect. I was the patsy.

I cabbed back to my cell, crammed my stuff into my bags, grabbed my briefcase, and shot to the airport.

Destination? Ann Arbor.

possibly since the Pleistocene era. It wouldn't surprise me if the stroganoff were made from mastodon.

For the life of me, though, I can't figure out why anybody would want to lunch at a chain restaurant named Pickle Barrel. Today's specials are: pickles. I like a good cucumber soaked in brine and dill as much as the next guy, but to have chosen that as their namesake gives the wrong impression. Their tour de force is not pickles, in fact, but diner food, not too unlike the Greek places in New York. Perhaps the marketing department felt that pickle barrels—an old-timey touchstone redolent of Mr. Drucker's General Store and a game of checkers between slow-witted farmers—were synonymous with good food. The association seems mighty flimsy to me.

The menu at the Pickle Barrel was predictably brief and heavily laminated. I ordered the club sandwich and a coffee. Even the most ordinary restaurant on a bad day has a hard time screwing that up. And I needed the coffee. My trip hadn't been easy. I'd managed to bag a seat on standby to Cleveland, and from there had gone to the long-term lot to retrieve the Lincoln, where it was waiting to be shipped to New York. I pulled up to the Ann Arbor Arms Motor Court at exactly 2:00 A.M. I'd called Angie from the airport, got the machine, and left her a message about where I was headed. I'd also left a message for Stella, telling her the FBI said I was no longer needed as part of the investigation and would no longer be privy to how the case was proceeding. Which was true, more or less.

"Garth, I asked you to call—you didn't have to visit." At the risk of being unkind, Gabby looked much better in sweats than in the buff, and it was a relief to talk to her in more familiar surroundings. Her long white hair was out of the braids and fanned across her shoulders. She stirred her Cobb salad distractedly.

"You may have told Angie that you needed to speak with me, but I needed to see you. Something very odd is going on that I need to discuss. But you go first."

She raised her eyebrows in curiosity.

"Well, I read about your trouble in the newspaper, about that football player. I wanted to make sure you were all right..."

"Well, that has to do with why I'm here."

"And I wanted to say I was sorry for getting in a huff, and that I wished we'd spent more time together on your last visit, and that I'd be delighted to come to Nicholas's handfasting."

"I'm sorry, too, Gabby. I didn't mean to offend you. I admit I'm not comfortable with your naturist lifestyle. But I don't have to be. Nicholas will be delighted."

"Thank you, Garth." Gabby's pale eyes softened, and she patted my hand. "When is this happy event?"

"Next week, Saturday. I know it's short notice, but it came about suddenly." That wasn't exactly true.

Nicholas's desire to have her there was short notice. "You can stay with me and Angie."

"I have a friend at The Sunny Gourde, he's an airline pilot and can get me a cheap flight. Now..." Her eyes sparked. "What's so odd that you needed to come all the way here and take me to lunch? Hmm?"

"Well, part of the reason I needed to see you in person is that what I have to discuss with you is going to be something you don't want to discuss."

Gabby stiffened, but maintained her serene smile. "There's nothing I'm afraid to discuss, Garth, you should know that."

"It has to do with the past, with my grandfather on the Carson side."

Her posture remained alert, but I saw her eyes dull over, which meant that she was unhappy with the subject already. Knew she would be.

"But this is important, Mom." I only used the "M" word to signal Gabby that I was calling in a favor. "I'm a suspect in the murder of that football player, and there's some kind of tie to Dad's father, Julius 'Kit' Carson."

"Oh, how could that possibly be? He's been dead such a long time."

"And, maybe, to J. C. Fowler."

She shifted uncomfortably, and said to her salad: "This is silly, Garth. Who thinks you're a murderer?"

"The FBI thinks I may have killed that football player in Chicago, and another man in Texas."

"Phooey! Did you tell them you didn't do it?"

"Yes, Gabby."

"And you didn't kill these people?"

"Of course not."

"Well, then they have to prove you did something you didn't, which in the end will make them look pretty silly."

"C'mon, Gabby, you know better than that. It's the FBI. If nothing else, they can make my life miserable until they find the real guy. Look, some nut out there has killed two of my clients with their own taxidermy. And with the football player, the killer called me himself pretending to be the client and drew me out there to discover the body. He's trying to make it look like I'm committing these murders, to make me the common link. And somehow and for some reason, I am the common link. There's been some suggestion that it has to do with our family history. For example, J. C. Fowler tracked me down, wanted me to help him find this killer, and when I told the FBI, they threw in my face the fact that you and Dad knew him."

"Fowler is a goofball. Don't pay any attention to him. Him and that crazy javelina fraternal order he was always pestering your father about. Honestly."

"Yeah, he was on about javelinas when I met him. Well, he somehow got wind of these serial killings. People like him around is the last thing I need. So will you help me here? I need to know more about the Julius Carson character, my grandfather."

"There's no dark secret, Garth." Her eyes were

still trained on her salad. "You know your grandfather on that side was a big-game hunter. Where else did all that taxidermy come from?"

"You can do better than that, Gabby. Where did he live? When did he die? Did he have a job?"

"I only know what little your father told me." She sighed like I was wasting both our time. "He was an outfitter in Wyoming, ran his own camp. He became famous for having killed a mountain lion with only a knife. Lost an eye in the battle. He went to Africa, where he rubbed elbows with well-heeled hunters and made a lot of money. That was just after World War I, I think, when he married. Your grandmother died from influenza when your father was a baby. Your father was an only child and grew up mainly in boarding schools here in the States. His father married again and was off killing animals on the other side of the planet."

"When did Kit Carson die?"

"Garth, I really don't know. I don't see how any of this could have any bearing on your troubles. Really. The very idea."

"So how do you know Fowler?"

"He was a friend of your father's from childhood. His life is public record, so I'm sure you could find much more at the library than I could ever tell you. Years later, as I said, he became mixed up with some fraternal order when he was researching a documentary topic, and was always pestering your father about it. He was such a nuisance we had to tell him to go away and leave us alone."

I considered my next question carefully, but decided it couldn't hurt to divulge the detail to Gabby.

"Does a gecko mean anything to you?"

Her eyes met mine. "It's a lizard, if I'm not mistaken."

"A white gecko."

She sighed. "Honestly, Garth, you were always such the serious one. Well, both you boys were. I don't know where you two got it, I really don't."

I waited.

"A white gecko?" Gabby repeated the words incredulously. "What's that have to do with anything? Do you take supplements?"

"Vitamins? I take one of those all-in-one pills."

"Those are garbage, I'd think you'd know that. You have health food stores in New York. Get yourself some arrowroot."

"So a white gecko means nothing to you?"

She gazed to the left, out the window to the parking lot. "It's a sign, Garth."

I knew that—the killer was leaving his calling card. And that the critters turned white every hundred years. And that the Native Americans thought they were special. But I knew the sign Gabby was talking about had to do with her paganist beliefs. I waited for more.

"The white gecko is an ancient symbol of five evil spirits of the earth that must never be united." Her eyes were clear and bright. "That's what Fowler was on about all those years ago. Stay away from him, Garth."

"He said he wanted to help me—something about a fuka."

"A *vuka*, yes."

"And a vuka is..."

"Fowler thinks you're possessed with this spirit called a vuka."

I sat there with my mouth open a minute as Gabby nodded solemnly.

"How so?"

"I don't entirely understand it myself. My sense was that he didn't so much want to exorcize the spirit as to capture it. But we had to put a spell on Fowler to make him stay away." She said this rather wistfully.

I found my mouth hanging open again. "A spell?"

"Mm hmm."

"A *spell*?" I knew she was pretty out there with the paganist stuff, but this was the first I'd ever heard of her practicing witchcraft. "What kind of spell?"

She straightened in her chair, and I could see she was about to clam up on me.

"Come on, let's have it."

"Just something simple."

"Uh huh, like?"

"If he ever came near our family, he would lose his human form and take another."

"Another? Another what?"

"Animal."

My mouth was hanging open again.

"You turned Fowler into a *werewolf*?"

A conversation three tables down came to a sudden stop.

"A lycanthrope, not a werewolf. They turn into all kinds of animals." She rolled her eyes like I was overreacting. "Our garden was planted with plenty of aconitum. Wolfsbane. Such nice blue flowers. The red admiral butterflies liked it, too."

It's a sad day when you realize your mother is not only insane, but certifiable. Sadder was that not only did she believe she blinked Fowler into a werewolf, but apparently so did he. Unless Fowler's coyote, pig, and snake routines back there at the Space Needle had some other explanation.

After dropping Gabby back at The Sunny Gourde, I stopped at a filling station to make a few calls.

First: Stella. I felt guilty about cutting and running. I knew she wouldn't find the short message I left her an acceptable excuse for getting the hell out of Dodge.

"So." That's all she said when she picked up.

"Sorry, Stella, but I can't do what you want me to do. It's not whining, it's not groaning. I can appraise for you, but I can't be a hockey puck for the Air Force and FBI."

"OK, Garth. So where have you been?"

"Pretty simple, really. I went to Ann Arbor to ask

my mom about my grandfather. That Colonel Lanston seemed to think my grandfather was the link to why the serial killer has involved me in this. And then I ran into this kook named Fowler at the Space Needle. He seemed to think I could help him find the killer."

"Who?" I heard her lighting up, and could picture her pale face in a cloud of cigarette smoke grimacing with confusion.

"An old relic named Fowler. Colonel Lanston knew about him for some reason. That he knew my parents. And now she and the FBI seem to think I'm a suspect."

"Not J. C. Fowler."

"One and the same." I paused. "Don't tell me you know about his connection to this?"

"Know?"

"You said his name like you already had some idea he was involved."

"He's your uncle."

"Howzat?"

"He's your grandfather Kit Carson's son. Your father's brother. That makes him your uncle. And he's a dangerous lunatic. A clinical lycanthrope."

"Oh, come on. Why wouldn't my mother have told me Fowler was my uncle? This is absurd."

"Fowler's connection to this is more complicated than you know. Are you still in Ann Arbor?"

I paused again.

"I think I'd better not say."

"Look, Garth, you better get back to New York. Wilberforce/Peete can protect you. We have lawyers, expensive ones."

"Protect me from whom? Lanston? Fowler?"

"Garth, I know you're confused..."

"How do I know the FBI, the Air Force, and perhaps Wilberforce/Peete won't use me as bait to find the killer? That's what was going to happen to the other people I did appraisals for—am I right? Or would it be more convenient to just hang the murders on me?"

"Well, who are you going to trust, Garth? Your brother? Ha!"

She was right. The only one I could trust was Nicholas. But I wasn't going to tell her that.

"I'm hanging up now, Stella. You can fire me or whatever. Because no matter what, I'm not going to let all you people make your problems mine."

I clacked the receiver back into its cradle with no little satisfaction. I felt quite proud of myself. This was the right thing to do; I had absolutely no doubt of it. I was not going to let the Air Force, the FBI, and Wilberforce/Peete thread me on a hook like a worm.

I dialed again, this time to home. Otto picked up.

"Alo. This Garv Carson Critters. Please, tell to me if help."

"I miss you, too, Otto. Put Angie on."

"My Got, Garv! Must come home before soon!

Very, very important to come before soon. KGB vas here..."

"KGB?" That was Otto's word for bad guys or the police, which on occasion had been both.

I heard the phone change hands.

"Garth?"

"Nicholas?"

"Do exactly what I say and don't ask any questions. Get away from where you are, as far as possible. You remember the bar where I last saw you?"

"What's going on? Where's Angie?"

"The bar. Do you remember?"

"Yes, the—"

"Don't say it! Just call me there in an hour. Stay off the interstate. And don't call back here."

The line went dead.

chapter 9

Next thing I knew I was in Hell. And like some people, both figuratively and literally, I found myself in Hell completely by accident. I took Nicholas's advice and left the highway, hoping to follow local roads instead, but I became all turned around when I rounded a bend and saw a huddle of wooden establishments painted red with flames and topped with billboard devils. Yes, I had accidentally found myself in Hell, Michigan.

I swung the Lincoln to a stop in front of the largest establishment. It was part café, part post office, part souvenir shop; the only other store was all souvenirs. Had I any need for satanic paraphernalia, I would have been well supplied by the merchants in Hell. Light-up horns, "devil made me do it" shot glasses, red tridents, you name it, it was all for sale here. All I needed was a pay phone, though, and I found one next to the café, an old-timey wooden booth outside the bathrooms marked HELLIM and HELLER.

"Gravy's Tavern," the bartender answered.

"Hi, Judy, it's Garth."

"Hey, Garth. Where are you?" I could hear the tinkle of glasses and ice in the background as she poured someone a drink.

"Um . . ." I looked up at the café's specials board: WELCOME TO HELL! FRIDAY NIGHT FISH FRY $6.95 ALL YOU CAN EAT. Nice that they observe Lent in Hell, and in June. "Just some town."

"You better get your butt back here in time for the wedding. We can't have a wedding without the best man."

"I'm working on it, Judy."

"Nice chatting. Here's Nicholas . . ."

"Garth: don't tell me where you are, can't be sure of this phone, either."

"You wouldn't believe me if I told you. So what the . . . heck is going on? Is Angie OK?"

"She's fine. But the FBI have her down at Federal Plaza, and they came to your apartment with a search warrant. They questioned me, too. And Otto."

"What the . . . heck? She has to leave for Chicago. Nicholas, what's going on?"

"You know a man named Bronte Jones?"

"Sure, the actor who had that TV private eye show *McGlaggart* in the seventies. Big-game hunter, lives outside Seattle. I appraised his collection a few months back. Uh-oh. Don't…don't tell me." My heart felt like it had been stabbed with a Popsicle.

"Reconjugate the verb 'to live.' He was run through the chest with an elk horn just before you left Seattle without saying good-bye."

"Why didn't Stella tell me that?" Why didn't Gabby tell me about Fowler being my uncle? Why was everyone keeping me in the dark? The frustration of my predicament was giving me prickly heat. "So, I guess now they think I killed TV's McGlaggart, too—is that it?"

"Bingo. Yet another person whose collection you appraised is dead.…*Stella?* Christ, you didn't tell Wilberforce/Peete where you are, did you?"

"I spoke to her just before I spoke to you last. I didn't tell her where I was. But she wanted me to come back to New York, said Wilberforce/Peete would protect me. I said I'd look after myself."

"Atta boy. There's good money to be made in appraising, but don't kid yourself—the insurers look out for themselves first and foremost. And Stella is sly, probably throw you to the wolves as soon as she could. You're a liability to them now. To the FBI, you're the common link. You not only were in town during each of the murders, you had entrance to the victims' homes. Now they only need a motive, and maybe a witness."

"How do I get into these things?" I massaged my forehead. "When the FBI questioned you, did they mention anything about our grandfather?"

"Yup. Didn't know what that was about. Do you?"

"No. And about Fowler?"

"Who?"

"J. C. Fowler. Just look him up, you'll remember. Seems he knew Gabby and Dad."

I held back on the Uncle Werewolf fantasy for the time being. The uncle part, well, I wanted to see if Nicholas's research came up with anything on that independently. If it was true, he should find it pretty quickly. And the werewolf part...well, that was just too nutty to repeat.

"I just finished seeing Mom again, trying to find out more. She didn't know much, just that Grandad was a famous big-game hunter and that Fowler was bothering Mom and Dad back when we were kids. Fowler somehow tracked me down, was babbling about coyotes and javelinas and spirits...Gabby seems to think Fowler believes I'm possessed with a demon of some sort. Just insane stuff, Nicholas. I'm hoping you can make some sense of it."

"Yes, Garth, how do you get mixed up in these things?" I heard Nicholas chuckle. "Let me have someone look into it. We're going to get you out of this, don't worry."

"You going to have Mel research it?" A cute brunette with an even cuter little daughter, Melanie was once his skip tracer—she could hack her way into anyone's past. Now she was his fiancée.

"She's pretty frazzled these days, what with the

wedding," Nicholas said, clearing his throat. "I have someone else in mind, at least for some of it."

"Nicholas, there's something else you need to know about the murders. Maybe you can dig something up on this. What's the significance of a white gecko?"

"A white gecko? You mean the lizard?"

"Yup, the lizard. Each of the previous victims was found with a dead white gecko. And these geckos only turn white every hundred years or so. The FBI wants to keep that a secret. Gabby said that five geckos together were some kind of bad mojo, and Fowler had a medallion with five white geckos on it around his neck and seems to think they're the key to all this."

"So, let me get this straight. You want me to research the connection between our grandfather, J. C. Fowler, the murder of three big-game hunters, and five white geckos?" He snorted. "Can I get you something else with that, sir? Fries? A shake?"

"I'm just giving you what I've got. But what do I do now, Nicholas? I can't come home."

"We have to get you to a safe house."

"Who am I: Machine Gun Kelly? I haven't done anything!"

"The FBI has an all-points out on you, buddy boy. If you get picked up, the local cops will lock you up until the FBI can get their hands on you, and then you'll be arraigned..."

"But I haven't done anything!" Now I was sounding like Gabby.

"Doesn't matter. They're convinced you're their man, and they'll want to put you under wraps until they get the goods on you. Your departure from Seattle was ill-timed. They think you flew the coop and they'll most likely be able to convince a judge that you're a flight risk. So unless you want to spend a couple weeks in prison until they clear this up, I suggest you dig a hole and climb in. Don't use your credit card, or your cash card—they can track you with that."

"There's forty dollars in my wallet, and the Lincoln needs gas. Any idea how much it costs to fill her tank with premium? What am I supposed to do, sleep in the car, eat roots and berries? Exchange dirty underwear for bark?"

"I have a friend in your vicinity. He owes me. Got a pencil?"

"Sure, but is it safe to say it over the phone?"

"Remember the code? Frick Frack?"

"How could I forget," I said dryly. Frick Frack was a code system used on a kids' TV show we used to watch called *General Buster*. The show's host worked with puppets and was supposed to be some kind of heroic pilot living on a military base. He would relay coded messages to us kids during the show, which usually translated into something about brushing our teeth or washing our hands before meals. My memories of the show were fond but tarnished since, years later, General Buster had tried to kill me. No lie.

"Ready?" Nicholas cleared his throat. *"Fricka fracka, quacka fava, massa mat moot. Waza waxa pixa fassa laxa ipso croon."* I jotted down the number. If the song began with "Fricka fracka," it meant that what followed was a number, and if reversed meant that what followed was a series of words. And the words "ipso croon" always signified the end of the message, whether it was words or numbers. The code sounds terribly complex, and as an adult I'd have to go through rigorous training to learn it. But as kids we had a natural facility to absorb things like that. Maybe our brains had space in them that has since been taken up by sports scores and tabloid news.

Anyway, I doubted very seriously that the FBI's encryption department kept a file on General Buster's Frick Frack code. If they were listening in, at least they wouldn't get the phone number Nicholas had just recited.

We signed off and I stood to leave. Through the glass of the phone booth I could see the front entrance to the store.

I did a double take.

It couldn't be.

But it was.

Colonel Lanston was entering Hell, and she had two MPs in her wake.

chapter 10

Like the Amazing Collapsible Man, I melted down in the phone booth, out of sight.

Lanston was even more compact than I remembered. She was only about five feet tall and packed tightly into her uniform. Her gait was all business, arms straight at her sides, folding garrison cap under her epaulette, hands knotted into fists, and feet stepping like they were following orders. She looked like some military attaché from the Lollipop Guild.

By comparison, the two MPs were towering and lanky as scarecrows. But why was Lanston here—and why with MPs and not agents Brickface and Stucco? Which begged the question of why the Air Force was hounding me in the first place.

How Lanston had tailed me to that spot I had no idea—but one could imagine. Perhaps the local police had seen my car and plates and called them in. Maybe the Feds had put a tracking device in my luggage or on my car. It was the federal government. Weren't they capable of just about anything?

Of course, how they found me didn't matter now; how I was going to slip out of Hell did. It was dawning on me that there was no way to keep these people from making their crazy serial killer problems mine.

The idea of just staying in the booth and waiting for Lanston and the MPs to leave was an attractive idea. Except, of course, that my car was out front and they had to know I was around someplace. And if they asked the clerk if he'd seen me, a finger might well point toward the phone booth.

I had little choice but to get out of there, pronto. I snuck a look out of the booth's window and saw the backs of three uniforms trailing away from me toward the far end of the shop.

Crouching again, I slid the door open and started to crouch-waddle into the men's room like some gnarled elf. But the men's room would be the second place they would look, so I veered into the women's room instead.

Thankfully, it was vacant.

I locked the door. Figured I'd better take a quick whiz while I was in there. Panic had reached my bladder.

Now what? I stood in front of the bowl, looking around. The only window was small and had bars on it. Right: a common place of forced entry after hours, even way out in Hell. But I couldn't stay in the women's room, either. Eventually, Lanston would check there, too. Either that or some Heller who needed to use the head would contact management when she couldn't gain access. Maybe I could pry the bars off the window.

I zipped up and almost flushed, then thought better of it. Quiet.

The absurdity of my situation bounced around inside my head as I paced. Here I was like a trapped animal, like a tiger in a pit. I recalled a story one old-time big-game hunter had told me about tiger hunting. This guy had the stereotypical overly elaborate mustache and was a veritable Commander McBragg. According to this blowhard, it was common, back when, to merely dig a pit for the tiger to fall into when he pounced on a dead goat used as bait. All the hunter had to do was sit in a tree and wait, then shoot the tiger once it fell in the pit.

Here I was, a tiger in a pit. A fish in a barrel. A frog in a puddle.

I'd asked McBragg what would happen if the tiger saw the hunter in the tree before it fell in the pit. Wouldn't it be scared off? Or attack him?

I could still smell the scotch on his breath and see the tobacco stains on his white mustache when McBragg leaned in close with a confiding and sapient air: "A tiger never looks up."

So I looked up.

Just the ceiling. And a hatch.

I silently thanked McBragg for this crumb of hope.

Much like hatches in the roofs of New York apartment buildings, this hatch was simply a lid to a square portal. Two buckle-like hasps held it in place. No locks.

Standing on the small sink, I could just barely reach the hasps to unbuckle them. But I wasn't high enough to lift the hatch itself.

Moments later I found myself precariously balanced atop a metal wastebasket atop the sink, pushing on the hatch. Then shoving.

The hatch gave suddenly, the springs on the hinge opening it wide to the sky.

That's when the trash can popped out from under my feet, clattering to the floor.

I was dangling from the rim of the hatch by one hand, gasping with surprise and frustration. My left foot found the faucet, and I pushed off with enough force to get my other hand to join the one on the lip of the hatch.

That's when the entire sink came off the wall, crashing to the floor in a geyser of water.

So there I was dangling by two hands, a gusher of water drenching me, my feet kicking in midair, as I attempted to do my first chin-up in twenty-five years.

Vainly, I prayed that nobody had heard the ruckus. But how long before someone noticed the water gushing out from under the door?

I scrambled to get a toehold on the top of the

mirror, then straightened my leg, hooking one elbow over the edge of the hatchway before the mirror popped off the wall and smashed onto the floor with the sink and trash can.

Someone must have heard that.

But moments later I was standing on the roof, sopping wet in the hot June sun, with extremely sore armpits and wheezing like a leaky bagpipe. If this sort of episode were to keep recurring in my life, I was going to have to go into training. I know, the life of this particular taxidermy renter and appraiser must sound strenuous enough to have prepared me for the Marines, but such was not the case. I was ready to collapse from the exertion.

Pounding echoed up from the bathroom door below—if I had a next move, now was the time to implement it. The roof had a very slight pitch, but was mostly a flat expanse of tar paper with a few drain risers and exhausts poking out of it. I trotted to the roof's edge and looked down at the parking lot.

An Air Force sedan was parked next to the Lincoln, which was backed into a spot directly below me, top down.

Colonel Lanston was talking on her cell phone while she paced between the two vehicles. The MPs were standing, arms folded, to one side. All they had to do was look up thirty degrees and they'd spot me. I held my breath, my lungs protesting.

The tiger never looks up. In this case, I sure hoped not.

"What do you mean Gibraltar is sending someone

in?" Lanston stopped her pacing long enough to stomp her foot. "I have this under control. Carson is here somewhere."

Gibraltar? What was that, some secret organization like SMERSH, THRUSH, or SPECTRE? Were they sending in a contract killer to bump me off?

"I'll find Fowler." She punctuated her remarks with a wave of a clenched fist. "I said I'll find him—that nut has been a thorn in my side long enough.... Yes, I think I have the FBI taken care of.... Well, who is it they're sending? An independent? Why can't they tell me?...Look, I've kept this bottled up for thirty years. I think I can keep a lid on these jerks for four more days. Hold on." She turned to one of her goons. "What's all the hubbub in there?"

He shrugged, and she finished her call. "Gotta go."

The three of them trotted back into the store to investigate the growing clamor.

I exhaled like a whooping crane with asthma. *Oxygen, sweet oxygen.*

The distance to the hood of the Lincoln's trunk looked to be about ten feet. Landing on it would likely put a major dent in the trunk, something I'd already had fixed the last time I was in trouble. And I'd just had all the bodywork done and a new paint job. I hated to do it, but...

Time to play stuntman; cue *The Six Million Dollar Man* zither.

I jumped, landing on the trunk, knees bent, judges about to flash me a perfect ten. But the hood and the rear shocks gave as I thumped down. I tried to maintain my balance but tipped forward as the shocks sprang back up. I launched like an acrobat off a teeterboard right into the red leather upholstery of the backseat. Headfirst.

With a squeak, my wet noggin wedged between the seats, my soggy scalp scrunching onto the rear floor mat.

Terrible dismount. Judges? *Five.*

No time to dally. In a mad scramble, I pulled my head from between the seats like a wet cork from a bottle. Clambering into the driver's seat, I juggled the keys from my pocket and cranked the Lincoln alive.

Of course, I wanted to make like the Batmobile and fishtail up the road, flames in my wake. But I had the presence of mind to drift as calmly as possible toward the exit. No sense drawing attention.

My eyes were trained on the rearview mirror—so intently that I didn't see the moving van coming around a bend as I exited the parking lot.

Booming air horns drew my attention to the impending collision.

Now, I might have applied the brakes and let the truck swerve around me. But driving a vintage powerhouse like the Lincoln gave me another option.

Under such circumstances, it's not enough to merely jam the accelerator forward. In the Lincoln, you needed to punch it and then bring your knee forward and pivot the accelerator pedal to the floor.

That's what puts the spurs to the V8 and transmission.

Gotta love a powerful old car—she paused a split second before the 460 roared gleefully to life, my tires screeching. All 340 whinnying horses bolted into full gallop. The truck skidded up close behind me, but the Lincoln lunged forward like Seattle Slew out of the gate and narrowly avoided a collision. The turbodrive transmission slammed into second, making the truck shrink harmlessly in my rearview mirror.

But I could see the moving van skid sideways—the truck's brakes must have locked up. I felt a *whump* and saw the van tip onto its side across the road.

So much for the nice quiet exit.

Now the problem was how the hell—literally, for a change—to get out of there? The roads into Hell had been so confusing I'd only gotten there by chance. I had intended to ask for directions back to the main secondary road.

My knees were trembling and my armpits ached, but I took the corners as fast as the Lincoln would allow, the tires complaining as we swayed this way and that along the little two-lane road. The canopy of trees raced away behind me as I kept an eye on the rearview mirror for the Air Force sedan.

But it never appeared.

Either the truck had blocked the road entirely so Lanston couldn't follow.

Or Gibraltar was taking over.

chapter 11

If you've never driven around the center of the country, it is quite remarkable how geography shapes land use. Ohio, Indiana, Illinois, and Michigan are largely a succession of red barns, silos, crops, Bob Evans restaurants, and an increasing number of cheese curd outlets. I didn't know what a cheese curd was, and wasn't sure I wanted to.

But almost as soon as you pass Omaha, *Green Acres* is replaced by *Bonanza*. Crops give way to cattle—twelve hours of cattle if you drive straight through to Denver. It is the wellspring of Big Macs. Unless you stray near the Great Lakes, that is, in which case you're likely to encounter oases of industry instead.

My destination was firmly in *Green Acres* territory as I meandered north into Michigan's Lower Peninsula, to a town with the unlikely name of Vargo. I had spoken with a man named Vargas. That's right, Vargas of Vargo. Once I told him Nicholas was calling in a favor, he became very quiet, and in a heavy Spanish accent gave me directions to my destination.

What kind of place was Nicholas sending me to? I dared not wonder. I was imagining a remote trailer park, or some Bates Motel look-alike. I only had a name: "Look for the sign that says SHELLY'S."

It was late in the day and I had been driving all night, taking back roads and hiding out. The setting sun an orange coal on the horizon, farmlands and white farmhouses glowing cerise on either side. Despite my predicament, I was enjoying the sizzling summer air rushing around me in the Lincoln, the convertible top down.

A stand of stalwart sycamores lined the top of the next rise; old trees were a certain indicator in that landscape that a house lay ahead. The only trees not cleared in farm country are those where crops aren't planted. Sure enough, built into the side of an embankment was a sprawling gray compound of wood structures with low, slanted roofs. Planted in the ground at the driveway entrance was a wagon wheel, and hanging from a post above it was the sign: SHELLY'S STREUSEL STOP.

I piloted the Lincoln down the drive and ground to a halt in a cloud of dust. *Streusel?* Or did they mean *strudel?* Whichever confection, it smelled like pies baking.

Well, of all the places I imagined for a safe house, a streusel stand was way down the list. For one, I'm not what you'd call a dessert person—I idly wondered whether the FBI dossier on me included that epicurean Garth factoid or not.

The screen door to the shop was surrounded by scattered antique agricultural hardware, like two-man saws, threshers, sod busters, and barrels. Across from the entrance was another set of buildings that looked like wooden coach houses. Between was the empty dirt parking lot.

The screen door wouldn't budge. That's when I noticed a sign hanging on the other side that said CLOSED—COME AGAIN!

I stepped back to look for another entrance and nearly tripped over a dog standing next to me. It was a yellow dog with a white chest, about knee high. Tail wagging slowly, the dog seemed to be averting its glance almost apologetically.

"You wouldn't be Vargas, would you?" I reached down to pet the mutt's head.

There was a flash of white teeth. Had my reflexes been slower, my hand would have been Alpo. The dog smiled, resuming its unassuming composure. Great. Was this what I had to look forward to when Angie and I returned from the breeder?

"That's Wilco." A swarthy man in a baker's cap, cheek dusted with flour, was hanging out of a side window. "I am Vargas. You must be Garth."

"How did you know my name?" I hadn't mentioned it when I phoned.

"Nicholas called. Wait there." He disappeared, adding: "And don't pet the dog."

I watched as Wilco sauntered away, looking for someone else to eat.

The screen door opened, but it wasn't Vargas who appeared. Instead, it was an attractive, middle-aged woman in a yellow print dress that looked like it had been made by hand from a pattern. Her black hair was stacked high, country style, and she smoothed her dress on her hips as she stepped off the porch and approached me.

"Are you Shelly?" We shook hands.

"Heavens, no. Shelly is a dog." She looked me up and down, from my running shoes up the chinos, white oxford shirt and sport coat, finally stopping at my unruly blond hair.

"I thought his name was Wilco." Self-consciously, I tried to tame my hair.

"Not that dog, another one."

I kept smiling. "A pastry shop named after a dog?"

"C'mon in, I'll show you."

I followed her print dress through the screen door to an entryway, where tucked in the corner sat a dusty horse wagon. Resting on a blanket on the cracked leather upholstery was a collie looking intently out the window as if she sensed the barn was on fire. The dog sat very still. Too still. A placard around her neck read: SHELLY.

"That's Shelly. People come from miles around to see her, and get their streusel."

The dog remained steadfast. Deadfast, to be exact. She was stuffed. *Now, this is my kind of dog.*

"Stupid question: what is streusel?"

"Pie, with, like, a crumb topping. Michigan favorite. Shelly died in 1938. Was a local hero several times over. She saved some kids from drowning when they fell through the ice on Green Pond, alerted the police once when Dillinger was hiding out in a person's barn, and could predict rain. She wasn't real busy during the Dust Bowl days. My name is Amber. I own this place."

Amber was still sizing me up, and I wasn't sure why. Perhaps she was wondering what I'd done to need hiding out. Maybe she was trying to tell if I was violent. Then again, she had a twinkle in her eye that made me wonder if she didn't take a liking to me as a man.

"Nice place it is, too. Is Vargas your ...?" Husband? Boyfriend?

"Gosh, he's just my partner here at the streusel shop. Whodathunk that a wetback baker would be so good at making blueberry streusel? C'mon in."

We stepped from the porch into a dimly lit dining room.

"We have a full menu. Lunch and dinner. About half our business now is mail order streusel. That ad in the *New Yorker* really paid off."

"Let me ask you something else. What exactly is a cheese curd?"

"They're yummy. Itty bits of cheese the size of your little finger."

"What kind of cheese is it?"

"They come in all flavors."

"Gouda, Swiss, Jarlsburg, Emmenthaler, cheddar...?"

"No, more like smoked, bacon, jalapeño..."

"Surely it must be some specific type of cheese?"

Through the swinging kitchen doors came Vargas, wearing an apron. A stout man with a big white grin and black crew cut, he was decked out in Boy Scout shorts and had a rolling gait. One of his large hands reached out and grasped mine.

"I am Vargas."

I knew that. But he seemed to like saying it so I didn't complain. "Thanks for having me on such short notice."

"I owe a debt to Nicholas." He closed his eyes and bowed his head in reverence. "He was very kind to me, when it was not required."

Amber looked me up and down. Maybe my fly was open. "Want something hot to drink?"

"Only if—"

"Yes, Amber, let us have coffee," Vargas interjected. "Please, Garth, have a seat."

Amber sauntered into the kitchen while Vargas and I slid into a rough-hewn booth that I hoped wouldn't result in an ill-placed splinter.

"Nicholas is your brother, yes?" Vargas's gaze was

leveled seriously, his meaty hands folded on the table before me. "You are lucky to have such a brother."

"I suppose I am, at times. Should I ask how you know him?"

"Do not ask, I will tell what there is. I stole paintings for a living, Goyas a specialty, on spec. But that clever brother of yours tracked me down. For help to recover the paintings, I did not go to prison, and he even gave me a percentage of the bounty from the insurers on the art. I used that money to come here, with Amber. He caught her, too. She was my courier, my assistant. This is her hometown. She knew of this place, where the dog lived, where an old farm couple sold streusel on the side but had died. It was time to retire anyway, before our luck ran out. Streusel are about as good as anything else in this world to sell. We like it here."

"What's not to like about streusel?"

"I am also a scoutmaster."

"The shorts gave it away." I actually felt better knowing he and Amber were criminals. If they were straight, there was the chance they would turn me in. Even if he was a scout.

Amber returned, setting down a tray with three steaming mugs, a sugar bowl, cream, and a bottle of Tia Maria. She sidled in next to me. Close.

"So I have told Garth of our adventure with Nicholas. Now, we need to know a little about your situation. Not everything, just some details. It will help us to hide you. I will ask questions, you tell me yes or no. Yes?"

"OK."

Amber's foot brushed my shoe and I shifted my feet. She poured the coffee, then held out the creamer.

"Cream and sugar?" She eyed me sidelong, lashes batting.

Was I imagining it or was she flirting?

Vargas held out one hand and pointed to a finger on the other. "Have you escaped from prison?"

"No."

There was Amber's foot again. I stayed put. Maybe she thought she was bumping the leg of the table.

"That is good. Very good. Are the people who want you the good guys or bad guys?" He pointed at the next finger.

"Good guys, I guess."

Now her knee was touching mine. I couldn't move over as I was at the edge of the booth. I grabbed the bottle of Tia Maria and dumped a hefty shot into my coffee.

"Excellent. Much better than the Cosa Nostra. State police?"

"Probably."

"Ah, not just state police. Feds?"

"Them, too."

"I see, I see. Did you kill a cop?"

"I didn't kill anybody. Look, I'm only a suspect."

Now Amber's hand was on my thigh. So it was safe to say she'd been checking me out as a man in the parking lot. But I still wasn't sure what her relationship with Vargas was. Were they "partners" or *"partners"*? Vargas's large brown hands looked very strong. As suited to kneading pie dough as to strangling a perceived interloper.

"A suspect." He closed his ten little Indians into fists on the table, gazing thoughtfully at the wall. "Ah, yesss!"

"Vargas, doncha know who he is?" She gave my thigh a little squeeze under the table.

"Hmm?" Vargas looked startled.

"Gosh, but I recognize him now. He's that guy from Chicago. Discovered that football player who was dead."

"Hmm?" Vargas looked startled again.

"I saw him on TV. Remember?"

"I only watch *lucha* on TV."

"Well get your head outta the sand. There was this murder, in Chicago, of a football player. He was killed with a stuffed bear."

"Is this true?" Vargas eyed me.

"Yes. And there have been two more murders, of other big-game hunters I've met. But whoever is killing them has succeeded in making the authorities think I did it. I'm being framed." I put my hand on Amber's, stopping its advance up my leg. I followed that with a little nudge from my elbow, a signal to cease. She smiled impishly.

"You are sure you did not kill them?"

"I have never killed anybody." OK, there was that thing a few years back with the carnies, but I didn't actually kill anybody, not technically. "And I have a home, and a wife, and a Russian."

"A wife?" Amber said playfully. "There's no ring."

"A Russian?" Vargas added. This detail both fixated and eluded him—I only blurted it out as evidence of my stable home life in an attempt to thwart Amber's advances.

"Angie and I have been together twenty years, and we have Otto, our helper."

Vargas put a heavy hand on my forearm and nodded. "Very good. Believe me, killing only leads to more killing. They know this car you drive?"

"Most likely." I was now thumb wrestling with Amber under the table.

"We must hide your car immediately. The local pigs come here for our cinnamon apple streusel. And at all hours."

"Great." I half stood, making clear my intention to escape the booth.

Amber rose and let me out, a playful spark in her eye as she smoothed that yellow dress around her figure.

I wanted to hide the Lincoln and she wanted to hide the salami.

Fortunately, Amber had to go to town to pick up a shipment of baking supplies, so I managed to avoid her for a while after that first encounter. As a heady blue twilight descended on Shelly's Streusel Stop, Vargas made us some Mexican pizzas: a tortilla topped with bean paste, cheese, peppers, onions, chorizo, and another tortilla. While they were baking, he led me into his apartment upstairs, where he cracked open a couple Dos Equis and flicked on the tube. He began pecking at the buttons on the oversized remote with his thick finger.

"You like *lucha libre?*"

"*Lucha libre?*"

"Wrestling."

"You mean like WWE?"

"Bah. That is not wrestling. *Lucha libre* is real wrestling!"

An image popped onto the screen of a sweaty man in a glittery black mask strangling another sweaty man in a green glittery mask. In the same wrestling ring, a different masked man flew at another competitor, knocking him flat.

Of course. Mexican wrestling.

"In Mexico, it is very popular with a long tradition." Vargas raised his chin to indicate the nobility of the sport. "They say it is very ancient, from the Aztecs. Like in Mexico, the wrestlers were an elite society of soldiers, with many hidden rites, and were revered above all others. It was said when they wore their masks they could project their souls."

"Didn't know that. I always assumed it was sort of…" I wanted to say "a goof" but finished with "…playacting."

"*Lucha libre* is many things. It is tradition, it is drama, it is acrobatics, it is comedy, it is allegory, it is gladiators. You know, the most famous *luchadores* have passed their masks from one generation to the next. There are even mask matches, in which the winner unmasks the loser, revealing his face for the first time and taking away his fighting spirit, his *lucha* soul, right before your eyes!"

"Really?" On the screen, a wrestler in a sparkly yellow cape and green mask with rubber devil horns leapt from the ropes, flew ten feet in the air, and landed on his opponent.

"You know, in my younger days," Vargas began, puffing out his chest, "I was a *luchadore*. *El Gallo de Muerte*. Then I hurt my back. So I stole paintings instead."

"Of course." Great. I was lodging with the Chicken of Death.

"Here!" He bounced out of his seat and set upon a shelf of dusty VHS tapes. He yanked one out and shoved it into a vintage Goldstar tape player. The TV went blue for a second, and then a slightly blurry brown-and-white image popped onto the screen— we were midtape, in the middle of some hot wrestling action from back when TVs had horizontal control knobs.

"You see?" Vargas tapped the screen. "This is me, in a match against *Pepino Malo*."

I watched the wobbly image of a man in white with a coxcomb on his masked head battle some guy in a dark outfit with what looked like pickle imprints on his leotard.

"Watch! Right here is where I—*El Gallo de Muerte*—perform my very own special takedown. It was mine, I invented it!"

The blurry image of the chicken man leapt across the stage, his legs scissoring midair so that they pincered the pickle man and drove him to the mat. The crowd roared, and Vargas's chest inflated with pride.

I took a sip of beer and said, "Wow. That's something, all right. What do you call that move?"

"*El Huevo Podrido!*" He said this like he was announcing the arrival of a famous matador.

"My Spanish is a little rusty. I know it means something about eggs..."

"The Rotten Egg!"

I took another sip of beer, and it went down hard. The Chicken of Death lays the Rotten Egg? Does it get any more absurd? I felt like laughing for the first time in a week.

Vargas's reverie was mercifully short: "I must go make sure the tortillas don't burn. Put yourself at home, I will return." He popped out the tape and our regularly scheduled program of masked marvels continued.

So I was left alone in Vargas's abode. Instead of watching the bizarre spectacle of cheesy superheroes doing jumping bean imitations, I took a tour. It was an efficiency apartment, with a small kitchenette off the TV room, and a side room containing an overly ornate bed that looked like a miniature galleon. Everything was dark and accented with red in the old Spanish style. The room looked like it had last been redone in the eighties, with cheap wood paneling and discount black lacquer furniture with lots of chrome. On a side table were a number of faded framed photos of Vargas as *El Gallo de Muerte*. His white cape was sculpted to look like wings, and his white mask had a yellow beak and red coxcomb. Somehow I had a feeling that even if he hadn't hurt his back the Chicken of Death wasn't going to be the next big thing in Guadalajara. In several of the photos, he was posed in the ring, holding trophies and flanked by buxom bikinied faux blondes with octopus hair. You know, hair so blown out that it looked like it might just reach out and strangle someone.

There were also a few Goya prints hung on the wall, framed in heavy wood like portholes from the armada. But I soon lost interest in my surroundings, my mind sinking into the depths of my predicament.

I hoped Angie was OK. What with having the FBI question her, she was probably worried sick about me. Well, at least my situation wasn't going to bollix her plans to go to the Couture show in Chicago. I guessed I shouldn't worry too much. Nicholas would reassure her, and if the FBI was lurking around, the murderer would probably stay away. I had no reason to think the killer would go after her, but I wasn't sure of anything.

Then there was Fowler. I'd given both the FBI *and* him the slip. *Let him try to find me here.*

I'd been in a bit of a trance since speaking with Nicholas, numbed by exasperation of my circumstance. Me, on the lam. Me, a suspected serial murderer. Me, holed up in a pie shop, waiting for Lord knew what. Amber's next advance, probably. Or a dog bite. I determined that I was just going to tell her to back off. And if that didn't work, I was going to tell Vargas to ask her to back off.

It occurred to me then that all in all I wasn't in such a bad way. My respite at Shelly's would give me an airtight alibi should another big-game hunter wind up a victim of his victims. As long as circumstances didn't put me in the vicinity of the next murder, I was in line to be vindicated as a suspect. I relaxed some, with the help of the beer.

So I was sitting there, staring blankly at the screen full of parading Mexican would-be superheroes, hoping there would be another victim. Not very nice, I know. But what could I do to stop another big-game hunter from biting the dust? And after all, the FBI only needed to use my client list to stake out the potential victims and nab the murderer in the act. A cinch. If I just sat tight long enough, something would give. I hoped.

Now a wrestler in white sparkly tights, his belly sucked in, was striding down a ramp toward the ring, his white cape flapping behind him. The crowd roared louder for him than for any other wrestler who'd approached the ring since I'd been vacantly taking in the spectacle. When he took the stage, two pneumatic octopus blondes latched onto him, and he began shouting into the microphone. Regrettably, my fluency in Spanish ends with *cerveza* and a rudimentary grasp of Latin root words.

Vargas returned with a platter of food, and it wasn't until then that I realized I hadn't eaten all day. The smell of the hot tortillas, chorizo, and cheese suddenly rendered me famished.

"This smells terrific, Vargas, thank you."

His chest puffed, clearly pleased. "I brought you another beer. The food is spicy, as well as hot."

He produced two TV trays and set them before the couch.

As I carefully nibbled the edge of my tortilla, hedging against flaying the roof of my mouth, Vargas grunted and pointed at the TV.

"You know Draco?"

"Draco? Nope, I'm afraid I haven't been following Mexican wrestling recently."

"If you had followed it at all, you would surely know him. Draco is perhaps the most famous *luchadore* in the world. Ten times over. I wrestled him. He will soon pass his mask to his son."

"Did you win?"

Vargas dipped his head to one side. "I am afraid I did not. But it was an honor to lose to the best. And at his age, he still is in the ring. Not so much anymore, but still, the crowd loves him."

On the screen, Draco moved to his corner of the ring. Sewn into the back of his cape were the shapes of five silver lizards.

"Why the lizards?" I asked cautiously around a mouthful of pizza.

"He is Draco. The lizard."

"Yeah, but by the shape of them, those are geckos on his cape..." And the way those five geckos were arranged in a circle looked very similar to the design on Fowler's medallion. I choked a little, coughing nervously. There were geckos and lizards in commercials all over the boob tube, and they didn't have anything to do with serial killings, so why not some wrestler's cape? Sure. Didn't mean it had anything to do with white geckos and dead hunters. Nah. Couldn't be. Not a chance.

Then my appetite hit a brick wall. EL DRACO BLANCO flashed on the screen.

"He is magnificent!" Vargas enthused.

Swallowing hard, I dropped my tortilla onto my plate and took a gulp of beer before I asked.

"His name is the White Gecko?"

"Yes, but everybody just knows him as Draco. Is there something wrong with your food?"

This must, I thought, be a bizarre coincidence. I could suddenly picture the dead gecko hanging out of Sprunty's mouth, and it was all I could do to steer away from the memory of his guts spilling out like a bowl of fettuccine bolognaise.

"Garth, are you all right?"

"I...I'll be fine, it's just that..."

On the screen, the producers of the fight were airing a quick retrospective of *El Draco Blanco*'s personal life, in which he was out of costume except for the mask. There were more tenticular blondes, and then there was a brief series of clips that made me knock over my TV tray.

Draco on various hunting trips—kneeling next to a dead oryx, a moose, a bear, then showing off his collection of trophies.

"Garth, I will call a doctor! Sit..."

"I don't need a doctor! Oh, jeez..." I looked down at my food spilled on the floor, my beer gushing froth on the carpet, then back up at the screen, which had returned to the ring as an MC with a huge mustache announced the match. "I'm sorry, Vargas, I apologize..."

"You look like you saw a ghost! Sit, tell me, what is wrong?"

"He's called the White Gecko?" I pointed.

"Yes, that is his name." Vargas pushed me back onto the couch and started taking my pulse.

"And he's a big-game hunter?"

"One of the finest. Your circulation, it is very fast, my friend. Are you sure—"

"I need to tell you something that you must keep in strictest confidence, and then tell me if I'm crazy."

"Take it easy!"

"Promise?"

"Yes, whatever..."

"The three people that were killed? They were all

big-game hunters, and they all were found holding white geckos."

"I don't understand."

I repeated myself.

"You must be mistaken." He shook his head like he had water in his ears.

I locked eyes with him. Vargas suddenly looked grave.

"This is a coincidence." He almost whispered. "A very big coincidence."

"Very, very, very big coincidence. Either Draco is next, or he's the murderer, or whoever is doing this is a fan of his."

"But you do not know Draco." He scratched his stubble. "You say that all who have died knew you."

I thought about that a moment. Yes, I'd appraised the collections of the three that had died. But just because the first three were known to me didn't mean the next victim would be. Could my connection to the victims be a coincidence? Yes, and why not? I mean, if somebody was targeting big-game hunters, they'd be as likely to focus on one of my clients as not. Most of these hunters insure their collections, and Wilberforce/Peete was practically the only one that specialized in taxidermy. Perhaps I'd been called out to Sprunty's manse merely as a way to effect the discovery of the body sooner rather than later. I was floundering in doubt, trying to buoy myself with hope.

"Do you know why he has five white geckos on his cape?"

"Of course. His grandfather was part of an organization of big-game hunters called the Order of the White Geckos. It is to honor his very brave ancestors."

"Vargas, do you still know Draco?"

He was down on the floor with a sponge, mopping up the spilled beer and shoveling my pizza back onto the plate. "Well, many years ago . . ."

"Could you talk to him?"

He shrugged. "I don't have his number, I do not know how. All my old friends, I have lost touch."

I looked again at the screen. As the two masked men grunted and growled in the sweaty tango, a crawler scrolled across the bottom of the screen. There were names of cities, and dates.

"Vargas, what's that say on the screen?"

"It is a list of places where the *lucha libre* exhibition is traveling to next." He went off to the kitchenette to wring out his sponge.

"You mean this isn't taking place in Mexico?"

"No. This is the U.S. tour."

"What's their next city?"

"I will have to see."

We sat there in his dark living room intently watching the screen's blue flicker as we waited for the crawler to repeat.

Vargas slapped his knee. "The night after tomorrow."

"Where?"

"Omaha."

chapter 12

I was given the guest bedroom for the night. Guest of Wilco.

"The dog will not bother you," Vargas assured me as he showed me to the doggie's attic redoubt. "It is his room, but he will share it with a friend of mine."

The accommodations looked swank enough for the likes of me. There was a queen-sized bed at one end, along with a dresser, bedside table and lamp, and a small four-paned window. At the other end of the attic was a clutter of old trunks and boxes, in front of which sat a well-loved dog bed. In front of that sat Wilco, guarding it like I might opt to bunk there instead. He wagged his tail lazily, averting his eyes as before, a wry smile upon his chops like he was dreaming up some scheme to make a sandwich of my hand in the middle of the night.

The attic was just cooling down from the heat of the day, and I could smell the tar from the shingles.

"Just stay on your side of the room," Vargas whispered, so the dog wouldn't hear.

"Thanks, Vargas. I appreciate all your help."

"Think nothing of it." He closed his eyes and shook his head. "We all need a little help of this kind once in a while."

We? I guess I'd officially entered the realm of the fugitive. Could the membership card and secret handshake be forthcoming?

Vargas put a hand on my shoulder. "And tomorrow, we will speak with your brother about Draco and how we will proceed. Sleep well."

He clomped down the stairs, but left the door open, which was fine with me. I didn't want to be locked in with Wilco.

I'd taken the precaution of brushing my teeth and washing my face before I came upstairs so as to avoid naughty Amber. I'd heard her return and peeked through the bathroom window as she carted supplies from the back of her pickup toward the yawning yellow light of the kitchen. I figured she might still have designs on yours truly. I didn't know where her room was—there was no evidence in Vargas's place of any female cohabitation. Even in the bathroom, which I gave a careful inspection. That's where the fair sex always leave their mark, prominently or not. But Vargas's bathroom was all male. Scummy soap dish, aftershave, unscented soap, overused toothbrush, tortured tube of toothpaste, both seats up. Any co-habitating male would have been trained out of such barbarities. So I was well satisfied that he and Amber were not an item.

That was good and bad. While it meant Vargas wouldn't throttle me if he found her sneaking up the stairs, it also meant the fear of discovery might not be a deterrent to Amber.

Was I worried about my constancy? My heart, and all the attachments above and below, was fenced off for Angie. But that doesn't mean I enjoy taking pot-shots at would-be poachers. Most men have a natural inclination to please women, and a natural aversion to disappointing them. I hoped to avoid fending Amber off again.

Once I was snug in bed, I tried to read an article in the *New Yorker* about the lost art of Florentine pup-petry. But I was too distracted. I missed Angie and wanted to talk to her. I wanted to tell her about all that was going on, share my troubles. That's part and parcel of having a soul mate, a need not only to share the good but the bad.

Then, as if I didn't have enough to worry about, I found myself fretting about adopting a dog. Wasn't Wilco ample proof that some dogs are just bad seeds? I eyed the yellow curl of his body across the room. You get one like that, you can't just return it. You're stuck with it for however long it lives, which could be twenty years or more. But the more I thought about it, the more I realized that what put the ache in my belly was the feeling I'd had lo those many moons ago when, at age seven, I found that dog by the railroad tracks.

It was all white fuzz with little black eyes and a black pointed nose. Knowing I wasn't allowed to have a pet, I hid the puppy in the tree house. I brought it scraps, took it for walks on the sly. Nicholas was only five, but even at that age he had the smarts enough to warn me this would be trouble. But Arnold was my puppy, I loved him and I aimed to keep him no matter what. Then came the day that I climbed up into the tree house and found him listless and sick. I was so distraught I took him directly to Gabby, confessed everything, and pleaded for Arnold's life. She said she'd take him to the vet.

And she did. To have him put down.

Later she pointed out that Arnold wasn't so much a dog as an opossum. I'd thought his hairless tail was sort of odd, but when you think about it, opossums don't look that much different than a lot of the ankle nippers out there. How was I to know?

"He was a wild animal and it was illegal to own him, so the vet had to kill him," Gabby said, adding: "I told you, Garth. No pets. It's bad enough your father lets you boys have a television. But you took in a pet anyway. And in so doing, you killed it."

So why not get a dog with Angie? Now I could have that little white ball of fuzz with shiny black eyes if I wanted. One that wasn't a rat-tailed marsupial. All I knew was the notion of having a dog made me uneasy.

Turning the light out, I lay there looking at the roof joists, listening to Wilco do his impression of the Three Stooges asleep. Yes, all three. Damn dog was like a calliope of snores, hitting high notes, low notes, and walking bass all at once. I wondered if Wilco would let me put one of those Breathe Right strips on his snout. Not without a midnight snack of finger food, I suspected. But I eventually drifted off, counting the pops and creaks of the wooden roof cooling instead of sheep.

I don't know what time it was when I woke up, but it was still pitch-black except for the starry glow in the window. My arm was curled around something warm. At first I thought it was Angie, and then I thought it was my pillow. But when I snuggled up against it, it snuggled up against me.

"Holy..." I recoiled and almost knocked over the lamp while turning it on.

Pale brown eyes fluttered in the glare of the light, my bedmate gazing up at me furtively.

"Look," I began, "this is not going to work. I know this is your place, but I have to insist that you leave."

Wilco set his head back down and sighed sleepily. I didn't know whether to try to push him out of the bed or not. Well, I reckoned if he stayed on his side of the bed, he could remain. It had cooled down quite a bit (the attic was plainly not insulated), and the extra warmth was welcome. And frankly, I was too exhausted to care. As long as he didn't start farting, I wasn't going to risk an altercation. Dog farts are a line in the sand.

Great. Imagine Angie and me sharing a bed with a dog. Take a guess who'd get the small slice of the mattress pie in that scenario? I had to fight for half the bed as it was.

The next time I awoke, the gray of dawn was chilling the window. I realized what had woken me. Wilco was pressed up against my back, infringing on my side of the bed. You know, the way dogs slowly drive their bodies like a wedge between you and the mattress until you find yourself on the floor, the canine splayed across the bed like the Queen of Sheba in her barge.

I groused and started to shove Wilco back to his side with my butt. He growled. But what was he going to do, eat my spine? I drove him back farther. Damn, that dog was heavy. Then I felt his teeth gently bite my ear. I briefly considered abandoning ship and curling up in his dog bed.

But then the dog spoke, an imposter in my midst.

"Harder, baby..."

I flipped over faster than a burger on a Saturday night grill.

"Jesus, Amber...what are you doing here?"

She just smiled and hooked her arms around my neck, which I promptly removed. As I did so, I had an eyeful of her charms. She was stark naked. Stark? That word did not apply. Her copious black hair was down and spilling all over the pillow. A pair of comely round orbs emerged from the sheets.

"Look," I began, "this is not going to work. I know this is your place, but I have to insist that you leave." That little speech didn't work any better on her than it had on Wilco. In fact, she did the exact same thing the hound had, settling down with a sleepy sigh.

There are those who will tell you that a man's fidelity is no stronger than a trailer park in the path of opportunity's tornado. I consider myself very fortunate for having found refuge in the bunker of devotion. Fidelity is a conscious act and thus reversible; devotion visceral and thus involuntary. I'm not inhuman—libido's centaur did indeed caper about, playing his dissolute lute. But one can listen to the centaur's song without humming along.

I rolled out of the bed and pulled on my chinos. My teeth were chattering from the cold.

"What a shame," Amber purred. "Much warmer under the covers."

I heard someone coming up the stairs, and snatched up my shirt in my hurry to dress.

"Don't worry, baby, that's just Wilco," Amber purred teasingly. "He went out for a pee. Now would you get back in here and let me rock your world?"

"Amber, you're a very nice girl—woman—and all, very attractive, but really . . ."

My attention was drawn to the doorway, suddenly filled by the shadow of a man.

I heard Amber inhale with surprise.

Though my instinct was to put wings to my feet, I was a statue. Mercury buttoning his shirt. Curiously, though, the shape didn't betray Vargas's deportment. Amber's boyfriend? I sensed that whoever stood there was likewise frozen in place with surprise, taking in the scene.

There was nothing to do but hold our collective breaths until the figure spoke. But he didn't speak. He whistled a familiar sliding crescendo of astonishment.

Then he spoke.

"Could this be my straight-arrow brother? In a love nest?"

"Damn it all." Amber groaned. "You scared the hell out of us, Nicholas."

"Hi, Amber." He strode into the room, bent down, and gave her a kiss. Even at that hour he was wearing one of his tweed suits. I could just make out his sardonic eyes turning my way. "Helloooo, Garth."

Those who have no siblings have been spared the joy of perpetual brinkmanship.

I'd just been brinked. Then he said:

"We're going to Omaha."

chapter 13

Silos, red barns, budding cornstalks, and Phillips 66 truck plazas slid by as Nicholas captained our voyage across the sea of Iowa to the isle of Omaha, me riding shotgun, the Chicken of Death behind us on the poop deck reading a *lucha libre* magazine. Amber, thankfully, was back at the streusel stand. But I could feel Wilco breathing down my neck from the backseat next to Vargas.

The vehicle we were driving was neither mine nor Nicholas's rental, but the Vargasmobile, a white '68 Pontiac Catalina hardtop. It was equipped with a figurine of the Virgin on the dash, red fuzzy dice hanging from the rearview mirror, and an eight-ball steering wheel spinner. It had the familiar old-car sway and rumble, which was one small twinkle of reassurance as we headed off toward what I feared would be more trouble.

Unlike in the East, where semis tend to be lone

wolfs, big rigs in the heartland travel in long packs. In effect, they are like a train, nose to tail, and one wonders why the haulers don't just put their wares onto the rails and save some rubber. So to pass "a truck" takes about five minutes to get by the whole train, and just when you have them safely in your rearview mirror, there's another convoy around the next bend. But passing trucks becomes a way of passing the time as one sails west on the ocean of crops and grassy plains.

We'd left the Lower Peninsula an hour after Nicholas had made his appearance, and the conversation had been kept to a minimum. My brother obviously knew about Draco, so the preliminaries of why we were headed to Omaha were largely moot. As we grabbed coffee and pecan swirls at the gas station on the way out of town, I managed to shoot off a call to Angie on the pay phone, using my calling card, which would disguise the origins of the call. I got the machine, left a message that I was all right and that I was headed to Aunt Jilly's. That was an inside joke. We had a standing black bear mount at home we called Aunt Jilly, named after a relative with an abnormal amount of body hair for a human female. Long since deceased, this aunt lived in Omaha, Virginia. This was my roundabout way of signaling to my sweetie my destination. That way she'd know where to look for my remains when all hell broke loose, as it was apt to. Angie was good at puzzles, and I was confident she'd quickly figure out that I was headed for Nebraska, not Virginia, since last she knew I was in the Midwest.

Nicholas had said zero about the situation in which he'd found me at the streusel stand, for which I was grateful. But there was little doubt he was saving it for later. After passing a particularly long train of semis, I finally broke the silence.

"So, shall we lay our cards on the table?"

Nicholas shot me a glance. "Cards?"

"Yeah. Like what inspired you to come out here."

"To help you. Hey, I can't get married without my best man."

"No, there's something else, I can feel it."

He rolled his eyes. "Feel it?"

"I know you, Nicholas, and I know when something is up with you."

"My researcher uncovered the Draco connection." He shrugged.

"And?"

"And, well, my researcher revealed some other interesting little facts."

I merely waited, and under my scrutiny, my brother finally continued.

"There was once something called the Order of the White Geckos. A fraternal thing."

"Vargas mentioned that Draco's grandfather was one of the White Geckos. So are we talking about middle-aged guys in fezzes driving miniature cars in parades? That kind of fraternal thing?"

"Basically. And our grandfather, Kit Carson, was

also a founding member. It was him and four other big-game hunters, one of them Draco's grandfather, who formed the lodge, and it was open only to big-game hunters."

"You used the words 'was once.' Just a guess but sounds like they're no longer around. What happened to them?"

"The five founding members died while traveling to a South African hunting trip. Their boat sank. In 1949. Soon afterward the Order of the White Geckos disbanded."

"How did this lodge get started? What did the geckos symbolize?"

Nicholas rubbed his jaw. "Apparently it's an ancient Native American symbol of some kind that they latched onto, the same one Draco has on his cape. Symbolizes power in the earth or something, which is partially why Draco adopted it as his badge. But also to honor the legacy of his grandfather. *Lucha* fans love that kind of thing."

"Since when are you into Mexican wrestling?"

"A Web search for 'white geckos' brings you to Draco way before the fraternal order. When I saw the connection between the five White Gecko big-game hunters who were killed and the five on the cape of the big-game hunter wrestler, I had a researcher dig deeper. The inception of the Order of the White Geckos happened while the five founding members were on safari in Mexico in 1917 hunting something called a javelina."

Aha. Fowler babbled something about javelinas.

Nicholas fished in his jacket pocket and came up with a few sheets of folded paper. "Grandpop was quite a famous guy in his day, at least in the hunting world. Here. Something my researcher summarized."

I unfolded the paper and began to read while Nicholas left-laned past another queue of trucks.

Julius F. Carson was born in 1878 to a Lutheran minister in Minneapolis, Minnesota. At seventeen, he boarded a train west, abandoning his father's hope for college and a career in the clergy. The next five years were spent in a variety of odd jobs for outfitters in Wyoming, Montana, and Idaho, mostly caring for pack animals, digging latrines, fetching water, and the like. He worked his way up to hunting guide. A turning point came when he and another guide, hunting for pleasure, were ambushed by a mountain lion. The lion had the guide by the neck, pinned to the ground. Julius came running with his gun, took aim at the lion, and the gun misfired and jammed. Throwing his gun aside, Julius pulled his hunting knife. He leapt onto the lion and stabbed it to death, but not before being clawed about the face.

Julius, half blind from his wounds, carried the guide twenty-six miles over rough terrain to town.

Even though the guide perished, Julius F. Carson became a local celebrity, and it only helped that he was instantly recognizable the rest of his days by the diagonal scars across his face and the eye patch. Several nicknames were attached to him, but the one that stuck was "Kit" Carson, after the famous American frontiersman. It was the nickname attached to an article published in The Field about his exploits.

He traded on this reputation to become a guide with a top Wyoming outfitter—if nothing else, the well-heeled hunters wanted to hear him tell the story of his tangle with the lion and to say that they had been guided by the famous "Kit" Carson.

From there, Carson started his own hunting camp and befriended visiting hunters who urged him to go to Africa with them. He did, and thus began a core friendship with four of the day's most renowned hunters:

Charles Gateway III, of Gateway Munitions, manufacturers of some of the world's finest hunting rifles; General Raoul Ovando, late of the Mexican cavalry; Bartholomew Jones, a tool and die magnate from Massachusetts; and Titan Harris, publisher of a string of newspapers.

On a hunting trip to New Mexico the five founded a society called the Order of the White Gecko, a name taken from Native American cave paintings they witnessed. The order was open only

*to fellow big-game hunters, and reached a member-
ship of several hundred.*

*In 1949, Julius F. Carson and the other four
founding members of the Order of the White Gecko
died in a shipwreck off of Capetown, South Africa.
Carson was survived by his second wife, Amelda,
and his son from his first marriage, Stuart.*

"Titan Harris." I looked up from the summary,
studying the distant horizon. "Titan Harris III was
the one killed in Houston."

"The men killed so far are all grandsons of the
founding five members of the Order of the White
Gecko. Charles Gateway III, of Gateway Munitions,
manufacturers of some of the world's finest rifles—
his grandson was Sprunty Fulmore. Bartholomew
Jones—his grandson was Bronte Jones, the TV actor
living in Seattle. And Titan Harris's grandson..."

"Titan Harris III, scotch receptacle, Houston,
Texas—I get it. And Draco is the grandson of that
Mexican general."

"Then that leaves you."

"Me? Why me?" And why did I find myself constantly having to say "Why me?"

"The killer already has you involved, you own
taxidermy... Let's face it, I don't exactly fit the profile
here as a taxidermy collector. Stuff gives me the
creeps."

The notion that I was the one being targeted
didn't alarm me as much as one might have thought.

Against hope, I'd already come to the conclusion that I was a marked man in this whole mess. Just not by birth.

"Nicholas, this is way out there, doesn't make any sense. I mean, the three that have been killed were all people I did appraisals for. It must be tied to that."

"That's what the FBI thinks. And maybe it is tied to that. But the coincidences in the rest of it are too huge."

"Nicholas, wherever you mined this information, the FBI probably has it, too. They'll be headed to Omaha also."

"Not so sure about that. A lot of that information came from the library, not the Web. The FBI tends to rely on their own files and police computer databases. Electronic stuff. Not that I didn't have my own Web spy check those same sources. So I had to turn to this musty old guy who wears shorts and Birkenstocks year round, Lanier Frankly. He hangs out at the main branch of the New York Public Library. He practically lives there, so the librarians let him have access to all kinds of out-of-print periodicals like *The Field*. This guy lives to do research. In return, I only have to buy Lanier a steak dinner with all the trimmings at Gunther's. That's his other hangout. Also, once the FBI thinks it's a serial killing, they turn to profilers who look at behavior, not stray genealogy."

"They know at least some of this information about Kit Carson. I was at an FBI tactical meeting and there was a woman, tough old broad, a colonel in the Air Force and also a doctor of some sort. Named Lanston. She had a complete dossier on me, and apparently on Kit Carson. She was busting my chops like I knew about Grandad."

"That's interesting. We found that the government files on him are sealed."

"Sealed?" I briefly reflected on the penguin in the desert joke.

"Uh huh. And you'll never guess which branch of the government had them sealed."

I shuddered. "Air Force?"

"Right-o, buddy boy. Did this Lanston say anything else about Kit Carson? About what connection there was between him and these murders?"

"Nope. But this must mean the FBI knows all about it."

"Not necessarily." Nicholas wagged a finger at me. "She's with a different branch of the government. She may have an agenda all her own. I'll make a call and have someone check her out."

"Wait. Back there in Hell, I overheard Lanston on the phone. She said something about how she'd been working on this for thirty years, and that she was after Fowler, too. And she said someone was being sent out to come take care of me. That make any sense?"

Nicholas shrugged and shook his head. "Did she say who they were sending?"

I scowled, trying to remember. "She said a name, but I can't pull it back. Shoot."

"Angie was talking about canceling her trip to the jewelry show. I convinced her to go, told her that I'd be sure to have you call her at her hotel as soon as possible. Doesn't look like the killer is after her, but it's better she beats New York for a few days to be on the safe side."

"Oh, man . . . I hope she doesn't cancel on that show." Sure enough, I was screwing things up for her career again. I guessed it was a little much under the circumstances to imagine she could just forget my predicament and go about her business. But I hoped she would. If this had to happen, why not a week later?

"And then there's Fowler." Nicholas glanced at me. "He's a kook. Read all about his TV archeology career, how he went gaga."

"I actually remembered who Fowler was on my own. He found me somehow in Seattle, followed me to the Space Needle and ranted about my vuka, which Gabby tells me is some kind of spirit or something, I dunno. Fowler insisted he had a key or something to get rid of it, some sort of dog tag he was wearing. Oh yeah, and I think he thinks he's a werewolf."

"Come again?"

"You heard me. And get this: Gabby said she and Stuart put a spell on him to keep him away from them. He was after Dad about *his* vuka. She says they turned him into a werewolf. Find anything linking Fowler to Gabby and Stuart?"

"I'd think you were kidding if I didn't know Gabby so well." Nicholas shook his head. "I still have Mel looking into Fowler. There's a connection between him and the Order of the White Geckos. Somehow."

I suddenly felt that the moment was right to change tack, see if I could catch Nicholas off guard and get him to open up.

"You nervous about getting married, Nicholas?"

"Please, Garth." He gave me a withering look. "No head shrinking, OK? I get enough of that as it is. I might as well ask you if you're nervous about getting a dog."

"Who told you we're getting a dog?"

"Girls gab. Your girlfriend and mine do talk, you know. So how did you know Draco was a target?"

"Vargas." I jerked a thumb at the backseat. "Did you know he used to be a Mexican wrestler? *El Gallo de Muerte*."

"Rooster of Death? You're kidding."

"It sounds funnier when you say 'Chicken of Death.' Vargas is a big *lucha* fan, and Draco was wrestling on TV. There was a bio piece on him as part of the program. Showed him as a big-game hunter. Five white geckos on his cape, big-game hunter—it was just too coincidental. And the geckos on his cape are arranged the same way as they are on the medallion Fowler wears around his neck. In a circle, nose to tail. Perhaps Fowler's connection to the five white geckos has to do with something Stella told me on the phone. Fowler . . . well, she says that he's our uncle."

I watched Nicholas absorb this information with more genuine surprise than I'd seen from him in a long time. Then again, I'd seen a lot of changes in my brother over the last year. I mean, Nicholas married? His hard edges had softened, but not so much that anybody but his brother—or perhaps his fiancée—would notice. He still had the short hair with the flip at the front, the tweed suits even in summer, the eyes that could freeze glaciers, the intensity that could make lava from rock. He was always passionate about his "work," whatever it happened to be, but never about people on any kind of personal level. It's hard to explain, but I guess you could sum it up by saying that he was always very much in the here and now. Concepts like love, which in its best form embodies a sense of interpersonal destiny, and thus the anticipation of many years of intimacy, seemed beyond him. It was my guess that he'd always harbored deeper emotions but had them well subjugated.

"I assume that means he's Dad's brother, and thus Kit Carson's son and not Gabby's brother. There's the connection to the White Geckos right there. Fowler . . ." Nicholas let the name hang. He seemed to be running calculations in his head.

My ruminations on family history quickly turned to trepidation. By seeking out Draco, weren't we just baiting the killer? Putting me in closer proximity to the murderer? Two birds with one gecko. "Wouldn't it be better just to lay low for a while?"

Nicholas gave me a longer look. "A while?"

"I dunno."

"OK, so you lay low. Now what? Say the murders stop at four. And assume that the FBI suddenly sees the light and drops you as a suspect. Are you really going to feel safe back in New York, knowing the killer is still out there?"

I squirmed.

"Consider another scenario," he continued. "That the FBI and Air Force have different motives for solving this crime. The FBI is probably just trying to solve a serial killing. But, gee, last I heard the Air Force isn't in the business of solving crimes. So they're looking for something else. How much you want to bet it has something to do with, say, the military? Something that's in their interest, something that could be secret that they want kept secret. They may want to pin these murders on you—we don't know. Maybe they're even committing the murders."

"You're spinning quite a conspiracy theory here, Nicholas."

"If the Air Force grabs you for somehow compromising national security, who knows, you could be reclassified as some sort of foreign combatant and spend the rest of your days in a human kennel in Cuba. A few years ago that may have sounded like a conspiracy theory, but today it is entirely plausible. Since you're in hiding, Draco is the only one of the grandsons out in plain view—he's live on TV. You don't have to be Barnaby friggin' Jones to figure out that the killer is going to go right at him as soon as possible to stay ahead of the cops. If we get to Draco and keep him from getting killed, what does that make you?"

"Um..." My head was spinning again.

"The guy who *didn't* kill Draco. The guy who *saved* Draco. The guy who *isn't* the killer. That gets you out of this predicament right away instead of in who knows how long. Look, I want my best man at my wedding next week."

Perfect example of my earlier assessment of Nicholas. He said the "best man" line again, like he was trying to figure a way of delivering it like he meant it, but without any genuine hint of fraternal affection. It kept coming out like he was declaring his taxes would be in by the fourteenth.

"I get it, I get it. Whether the FBI or the Air Force are working together, or on the correct track, if we don't save Draco and find out who is at the bottom of this... Damn, Nicholas, why does this keep happening to me?"

He looked confused, so I illuminated.

"Maybe you're used to all this trouble, but I'm not. Well, I don't want to be."

Nicholas laughed. "Better get used to it, *muchacho*. Pretty obvious that the white gecko curse is just one of many the Carson family enjoys. So, what's Gabby look like naked?"

"Oh thanks, Nicholas." I put a hand over my face. "You had to put that image in my mind."

"Just watching after your virtue." An impish grin screwed his face. "Thought I'd try to replace the image of this morning's wake-up call."

I gritted my teeth and glanced into the backseat. Vargas was sawing wood with the wrestling magazine covering his face. "OK, let's have it."

"What?"

"C'mon..."

"I'm just razzing you, Garth. She once crawled into my bed. A frisky girl."

I heard the centaur's lute in the distance.

"Was she good?"

"You know what they say: practice makes perfect."

chapter 14

I don't know what I expected. Statues of Marlin Perkins? A skyscraper with OMAHA STEAKS emblazoned across the top? Billboards for Boys Town? But about ten hours and three Conoco filling stations after leaving Michigan's Lower Peninsula, we descended Council Bluffs, Iowa, and beheld Mutual of Omaha's namesake below.

The view was decidedly uninviting. The clouds ahead were doom itself, the Missouri River in the foreground a black moat of ill fate. Unlike an Eastern thunderstorm, the clouds roiled green around the edges like angry waves approaching a shore. The center of the storm glowered over the city, engulfing the metropolis in the depths of darkness. Perfect setting for evil troll armies or Vlad the Impaler's domain. No help for my sense of trepidation.

Behind us the sky was painfully bright, but ahead in Omaha the streetlights were on. I've never seen a tornado, or been in one, but one look at those clouds and I guessed those firsts were close at hand. Hail started pounding the roof and car hood. No, not the size of golf balls, but bigger than any I'd ever seen, and they were bouncing all around us on the roadway as if a tractor trailer of mothballs had flipped over somewhere up ahead.

I cleared my throat. "Vargas, should we pull over or something? Hail means a tornado, doesn't it?"

Vargas leaned forward between me and Nicholas.

"Yes. This is a bad sign. But not to worry. Wilco knows when a tornado is about to strike. Here, have a cheese curd."

"The dog?" Nicholas glanced in the rearview mirror. Even Nicholas looked a little concerned.

Vargas was holding an open package of what looked like malformed white cocktail franks. I gingerly took one and examined it closely as Vargas continued.

"Yes. Two years ago, a storm was approaching, and we heard Wilco howling. Not like a normal howl. Like a yodel. We look outside and we say, 'Shut up, you stupid mutt!' But he was not so stupid. We see a funnel cloud tearing up the neighbor's crops. I collected the dog and we sat in the root cellar until the howling stopped."

"What exactly is a root cellar?" I asked. "Is it called that because there are roots coming out of the walls, or is it because you keep root vegetables down there? Or is that where cheese curds come from?"

"Garth, please, must you ask ridiculous questions when you're nervous?" Nicholas sighed. "So, Vargas, the tornado missed Shelly's Streusel?"

"Yes. The dog, he stops howling. We come up, the tornado is gone. We keep canned fruit in the cellar."

"Wilco yodeled just that once? None of Granny's pickled hog jowls down there in the cellar?" I took a small bite of the white cheese. "It's just mozzarella."

"Sometimes once is enough. No, it is a cheese curd."

I was convinced this cheese curd thing was some Midwest inside joke, and like down east humor or mutterings from Lake Wobegon, the irony was too obtuse and slight for my sensibilities. But the mozzarella was tasty.

The windshield wipers were batting away what looked like a downpour of Ping-Pong balls. Captain Kangaroo's worst nightmare or Mr. Moose's wet dream, take your pick. I swiveled around to look at the mutt, who, as was his custom, was gazing nowhere in particular and seemed as content as ever in his quiet canine reverie about whether to eat my pinky first or go for all five at once. I hoped Vargas wasn't feeding him any cheese curds. Remember that line in the sand.

Nicholas and I exchanged glances. The cars and trucks all around us charged on toward darkened Omaha, so we did, too. The hail stopped abruptly, and I watched as we passed under the green edge of the storm. I could picture a twister corkscrewing down from the sky like a petulant Hydra, and flicking cars off the road.

"It is bad when the hail stops." Vargas grunted with apprehension.

I expected yodeling any second.

But we made it to the Missouri River, and the bridge, where waves of water suddenly crashed down out of the sky. To our right through the blur of rain, I could just make out a large modern arena with the glowing word QWEST emblazoned across at the top.

"It is good when the rain begins." Vargas grunted with satisfaction. "I don't think twisters happen in heavy rains. Much."

Well, Vargas was right, because it rained hard all the way to where we veered off the highway and pulled into a Best Holiday hotel.

Wilco never did sound his tornado warning howl. Thankfully.

I'd done a fair bit of traveling for the Wilberforce/ Peete gig and had become familiar with the conventions of most hotel chains. Fortunately, my employer—well, my former employer—was pretty good at placing me at the better chains. No Motel 11's for Appraiser Par Excellence Carson. Still, there's a certain tiresome routine to the hotel/motel shtick no matter where you go. To their credit, many of the chains have put brains to the grindstone in an

effort to dispel the disorienting experience of sleeping somewhere different each night. They want their
loyal business travelers to feel at home, and thus
they've added little hints of terra familius. Like
having the paper at your doorstep every morning.
Or having toiletries handy, and an iron and ironing
board, and a clock radio. Yet nothing makes me feel
less at home than the search for the ice machine. I'm
a big fan of ice and like great chilly heaps of it around
for any and all beverages, even beer on a really hot
day. Nowadays, many hotel rooms have fridges—why
can't they just put ice trays in there? Cracking a few
ice trays would go a long way toward making me feel
at home.

We took two rooms: Nicholas and me in one,
Vargas and Wilco in the other. I had the ice bucket in
hand, about to begin my quest.

"No time for that." Nicholas extended a glass
containing a couple fingers of brown fluid. He had
his own glass in the other hand, and a bottle of
Macallan sat atop the TV. A reporter on the tube
was talking excitedly about a twister that struck just
outside the city, and a crawler along the bottom
boasted many more throughout the county.

"The ice machine is just down the hall somewhere," I said.

"Take a snort and let's get to the arena. The *Lucha
Libre Mucho Grande Spectaculare* begins in two hours."

I plunked down the ice bucket and took the glass
hesitantly. Well, if there ever were a time to start

drinking scotch, this would be that time. Bolting the scotch, I felt my throat seize.

"Damn, Garth." Nicholas gave my back a few hard swats as I coughed. "This is expensive scotch. You're supposed to sip it."

"Nicholas," I rasped. "I want to call Angie."

"Out of the question. The heat will be all over us within the hour if you do."

"I could call Otto. On his cell."

"Otto has a cell?"

"I could call Otto's cell phone. Angie's cell phone is being fixed and she was going to borrow his for the trip. I'll use my calling card."

"Getting it fixed? Nobody gets a cell phone... OK, make it quick." He jerked his arm and eyed his Timex. "Very quick. And for God's sake, don't give her any particulars. Not where we are, not where we're going..."

"Alo. This Garv Carson Critters. Tell to me, please, if help."

"Otto?"

"Luba?"

"Otto, it's Garth, not your estranged wife. Didn't Angie borrow your phone?"

"Oo my Got! My friend! *Dyepdeyavoga*...I very glad eetz not Luba. I go to nude beach for Fire Island, and vife Luba, she know, and like bear with a one eye and no shovel."

"Otto, no time for that. Did Angie get to the airport all right?" *One eye and no shovel?*

"Yes, but of course, Yangie here."

"What? Put her on the phone."

"Vy you call to me if you want Angie is to call?"

"Otto, I don't have time—"

"Vy not you talk of your friend Otto, eh? When to home you come, my friend? We drink vodka, I make cheeken—"

"Otto, KGB."

"Oo my Got! KGB!" That had more or less become the code word for "bad men are after me."

"Garth?"

Beethoven wrote symphonies of great passion. Strauss: waltzes of swirling splendor. Raspighi: tone poems of scintillating beauty. None held a candle to the sound of sweet Angie's voice over the phone at that moment.

"Angie—are you OK?"

"I'm fine, sweetie. Listen, there's something I need to tell you. We're not in Chicago. We had to give two FBI agents, Bricazzi and Stucco, the slip."

"The slip?"

"Yes. I guess I can't tell you about it if you think someone might be listening…"

I tensed. "So if you're not in Chicago at the show, where are you? Are you OK, Angie? Something's wrong…" I could hear all sorts of muffled, cavernous sounds in the background.

"I'm fine. You're the one who's in danger. I need

to tell you . . . Are you visiting Aunt Jilly the way you said you would?"

"Yes, I'm at her house now. But are you sure you're OK?"

"Yes, yes . . . oh, Garth. For the love of Pete, why is this happening again?"

"I wish I knew. But why didn't you go to Chicago? You'll miss the big reception and everything."

"Some things are more important. Please be safe. I've been told Aunt Jilly's is very dangerous, so be careful."

"Babe, I'm not in any danger . . ."

"You liar," she chided, only partly in jest. "I know that voice."

Can't hide anything from Angie. Doesn't keep me from trying now and then.

"Nicholas is here . . ." I looked over at my brother, who was waving his hands furiously. Oops.

"That makes me feel better. I think. But what's he doing there?"

"Again, I don't want to say anything except to tell you not to worry and that I'll hopefully be home soon, with this whole mess cleared up. Don't tell anybody that Nicholas is here—I mean, unless you have to."

There was silence on the other end, and then quietly: "Garth, you be careful. If you let anything happen to you . . ."

"Yeah, I know." I smiled. "I know, if I get hurt you'll kill me."

She laughed briefly, her voice quavering. "Hope to see you soon."

"I love you, too, babe."

Nicholas was drawing a finger across his throat, signaling me to hang up.

"Love you to pieces." Angie hung up.

I leaned on the phone a few moments, my back to Nicholas. His hand gripped my shoulder.

"Buck up, Garth. We'll get to the bottom of this and be back in New York in no time."

I wished I could believe that.

chapter 15

In high school, I was a wrestler. Varsity, in fact. That doesn't mean I was good, just the right weight. It doesn't mean I enjoyed it, either. At that age, it sometimes takes you a while to realize you've gotten yourself involved in something that you don't enjoy. Like AV club. Reduced to its elements, wrestling was all about close personal contact with another boy, and at a time when all a heterosexual male really wanted was close personal contact with a girl. And it was about crash dieting to make your weight class. There wasn't an ounce of fat on me, and I was muscular. Had I been a chicken, I'd have been dry and stringy fare. I finally bailed out of the sport after a match with a guy who was my same weight but about six inches taller than me. Like a crowbar, this guy simply pried me over and pinned me to the mat. In wrestling, you can be defeated by fulcrum and lever physics, and growing longer was not something I could achieve no matter how hard I worked out. I was perpetually starved, exhausted, and physically disadvantaged. No fun memories.

So given my experience with the Greco-Roman sport, I was not a fan of wrestling. Not even the show-biz kind with fireworks, strobe lights, and the seething, vein-popping, scowling, gnashing, and trash-talking musclemen pinballing off the ropes and hitting each other with folding metal chairs. I'm not immune to the occasional joy of gratuitous fictional violence. I'd choose to watch pro-wrestling over bowling, boxing, or competitive bass fishing any day. But that's just me. To each his own.

Sitting there in the Qwest Arena among throngs of cheering Latinos, I wasn't expecting a much different spectacle than American wrestling. But I immediately ranked it higher for the masks and costumes. I used to think the Americano version was over the top, but maybe it wasn't far enough over the top to engage me. *Luchadores* are like matadors, and there's a nobility to them that contrasts well with the circus of it all. And I mean *circus*. These guys were acrobats, balancing on the ropes and winging across the ring at each other like flying squirrels on espresso.

The masks in question covered the full head and were skintight, leaving only the eyes and mouth exposed. Many had racing stripes, chevrons, or designs evocative of the *luchadore*'s persona. Lightning bolts for *Electro*, swirls for *Miasmo*, daggers for *Stiletto*. Without the benefit of standard pro-wrestling facial expressions of rage, triumph, and pain, these guys had to carry off their prowess with their bodies, with deportment, with controlled motion. They almost seemed to move like dancers, not brawling lumberjacks. Makes it sound effete—anything but.

And there's something about the experience of watching *lucha libre* live that made it exciting. Perhaps the enthusiasm of the faithful fans who had braved the terrible weather was catching.

There had been two bouts, and still no sign of Vargas. He'd gone backstage to talk with Draco. We waited, and he hadn't returned. Maybe he'd gone to check on Wilco? We'd left the mutt hitched to the bumper of the car so he wouldn't soil the Vargasmobile upholstery.

Nicholas was next to me, and he seemed indifferent to the show, more intent on the crowd. I gave him a nudge.

"Gibraltar. That was the name Lanston said on the phone."

"Hmm?"

"When I overheard Lanston on the phone, she said something about them sending someone to replace her. And I now remember the name. Gibraltar."

He just glanced at me.

"Gibraltar mean anything to you?"

His answer was a shrug.

I was about to say more when the crowd roared in response to whatever was being said in Spanish over the loudspeakers. As I said, the audience was mostly

Latino, but to our right, moving up the aisle to the exit, was a trio of gringos. Nothing odd in that, except that I recognized them from somewhere. One was tall, with short, burlap-colored hair and gray eyes. There was a littler one, stooped, with an ill-advised mustache, weak chin, and nervous walk. Lumbering last was the largest of the three, a man of substantial girth and obvious strength.

Nicholas noticed me noticing them.

"Friends of yours?"

"Not exactly..." I began absently, searching my mental mug shots. "I know them, though. They're from a fraternal order. Rented a pronghorn from me a couple weeks ago. Tupelca."

"Tupelca?"

I nodded. "Mystical Order of the Tupelca. There's a lodge—or I think they call them 'dwellings'—in New York. Angie told me on the phone that they were coming by the other day to rent something else."

"Pronghorn?"

"A Southwestern antelope with sharp, hooked horns. Their lodge was the Pronghorn Dwelling. Seems each lodge is named after a different animal."

"Where the hell is Vargas?" Nicholas resumed his survey of the arena.

My gaze was just turning from the Tupelcas when the tall one caught my eye and quickly looked away. Almost imperceptibly, I saw him nudge the one with the bad mustache next to him, who glanced in my direction just before they vanished out the exit.

"You want some popcorn or something before the next match? I'm starved."

Nicholas looked at me like I'd suggested pouring gravy into his shoes, and disdained replying.

"I'll be right back."

"Garth: don't talk to any strangers."

I dismissed that comment with a roll of my eyes and headed up the aisle. My mission wasn't popcorn, of course, but to buttonhole those Tupelca and make sure the coincidence of them being at the match was just that. But when I stepped into the corridor surrounding the perimeter of the arena and scanned the throngs of *lucha* fans milling in and out of the eateries, my three amigos were nowhere to be seen. I turned right, scanning the heads for the tall, burlap one.

The crowd was so thick, I quickly lost hope of finding those Tupelcas. But I was uneasy at having seen them. Especially since Angie had mentioned on the phone that they'd called again recently. Coincidences, under these circumstances, were unwelcome and warranted scrutiny.

I stepped out of the flow of the crowd into the Creamy Pebbles stand to make my U-turn. Stadium culinary delights sure have changed. Used to be it was all popcorn and hot dogs and "pop." Maybe the stray snow cone. Now there were fast-food chains dishing out the empty calories. But I had no clue what a Creamy Pebble was.

My curiosity got the better of me. Could this culinary discovery be on par with cheese curds? I felt like the Marco Polo of the American heartland in search of my spaghetti in a strange land harboring exotic delights.

"So what are Creamy Pebbles?" I inquired of the clerk.

The answer came from behind me.

"Flash-frozen pebbles of ice cream in forty-eight flavor combinations."

Like the inimitable Marco Polo on the cusp of the Gobi Desert, I turned to find the Hun at my back: J. C. Fowler. And he was holding out a spoonful of multicolored Creamy Pebbles from his plastic cup. He eyed me speculatively. I didn't like it.

"Following me?" That was obvious enough, but I didn't know what else to say.

"Just looking after your vuka. Three down, two to go. The only way to save yourself is to go to the mound, and use this to remove the spirit." He dangled his medallion at me.

"Sir, did you want to order something?" The kid behind the counter was alternately eyeing me and the queue developing behind me and Fowler. We were gumming up the Creamy Pebble works, so I stepped out of line. Fowler followed me intently, like a dog follows a butcher.

"Fowler, just tell me what you want."

"I want you to follow me to the mound." Fowler started squirming as before, but more so, like he was trying to crawl out of his skin. I'd seen similar things in New York, particularly in a certain sector of creeps who lurk on the periphery of parks huffing glue. The solvents were literally dissolving their neurosystems. Customers in line for the Creamy Pebbles were giving Fowler and me wary sidelong glances.

"Fowler, you are not a werewolf. Gabby is not a witch. I am not possessed of a vuka. You need a psychiatrist."

"What did Gabby tell you?" He was running his tongue along his teeth like he felt the fangs growing.

"Just enough: I should stay away from you."

He paused, absorbed that tidbit, and then seemed to ignore it as another thought gripped him. "There's an excavation at the mound—I worked there for years as an archeologist before the government chased me off. They knew what was in the ground and didn't want me to find it. I haven't been able to go back there until now. They won't recognize me, nobody will. We can go together. We have to go soon. It is the time of the white gecko, the stars are aligned for the trip home."

"Are you my uncle?"

He just smiled, and twitched.

I heard the crowd cheer in the distance, a sure sign the next match was to begin soon. I figured I'd better get back to my seat and Nicholas. And away from this Testor's addict.

"I'm not going to say this again, Fowler." I pointed a stern finger at him to let him know I meant business. "Stay away from me."

Because of the crowds, it took me about ten minutes to hack my way back to my seat.

"Where's the popcorn?"

"No popcorn, just Creamy Pebbles. And Fowler."

"Here?" Nicholas stood up in alarm.

"Yup. At the Creamy Pebbles stand."

"Creamy Pebbles?"

"Flash-frozen pebbles of ice cream in forty-eight flavor combinations."

Nicholas pushed his way up the aisle to the exit. He was back in ten minutes.

"Find him?" I asked, but I knew the answer by his scowl.

"No."

The boom of the announcer commanded our attention to the ring. His staccato was familiar to anyone who has paused on a salsa station while spinning the radio dial. I didn't catch any of it except the final words: *"El Draco Blanco!"*

Everyone stood to applaud, hands and chins held high, and we followed suit, joining the din. From the wings, a *luchadore* in a familiar white cape and glittery white cowl strode down through the curtain and down the gangplank to the ring. His thick arms swung with the machismo of a king, eyes steeled like a conqueror, his chest thrust forward like an armored knight. The tights revealed considerable muscle, but also a ripple of excess around the lower rib cage. Caesar obviously likes his pasta course as much as the next guy.

Nicholas and I exchanged glances as Draco swirled center ring, displaying the five white geckos on the back of his cape.

A spotlight swung to the opposite side of the ring, where curtains parted wide enough to accommodate the arriving contender's antlers.

This *luchadore*'s mask was black, and his black leotard had white racing stripes. Real antlers were affixed to the helmet atop his head. They looked like mule deer antlers, but I couldn't be certain. His hands were out to his sides as though ready to draw on Wyatt Earp.

"*El Macho Venado!*" the announcer boomed—just like some game show announcer unveiling "A New Car!" behind Curtain Number One.

Clearly Antler Man was the villain in this match, but the crowd didn't boo or hiss. They afforded the challenger polite applause and nods of approval. What's the point of a hero without a nemesis, after all?

Arms swinging high, *El Macho Venado* strode down the gangplank, and as he approached the ring, one could see that he was not well built. In fact, his stride was more of a lope that seemed amateurish even from my limited exposure to *lucha libre*.

As he approached the ring, he began to run, antlers lowered, and vaulted over the ropes at Draco.

The crowd gasped and sprang to their feet. We all

expected him to remove his antlers before the match, as a wrestler named *Diablo* had removed his horns in the previous match.

Draco lurched out of the way, unprepared, and the antlers caught in his cape instead of his gut. He whirled, swinging *El Macho Venado* into the ropes.

"Dammit!" Nicholas spat. "He's trying to kill him right here!"

"What?"

"That's not a *luchadore*, Garth! It's our killer. Wanna bet those antlers came from one of Draco's trophies?"

I wanted to utter some expletive, but gulped instead.

The referee tried to intercede, but was stuck in his side with an antler and flipped over the ropes. *El Macho Venado* was suddenly free of Draco's cape, and the opponents took to opposite sides of the ring, sizing up each other. The crowd was in tumult, confused, surging into the aisles for a better view. They knew this wasn't right, that something was wrong. A knot of security guards tried to fight their way toward the stage, but the battle was on.

I could see Draco's huge chest heaving, but he hadn't lost his composure in the face of actual combat. He let his cape drop, ready for the challenge, if not welcoming it.

Macho Venado charged. Draco dodged. An antler point caught Draco's side and pushed him to the ropes. Draco grabbed hold of the antlers, wrenching them clockwise like he was bolting shut a vault. Macho Venado spun and landed hard on his back.

Blood soaking his white flank, Draco hesitated. He put a hand to his wound, his eyes wide at the sight of the blood staining his costume. The realization that this was no game, no show, seemed to drain the Caesar out of this *luchadore*. Bravery and honor had been replaced with the flight instinct. He turned to the ropes. Clearly he intended to hop out of the ring and flee.

But he shot a glance across the audience, and even with the mask, you could see his jaw tighten, his eyes narrow with resolve, and the grandeur return. He'd forgotten, briefly, who he was, and what it was to be *El Draco Blanco*.

Draco turned and dashed at his opponent. He latched onto Macho Venado's lowered antlers and slammed him into a corner post. Draco then spun his opponent on the rebound into center ring and kicked Venado's legs from under him, sending the antlered fiend tumbling to the other side of the ring.

A wave of cheers crashed down on Draco from the sea of fans as security guards approached the ropes on one side of the ring.

Like some miraculous man-bird, Draco leapt onto the rope, balanced, and spun to face the ring. He hovered there, glorious in his glittery tights, our hero on the cusp of victory.

Our champion on the brink of vanquishing his foe.

Our demigod on the verge of expunging evil.

Bouncing lightly on the rope, Draco catapulted himself at his opponent. He seemed weightless, arching gracefully through the air.

Midair, his legs shot forward, scissoring toward his opponent.

By God! It was El Gallo Muerte's *signature move. The Rotten Egg!*

Macho Venado was just clambering to his knees, antlers swinging toward Draco.

Gasps and breathless exclamations of *mi Dios* cascaded across the arena, followed by a thunderous shout: *No!*

It is written: *Show me a hero and I will show you a tragedy.*

The antler tines had plunged deep into Draco's chest.

chapter 16

The slash of the reaper's scythe cut a gash of despair through the audience.

And shock.

I wasn't sure if they were about to riot or explode into mass weeping. Many were probably playing back in their minds what they had just seen, wondering if they had seen what they thought they saw. Others may have been trying to convince themselves it was part of the show.

During this moment of mass indecision, a mob of security guards topped the ropes from all four sides and converged on the combatants like a rugby scrum. Draco was quickly heaved up above their heads, his whole torso bloodied, and handed over the ropes to the audience.

Though unscripted, this move by the security guards couldn't have been more timely. Instead of erupting into a riot or panic, the audience moved the body mosh-pit style over the top of the crowd toward the exit where an EMS team had just entered. They had become part of their hero's rescue. Or at least his funeral.

The entire arena began to chant *Draco! Draco! Draco!* as the body of their fallen knight moved from one level to the next. It was like an incantation to sustain Draco's life, and it became louder as feet began to stamp. The stadium rumbled with admiration.

"He escaped!" Nicholas pointed to the ring.

The helmet with the bloody antlers lay in the ring.

But Macho Venado had vanished, and the escape had the guards arguing with each other and peering under the ring and into the crowd helplessly.

Had they been so preoccupied with moving Draco that they failed to notice the culprit slip away? Was the audience so transfixed by the spectacle of Draco's bloody white form gliding across the horde of fans that they didn't see Macho Venado dash into their midst?

"C'mon." Nicholas grabbed my arm and we bullied our way to the nearest exit, where we were literally propelled from the mob like a banana squeezed from its skin into a nearly vacant passageway.

"Where are we going?" I trotted after Nicholas.

"See if we can find the killer."

"Find the killer?" I skidded to a stop. "You mean find the guy who wants to kill me?"

Nicholas wheeled in my direction, shooting me a

look of derision. "I'd say this would be the best time, wouldn't you? He's focusing on escape, not killing you. Besides, he doesn't have a piece of your taxidermy to kill you with. Unless it's small enough to put in his pocket."

There are few things more annoying than a little brother who's right all the time.

So we resumed our trot around the curving corridor, skipped down a couple escalators, and burst through the doors into the parking lot.

We scanned the lot, which was slick from rain. Lightning still tickled the horizon, perhaps in Kansas where some other lucky campers were getting the tornado treatment.

"There." Nicholas pointed toward a parking area cordoned off from the main lot by police barriers.

We ran to the barriers and found the two cop cars by the entrance were empty.

"The fuzz must have gone inside." Nicholas winced in the direction of an open door that read STAGE ENTRANCE. "The killer could have slipped out already."

Nicholas began to sweep the parking lot with his eyes for the fleeing Macho Venado.

"Garth!"

I turned at the sound of my name being shouted from the stage entrance.

"So here you are," Stella said accusingly. She emerged from the doorway and paused just long enough to flare up one of her long brown cigarettes.

"What the hell is going on? Where have you been?" She lifted her sunglasses and took in the night sky's gloom with approval.

"I've been kinda busy trying to stay alive, that's what I've been doing."

"No whining, Garth."

"That was not a whine. And even if it was, I'll whine if I want to. I kinda assumed you didn't want me in your employ anymore."

Nicholas stepped up to our tête-à-tête with a wry smile. "Dearest Stella."

"Nicky." She flicked an ash at him by way of greeting. "What brings the both of you here?"

"If I had to guess I'd say the same as you. Draco. So was it you or the FBI or this Air Force woman who figured out the Order of the White Geckos?"

"I'm not at liberty to discuss company business," she said with a reptilian smile.

"Did you see Macho Venado in there? We figured he might have tried to escape this way."

"Who? The killer?"

Nicholas and I looked at each other, then he said, "Some wrestler with antlers just gored Draco. Didn't you see it?"

"Christ." She dropped her cigarette with disgust and squashed it like a bug. "I heard a bunch of commotion from the bathroom, but thought it was just cheering. They're not going to like this back in Hartford."

"If you were here to protect Wilberforce/Peete's

interests, you blew it. I'm not certain but I don't think Draco can survive those wounds. Where were you when this happened?"

We eyed her as she eyed us, like two dogs and a cat. Raindrops crashed onto the macadam from a fender. Leaves slapped together in the distant trees. The filament of a streetlamp bulb thundered overhead. We were all wondering the same outlandish thing. Could one of us have been Macho Venado?

"In the bathroom. How did the killer escape, in front of all those people?"

"Slipped away somehow," Nicholas groused.

"Or maybe he's right here." Stella waved her cigarette at me. "It's pretty suspicious, Garth being here. Once again at the scene of the crime."

"Yes, it is" came a voice from behind us.

The compact form of Colonel Lanston was stomping toward us from the stage entrance, the two MPs towering in her wake. She was wearing her folding blue garrison cap, the silver oak leaves twinkling in the streetlamp glow.

"Gang's all here," Nicholas muttered.

"Who's this?" Colonel Lanston jerked a thumb at Nicholas, eyeing him shrewdly.

"Nicholas Palihnic. An insurance investigator," Stella said.

"My brother," I said.

"My son," Fowler said.

We all froze, turning slowly to where J. C. Fowler

approached from amid the parked cars, his arms swinging like he hadn't a care in the world.

Had he just said *my son*?

"Fowler." Colonel Lanston betrayed a reptilian smile. "Glad you could join us. We've been looking for you, too. You're all coming in with us."

"What's the charge, little woman?" Fowler joined our circle, jauntily adjusting his sunglasses at Lanston. "Hey, like the hat."

"This is not my father," Nicholas snorted.

"You're all people of interest to the government. You're coming in for questioning."

"Not so fast." Brickface and Stucco emerged from the stage door, guns drawn but down. "This is the FBI's jurisdiction, Colonel. We'll take them in for questioning."

"Ha! The big pig versus the little blue pig. I love it." Fowler showed us all his little white teeth.

"This is definitely not my father," Nicholas repeated.

"Shut up," Lanston snapped at Nicholas, turning to Bricazzi. "I thought we were conducting this investigation jointly?"

"Then how is it you came here without coordinating with us?" He afforded her a patient grin. "My instructions are to conduct this investigation as we do any other. If you want to discuss that with my superiors, that's your privilege. Stucco? Bring the car around. We're taking them to the Federal Building for questioning."

Stucco cleared his throat. "All in one car? Maybe I should ride with them in their car."

"You know, you always seemed different," I whispered to Nicholas. "Maybe Fowler and Gabby...you know."

"No, I don't know," he whispered angrily. "Why did he say he's my father?"

I shrugged. "There is a resemblance."

Nicholas shivered and looked at Fowler.

"Listen, piggies..." Fowler started getting visibly itchy, beginning what was becoming his familiar Lon Chaney act. "There is no way I'm going downtown with you and the two flatfoots unless you get a warrant. I know my rights."

"Garth! Nicholas!" Vargas emerged from the stage door at a trot, his shirt soaked with sweat. "Did you see what happened? To Draco? A *luchadore* with horns—"

"We know," the assemblage chorused.

"Who's this?" Colonel Lanston jerked her head at Vargas.

"We may need more than two cars," Brickface said to Stucco.

"That's Vargas," Nicholas and I said in unison.

"Who is this woman?" Vargas said warily, looking like he might just take flight.

"Little blue piggie!" Fowler made his patented question mark in the air with his hand.

"And him?" Vargas pointed at Fowler, who was beginning to go into his snake pantomime.

"Nicholas's father," Stella answered, smirking.

"That weirdo is not my father." Nicholas didn't sound so convinced anymore.

"And the white one?"

"Stella, from Wilberforce/Peete," I said. "I work for her. Well, I did, but—"

"All of you shut up." Colonel Lanston spread out her arms like an umpire calling safe at the plate. "We're going to get to the bottom of what all you people are doing here. Stucco, you go with Vargas and these two." She gestured at me and Nicholas. "Bricazzi and I will take Stella and Fowler. The MPs will follow in our car."

"You don't seem to understand." Bricazzi stepped in front of Colonel Lanston, close enough that she had to look almost straight up at him. "This is an FBI matter. You're not coming."

That's when Fowler lit off into the parking lot, caroming between cars and howling.

Stucco and the MPs took off after him.

tucco rode shotgun, while Vargas took the reins of his Pontiac. Nicholas and I were in back, but Wilco was missing. Apparently he'd chewed through his leash and gone AWOL.

"That damn dog," Vargas fretted. "How will I ever find him? I should have left him in Vargo."

As cop cars poured into the parking lot, spectators had flooded from the stadium. We were following Bricazzi and Stella in the FBI sedan. Fowler had successfully vanished among the cars, and Bricazzi was furious.

Even with the red strobe, the black FBI sedan was fighting the riptide of traffic at the exits. It was slow going, and Vargas had been outflanked a couple times by exiting *lucha* fans, so that we were a few cars farther back.

"Agent Stucco?" I ventured. "What's Colonel Lanston's part in all of this, anyway?"

He glanced back at me, rolled his eyes, and resumed his previous blank stare out the windshield. None of my damn business, I guessed.

"You know," I whispered to Nicholas behind a cupped hand, "it occurs to me that it's possible one of this bunch is the killer. We don't know where any of them were at when Draco was killed. Stella had my list of clients, so she knew where to find them. We don't know where Vargas was, and he would know how to be a *luchadore* for an evening. And Fowler was both in Seattle and here when those two murders took place."

Nicholas pouted in thought, then leaned in and whispered in my ear. "Stella? I don't think she's strong enough to have done that. Vargas? The killer wasn't his build, and if so, why wouldn't he have killed you back in Michigan? Fowler? He's candidate number one. He's nuts."

"What a thing to say about your dad."

"You cut that out," Nicholas hissed. "I haven't forgotten about Amber."

"Touché." I winced. Had Angie witnessed the Amber incident, I'm sure she would be understanding. But I wasn't so sure my retelling of the scene would portray it accurately. That is, in a way that it might not bring my fidelity into question.

"You don't think it's really possible, do you?" Nicholas rubbed his hands together nervously.

"Nicholas, if you'd seen Mom at the nudist camp, I don't think you'd ask that question."

"Why wouldn't she have told me?"

"You know how she and Stuart never talked about the past. Hell, we lived in Uncle Lenny's house and never knew anything about him. Or about Kit Carson."

"This is a little different, don't you think?"

"Sure I do. Doesn't mean Gabby does."

Nicholas sulked a moment, but I didn't let him do it for long.

"Why did you want her at the wedding, anyway?"

He went from frustrated to annoyed. "Why do I have to keep answering that question?"

"It wouldn't be because you suspected you might not be Stuart's son, is it? To try to get her to tell you?"

"Now, what would make you say that?"

I shrugged and looked out the window at the jostle of SUVs ahead of us, their exhaust wafting in the window.

"Did Mom tell you something?"

"Gabby? Same as always. Trying to talk to her about the past is like opening a clam with a toothpick. So come on, Nicholas. Least you can do is tell me why. I did you a favor and invited her, after all."

He looked out his own window and said nothing.

"I am your best man."

He didn't budge.

"Nicholas, this isn't about one-upmanship. I'm

your brother, first, foremost, and always. If you can't tell me, who can you tell?"

He half turned from the window, and I could see he was on the cusp of caving. I just needed to give him one more tiny little sentimental nudge.

Growing up, even though we were just a few years apart in age, we'd been very different people, with radically different perspectives. We got along, even teamed up, but there was always a barrier between us: we never shared any kind of intimate bond where we confided things. Perhaps boys don't do that. There were times when I'd wished we were more open, that I could have helped him when he got in trouble, guided him. And that when I was unsure or worried or whatever, that I could have confided in him. Maybe we were too much like our emotionally distant parents.

Takes two to tango, I guess. I'd always been afraid Nicholas would have responded with derision or sarcasm had I showed any weakness. And no doubt he'd always thought that his big brother would interpret any emotional openness on his part as a green light to tell him what to do. But as I'd grown to know him better since he resurfaced from his self-imposed exile from the family, I'd found that he'd matured, mellowed. I'd recently started to hope that we could at some point put aside the sibling jousting and be more open. Angie's overtures toward warming his heart to us had also found some purchase—she could actually guilt him into showing up to Sunday dinners. And the impending wedding was certainly evidence that there was more emotionally to Nicholas than met the eye, that he was capable of letting someone beyond his heart's sentry.

"Well, Garth," Nicholas began, still staring out his window at the creeping traffic. "It's like this... there's no birth certificate on file for me with Gabby and Stuart. I think I'm adopted. Yet there's no adoption papers, either. So was I left on the stoop in a basket? I've known this for a long time. That's why I changed my last name to Palihnic all those years ago when I applied for a passport to go overseas. Picked the name out of the phone book."

When he turned, there was a new look in his eyes. Not sarcasm. Not the affected foxy squint.

His eyes were filled with alarm: "Watch it!" he shouted.

An arm circled around my neck and I was suddenly being dragged out the window. The last cogent thing I saw was a second, ill-defined assailant punching Stucco in the face through the front window. Lights were everywhere and nowhere, my body was being dragged, horns were honking, there were isolated shouts. The arm gripped my neck like a nutcracker, and I clung to it for dear life. The sudden plunge into icy panic made survival my body's number-one priority, shutting down such unnecessary bodily functions as seeing and hearing. All my resources were directed toward trying to keep a slight supply of air to my lungs and blood to my noggin. I tried vainly to keep my feet under me as I was hauled backward, each stumble threatening to collapse my esophagus. I had little idea where I was being taken until I found myself in the back of a dark panel truck with three figures looming over me, the truck engine racing, the gears churning, the sear of streetlights burning across the windows.

I was on my back, wheezing, and I think I implored my captors not to kill me, though with my neck and vocal chords feeling about two feet longer, I can't imagine I was able to speak. Maybe my brain was imploring all by its lonesome.

"You could have killed him like that," one said.

"Yeah, well, we had to hurry," another voice boomed.

"We're just lucky we grabbed him when we did," a third admonished. "He'll be OK. Anybody following? Here, sit him up. Get some water."

"I got some sports drink."

"It'll have to do," said voice number three. "Sit him up. Against the side."

I was dragged by my arms, for which I was grateful, and then I felt a plastic bottle pressed to my lips. I drank greedily, even though the liquid burned my raw throat.

That's when the lights came on, and my eyes hurt almost as much as my neck.

It took me a second to make out the three goons in front of me through my fingers.

It was the three men from the Mystical Order of

the Tupelca I'd spotted in the arena and seen in New York weeks before. There was a tall one with the burlap hair, flat nose, and wide lips. He was leaning over me, his gray eyes inspecting my neck. The linebacker, the guy who must have dragged me, had big worried brown eyes and a hairline a step away from the baldness goal line. The third had a droopy mustache, weak chin, and an Adam's apple you could have used to tee off for a par four at the Masters.

And they were dressed in what I'd classify as box store chic: sport shirts, jeans, Windbreakers, and white tennis shoes. For captors they certainly didn't look very threatening.

"Did I hurt you?" Linebacker looked genuinely worried.

"He's OK," Droopy simpered. "Aren't you?"

Flat Nose tilted my head to one side and looked at my neck. Then he gave a disappointed glance toward Linebacker. "You know, you could have opened the door instead of dragging him through the window."

Linebacker looked ashamed.

I cleared my throat, testing whether my vocal cords were still there or whether I'd somehow swallowed them.

"Don't worry." Flat Nose put a hand on my arm. "You're safe with us."

"Safe?" I croaked. They looked apologetic.

"It was the only way." Droopy shook his head. "You're not safe out there. You're the last one. If they get you..."

I coughed for a few beats, sitting up straighter. I could feel a ripple of pain down my back where it had scraped over the car windowsill.

"We're Tupelca," Flat Nose said proudly. "Javelina Dwelling."

Clearly Flat Nose was their leader as the other two always looked at him before speaking. They all thumbed their Windbreakers and little silver pig lapel pins at me, like I was being badged or would recognize the import of what they were showing me. But it meant nothing to me if they were javelinas, Porky Pig enthusiasts, or bacon aficionados.

"Yes, I know, you rented my pronghorn. I thought you were from the Pronghorn Dwelling?"

"We just pretended to be pronghorns." Droopy reached down and put on a purple bucket hat with two tassels and a little pig stitched into the center. "See?"

I pinched my eyes closed. "I've been kidnapped by Shriners?"

"Not Shriners," Linebacker corrected, "Tupelca."

"Uh huh. And you're not going to kill me?"

"Goodness, no!" Droopy looked genuinely appalled, like I'd asked if his Granny wore edible lederhosen.

Goodness, no. Well, I couldn't imagine any of your usual murderous, felonious types would use the word "goodness."

"Then let's have it."

They raised their collective eyebrows, waiting.

"Tell me what the hell is going on, why you kidnapped me from the FBI."

"You weren't safe with them." Flat nose snorted. "One of them may be a Coyote."

"A Coyote?"

"Yes, from the Coyote Dwelling. They're the ones trying to kill you, Carson."

"Let me get this straight." I rubbed my throat and brushed the hair from my eyes. "Other Tupelca, not Javelinas, but Coyotes, are trying to kill me. They killed Titan, Sprunty, Bronte, and now gored Draco in front of ten thousand people at the Qwest Arena?"

"I'm afraid so." Droopy nodded.

"Let me ask you this: why didn't you just call the cops on them?"

"We don't know who they are." Flat Nose shook his head, clearly annoyed by this detail. "They're a stealth dwelling. They were expelled years ago, after the first killings, but some members from different dwellings are secretly still allied with the Coyotes."

I suddenly felt very weary and heaved a sigh.

I'll admit, in the past when I've been subjected to such humiliations as being kidnapped, I was at times alarmed, and then some. Even terrified. At the moment, I was just annoyed. Very.

"What is it with you people? Why can't I be left in peace? I buy and rent taxidermy, I do a little insurance appraising, I have a home life, a beautiful loving girl. You know, there must be all sorts of people who live their entire lives without being kidnapped by a fraternal order. There must be people who aren't the target of murdering Coyotes. There must be some people who haven't been chased by psychotics at every turn. Unfortunately, I'm not one of them. Now, can you tell me why that is? Is there a conspiracy? Are you all working together or something?"

They looked at one another cautiously, and with no little confusion. I continued.

"So what is it you people want with me this time?"

Linebacker knew the answer and raised his hand. "We can't let the Coyotes kill you. The Coyotes must not get all five vuka."

With a metallic bang, the door to the front of the truck slammed open. I couldn't have been more surprised if you'd poured a bucket of Jell-O down the back of my shirt.

"Garv! My friend!"

It was my captain of the taxidermy industry, in his little woolen suit and flowery silk tie, ready to tackle the business world head-on.

"Good grief," I whispered, and looked at my captors. "You kidnapped Otto, too?"

"Very heppy to see you . . ." Or tackle me head-on, more like it. Otto flung himself at me, wrapping his arms around my sore neck.

"Ow! Otto, get off me, you're hurting me," I rasped. He smelled of stale cigarette smoke and street-vendor aftershave.

I felt the van veer and jolt to a stop, the brakes

squealing. I was in for another surprise. A beautiful blond surprise.

"Garth!"

"Angie!"

She rushed from the doorway, grabbed Otto like a humping dog by the scruff of the neck, and threw him aside. Next thing I knew she was hurting my neck, which was OK, and the kisses didn't hurt at all.

My mind was spinning. Had the Tupelca kidnapped Angie and Otto, too? No, they'd been up front, driving the getaway van. So, I was kidnapped by Angie and Otto? And they were with the Tupelca?

I pried my love off me, gave her a kiss on the lips, and said, "For the love of God, would you please tell me what's going on?"

That's when I smelled something familiar. Dog breath. I turned and found Wilco at my side, like he was inspecting my jugular vein for a snack.

"What the hell?" I lurched away from the mutt. "What's Wilco doing here?"

"Wilco?" Angie leaned down and gave the hound a hug. "I found him wandering around the parking lot, lost."

"Angie..." I began an earnest protest.

"Garth, I couldn't leave the poor thing wandering around."

Wilco rolled his eyes at her, and then smiled fiendishly at me.

My mouth moved, but no words came. Everyone stood there looking at me as if they were farmhands and parents hovering over Dorothy after the tornado. Would that this Midwest Munchkinland was only in my dreams.

"The Tupelca came to me and explained the whole thing." Angie waved at my kidnappers like they were contestants in a game show. "We have to drive to New Mexico."

chapter 18

Angie did finally explain it to me as Timmy the Linebacker drove us west through the night toward Denver, the panel truck rolling and rumbling beneath us. The others—Flat Nose Norman, Droopy Brutus, and Otto—slept restlessly across the floor in the back of the panel truck, their overnight bags doubling as pillows. It was gloomy back there, mostly empty except for a few cardboard wardrobe boxes.

As I'd already surmised, the Tupelca hadn't dropped by our abode to rent taxidermy for the second time in one week, rather to seek me out. And when they pressed Angie for some information on my whereabouts, she managed to pry from them what was up: the upshot being that my life was in danger and that they needed to try to protect me. She became alarmed: was she sure I was going to Virginia? They told her the next victim was in Omaha, Nebraska, and that if I were going there, I'd be heading right into the waiting arms of the killer. Their apparent panic at this prospect made her seriously worried in as much as she knew I was going to Omaha, Nebraska. And if these guys weren't for real, she reasoned, how would they have known about Nebraska?

Flat Nose Norman then told her the whole story of why the murders were happening, and the effect was compelling enough that she picked up the phone to call the FBI.

But the Tupelca pleaded with her not to do so. The FBI agents could be the ones trying to kill me. They reasoned that the FBI hadn't been able to protect any of the others, so why me? Surely it was plain they knew the murderer was connected to me but that I didn't fit the profile—so why didn't they have me someplace safe and guarded? Either they were using me as bait or they were thinking of pinning the murders on me. So why should Angie put her trust in the FBI?

And she knew that I was now a suspect, which made the FBI's motives even more suspect.

It was in this state of mind and state of panic that they all agreed to go to Omaha, and of course if she was going, Otto insisted on going. They were Otto's clients, after all, and he had to look after their interests. She already had the two tickets to Chicago, and the other three managed to get seats on standby.

When I'd spoken with her that afternoon on Otto's cell phone, I never imagined she was at Omaha's Eppley Airfield.

As to what the Tupelca had to do with all this, it was a long story that kept us up for half a tank of gas. First I regaled Angie with my half of the story because she just couldn't wait. She knew all about my grandfather being a founding member of the Order of the White Geckos and how that fez fellowship folded. But she knew more backstory than I did.

"It seems that the Order of the White Geckos was founded when the original five were camping on a hill during a javelina hunt in New Mexico. The area is known to have been inhabited by an aboriginal people known as the Tupelca. Each hunter had a dream one night, the same dream, about five white geckos."

"The same dream?"

"Yup. They thought that was strange, too, and mentioned it to their hunting guide, who told them that there were hieroglyphs in the area depicting five white geckos in a circle, like a chain, that had been left by the ancient people called the Tupelca. And that's when the hunters decided there was something special about the five of them, like the five geckos, and that they should form a brotherhood of good fellowship and hunting."

"Just like that? They suddenly just thought this would be a good idea?"

Angie shrugged. "I said the same thing when Norman told me the story, but I guess it was kind of a fad in those days to form brotherhoods. I'm told that a lot of lodges started from seemingly odd beginnings. Did you know the Cooties were formed by soldiers from World War I because the bugs that bit them caused them to scratch, which often resulted in them ducking under the Germans' machine gun fire?"

I paused, blinking incredulously. "OK, go on."

"And some orders were formed to make fun of other orders, but then turned serious."

"Not about that, about this tribe, the Tupelca tribe."

"That's just it, they weren't an Indian tribe."

"But you said..."

"I looked them up on the Web and printed out a bunch of stuff for the flight. The Tupelca are an anthropological riddle. They were thought to be some of the first inhabitants of North America, but nobody seems to agree on where they came from or how. Some scientists argue that they came by sea from the Pacific and Asia, while others think that they crossed from Siberia on an ice bridge—even though there is no archeological record of settlements in Alaska or Canada. Still others think their cave paintings are a lot like those in France. And still others, such as psychics and uncredentialed researchers, contend that the Tupelca were humanoid extraterrestrial castaways. Nobody knows how they arrived there, or where they went. All of a sudden—*pft!*— they vanished."

"*Pft?* Is that the sound they made when they vanished? *Pft?*"

At a loss for words in the face of my flippancy, Angie just squinted and stuck her tongue out at me. I could tell she was really worked up about all this, the way she gets when she's focused on one of her double-sided jigsaw puzzles.

"But enough about little green Frenchmen from Mars." I rolled my hand in the air. "Let's get to the part about who's trying to kill me. And why?"

"They told me that Coyotes are a stealth dwelling of the Tupelca. They're the ones trying to kill you."

"Right. My captors mentioned that."

"Here's the thing. Supposedly the Tupelca were great hunters, and their spirits absorbed those of the animals they killed. They had powers, and the native tribes in surrounding areas feared these strangers. So the natives banded together and wiped them out in a great war. All except five remaining Tupelca, who somehow—through magic or something—put their spirits into jars and buried them in a hill in New Mexico."

"Let me guess. This was the same hill..."

"Right, where the five hunters slept and had their dream. That's the moment the five spirits jumped into them. That's where their spirits hid, until they passed it to their sons, and then to their sons waiting for the stars to align and the white geckos to appear. That's now, and one of these vuka spirits is in you. And not only that." Angie took a deep breath, getting winded from her story. "They left a sign for any of their people who might follow, to rescue their spirits. The sign was geckos that turn white, which do so..."

"Every hundred years. Which is now."

"Uh huh. And some—get this—think that the appearance of the white geckos every hundred years signals an alignment of the stars so they can go home to their planet. If all five spirits come together into one man, they can call for a ride home."

"Like calling a car service to Planet X?"

She froze. "You really are smart sometimes, Garth."

"Gee, thanks." I rolled my eyes. "So these lamps with the genies in them..."

"Well, the Coyotes want to use the spirits to return to their planet and become immortal. To free the spirits, they need to gather them from the grandsons of the original five members by ritualistically killing them with animals killed by their grandfathers near the mound. It was killing animals near the mound that opened the grandfathers to receive the spirits. Same works in reverse. If you are killed by the animal that moved the spirit into your grandfather, the spirit will leap from you into whoever does the killing—in this case the Coyotes' leader, the serial killer. As long as it's at the time of the white gecko."

"Ah, so this is one of those cults where people divest themselves of all their worldly possessions and wait for a saucer to take them to an idyllic life in the clouds." I gestured at Norman and Brutus snoring on the floor across from us. "So what's this to these three? What do they care if these Coyotes go back to Zontar? I mean, not the nicest way of doing it, killing people with their taxidermy and stealing their vuka..."

"These Tupelca from the Javelina Dwelling found this out from a defector from the Coyotes, and want to take you to New Mexico, to that mound, and put your vuka back in the jar where it came from for the next hundred years, to keep it safe, to keep the Coyotes from going back to their planet."

"I appreciate that, I really do. I'd rather *not* die just now. But so what if they go back to their planet?" Was I the idiot who just said the words "back to their planet"?

"They're afraid the Tupelca will come back from their planet in huge numbers, to avenge the massacre of their people and—"

"I knew it. I knew it. Someone has to explain to me why the aliens are always coming here and trying to wipe us out, or enslave us, or eat us. If they're so smart and advanced, with spaceships that can travel parsecs in seconds and all that, can't they have machines make pastrami sandwiches out of thin air like on *Star Trek*? I mean, even we've figured out how to make doors open automatically—*shift*—like on the *Enterprise*. Messing with us is like me arbitrarily declaring war on pill bugs."

"Well, rant if you must, sugar. I don't know if they're aliens or not. All I know is that's what this is about. The Coyotes are trying to get all five spirits into one being during the time of the white gecko, and the Javelinas are trying to stop them."

"And these are the men who will save the world from an alien invasion?" I gestured at the snoring

Norman and Brutus sprawled across from us. "Suburban warriors?"

She gave me a shove. "Joke if you want, but someone is trying to kill you because they *think* you have one of their vukas. Doesn't matter whether it's true or not."

"Would it be indelicate to ask how my vuka is going to get from me into this jar? I'm picturing myself squatting over a genie lamp in the high desert."

"Gross. There's some kind of ceremony. Garth, this is serious. You need to take it seriously."

"No, my sweet, this is idiotic. You don't really believe all this?"

"I keep telling you, dopey, it doesn't matter what I believe. *They* believe it. Enough to try to kill you if they think you have the vuka spirit." Angie rested her head on my shoulder.

"So who's the Coyote leader that's going to absorb all these spirits?"

"Someone they call *El Viajero*—that means 'The Traveler.' He's the one who came upon the original charter for the Order of the Five White Geckos that explained all this."

"That nut J. C. Fowler mentioned that name when he was babbling to me at the Space Needle."

I stewed a few moments. I had little doubt that this story was cooked up much in the same way that Shirley MacLaine knows what condiment a thirty-five-thousand-year-old Cro-Magnon warrior named

Ramtha liked on his hot dog. Some ding-a-ling channeled this complicated little history, and like those guru hucksters with their doomsday cults, they roped in a bunch of impressionable knuckleheads. Three of them were right there in the van with us.

"J. C. Fowler?" Angie lifted her head off my shoulder in surprise. "Is he that archeologist guy from the seventies?"

"Wow, that was fast. How'd you remember him?"

"Crossword the other day. Six across, begins with 'F,' *archeologist who digs it*."

"Uh huh. Well, it seems he knew my dad, and Gabby, and told them and me he was a nice Javelina. When I spoke to Stella on the phone she said he was my uncle."

"Your mother would have told you, wouldn't she?"

I tried not to give her a sardonic eye. "That's right, you've never met Gabby. But get this: Fowler claims to be Nicholas's father."

Angie gasped, partly from surprise, and partially—I think—from pleasure. Her mouth hung open and her beautiful blue eyes were bright and wide. She gets a kick out of weird stuff like that, part of her puzzle personality.

I nodded. "That's what he said. And when I needled Nicholas about it, he confessed that he hadn't been able to find any record of his birth—that's the reason he took the name Pahlinic all those years ago. Found it in the phone book."

"Wow." Hands to her face, she sank back into my

side, deep in thought. "Wonder if it's true. Now, you mentioned a Dr. Lanston. The lead FBI investigator. A woman?"

"Air Force."

"Air Force? What have they..."

"I don't know...but when I escaped Hell she was on the phone with someone who said they were sending someone from something called Gibraltar to help find me."

"I didn't see her when they brought me in for questioning, just Bricazzi and Stucco. Is she cute?"

"Cute?" I eyed Angie warily. "Yes, cute like Charlie McCarthy. You don't really think I have a wandering eye, do you?"

"You've been away a lot." She assumed a grumpy demeanor, arms folded, bottom lip out. "I worry sometimes."

I reflected back on Amber. I was this far from telling her about that, to bolster her confidence in me, but thought better of it. I know I don't like hearing about guys hitting on Angie. If a relationship was a car, something like that can be the little *tick, tick, tick* sound you hear from the rear axle. Could be nothing, just one of your suspension bushings squeaking. Or your wheels might be about ready to fall off.

"Babe, that's the last thing you need to worry about. We've got a vuka to flush."

chapter 19

It felt great to have Angie with me, so I was a little more willing to go along with the Three Musketeers' scheme than I might have been otherwise. Not that I really had a lot of choice. I have an inherent distrust of the police to begin with, so it didn't take much of a stretch to make me suspicious of Colonel Lanston and the FBI. Historically, the cops have paid me undue scrutiny— I've surmised it has something to do with genetics, or pheromones. As a lad growing up, me and my pal "Mushy" Mochulski were just bug collectors chasing luna moths in the moonlit backyards of suburbia when a string of calls buzzed in to the police about a pair of Peeping Toms. For a relatively innocent teen, I must have found myself at the police station ten or twelve times. Once out of college, that stopped for about twenty years, but I still attracted undue scrutiny by passing highway patrolmen and beat cops. Nicholas has the same affliction, though in his case their attention was and is often warranted, even though these days he no longer perpetrates Ponzi schemes or kites checks to buy penny stocks. The previous year I'd learned from my morning paper that he was a murder suspect and possible art thief. It wasn't true, but one detects a pattern just the same.

Anyway, I always end up being suspected of something. When there's the least sign of impropriety in my proximity, the Man sees fit to direct me toward the hoosegow. I've come to resent it.

So going to the cops was out. Going home was out because the killer would know where to find me. Would he think to find me out in the flat expanses of Kansas, in north Texas? At least I was a moving target, harder to hit. What I didn't like was that having Angie with me was more or less collateral damage waiting to happen. Of course, back home the Coyotes might have kidnapped her to get to me, so I supposed it wasn't all bad: at least here I could watch out for her.

And then there was Otto. In the past, he'd proved useful in the path of danger, once even taking a bullet in the heat of battle. You wouldn't know it to look at the runt, in his boxy woolen Soviet-era suit and flowery tie, but the guy was like a taut spring ready to snap at the first sign of danger. Then, of course, we had Flat Face Norman, Linebacker Timmy, and Droopy Brutus. Somehow, I felt Timmy and Brutus must have gotten their names mixed up. So I was flanked by a full contingent, safety in numbers and all that. How battle tested my three kidnappers were in the face of menace I had no idea. All I knew was that Timmy could do a mean choke hold.

But look at the alternative. I could have been with Nicholas and Vargas and J. C. Fowler, not to mention the FBI and the Air Force. I would have been in the midst of suspects. So by default, without viable alternatives, I decided to play along and appease this idiotic Tupelca trio. Angie was right: if the Coyotes were so deluded as to believe enough in this claptrap about vuka spirits in jars to kill, they were just as dangerous as if it were all true.

It was crazy, to be sure. Crazy as a goose sleeping on a down pillow. Crazy as a frog in a shower cap. OK, perhaps even crazy as a loon. But as I stared across the plains zipping by in the orange gush of the rising sun, Angie asleep in my arms, I figured the Tupelcas were no loonier than a lot of fanatics out there. People have to believe in something. And some beliefs are a little more out there than going to church on Sundays or believing nakedness is the solution to the human plight. And what with the cyberworld encroaching on the real world, I'd sensed mankind getting a little bit more estranged, a little more alienated, a little more delusional than before.

Of course, sitting there scrunched in the front seat of the van, looking at all the little drab houses spread so far apart, all the open space and seeming monotony, I was reminded that a lot of hoi polloi think guys like me are crazy just for living in New York. I have to admit that sometimes when I'm crossing the street, and the jackhammers are going, the subway is rumbling, fire trucks are wailing, helicopters and jet planes are zooming, horns and neon lights are blaring, I do look around and go: *Wow, this is kind of intense*. But I usually screen it all out. Maybe the prairie proletariat of these expanses screen it all in.

At the same time, the great void out my window was quashing my hopes and dreams about Middle America: where were the malls? I'd seen so many to the north. I admit that I have the New Yorker's typical disdain of the mall-centricity that is the backbone of most of America's culture, but my hypocrisy was seeping out. I longed for one now. For the megastore, the megamart, the mega everything that is the contemporary mall. My companions all had their luggage with them. Not steamer trunks or anything, just overnight-type bags, but mine was back in my hotel room in Omaha. As Angie slept, she was slumping lower and lower in my arms, and I was afraid if she reached my armpit, she might wake up thinking we were under an anthrax attack. I was due for a change of clothes and a shower. I felt pretty grungy. I couldn't see the collar of my white oxford shirt, but didn't want to, and I dared not remove my running shoes without proper ventilation. A shopping list was going through my head: socks, cheap long sleeve shirts, cheap chinos, underwear, toothbrush, toothpaste, floss, deodorant, foot powder...

"Timmy? I need to stop at the next mall."

"Whut?"

I think I awoke the hulking driver from a white-line trance. He blinked sleepily.

"And it probably wouldn't be bad to change drivers. I need to stop at a mall to buy some clothes, and if there's any way I could catch a shower somehow... Where does one go for a shower out here?"

"Truck plaza. There's one coming up."

"Shower at a truck stop?"

"Uh huh."

"In the gas station bathroom sink?"

"Real truck plazas have showers, rooms, all that. There's one up ahead."

We veered off at the next exit, and sure enough we spiraled in on a sprawling truck plaza as big as some small towns. It boasted of showers, bunks, and home-cooked meals. I always wondered who was fooled by the notion that anyplace that wasn't home could deliver to you a home-cooked meal.

We squeaked to a stop amid several dozen big rigs.

"*Dyepteyah* ... Garv, vere to be?" Otto stuck his head between me and Timmy, rubbing his eyes.

"Stopping for gas and a shower..." I caught a whiff of him. "You and I will both take a shower, *da*?"

"Ah very nice! With weemin?"

"No, Otto, with truckers."

"I dunno, Garv." He scanned the big rigs and shook his head. "Not lookink. Maybe veemin truck drivers?"

"Where are we?" Angie uncurled from my arms as I opened the door. Wilco spilled out and wasted no time in lifting a leg on the nearest truck tire.

"A truck plaza. Otto and I are going to take a shower."

Her eyes widened.

"Not *together*. I desperately need to bathe and so does he—in his own shower, far from mine if it can be arranged."

"At a truck stop?"

"So it seems. For the long-haul truckers."

I could hear the others in back moving about, then heard the back door open, saw the light spill forward.

"Good idea." Angie rubbed her nose sleepily. "You have PU pits."

I stepped out of the panel truck and for the first time saw it from the outside. On the side was a cartoon of a grinning elf, with the words: PIXIE CLEAN! DRY-CLEANING. COLD STORAGE. There was a phone number with an Omaha exchange.

Norman was just striding around from the back of the van.

"Where'd you get this van, anyway, Norm?"

He yawned, his irises sparking with streaks of gold. "Fellow Tupelca lent it to us."

"With dry-cleaning boxes still in back?"

"Those are empty, for cold storage. If you're going to take that shower, let's get a move on. I want to stay ahead of the game, reach New Mexico before anybody else, and get this over with. My wife is wondering where the heck I am."

Otto and I cruised the aisles of the truck plaza store. In truth, I could probably have bought my clothes there, except I would have ended up looking like one of your more avid racing fans. In New York, there's none of this Nascar fever. By contrast, Middle America seems awash in posters, endorsements, and hats for all kinds of race car heroes. At least I think they were. Some of them looked like country singers, of whom I am also utterly ignorant. This stuff just doesn't exist east of the Hudson, and it made me feel pretty out of my element. Which I was.

I grabbed two Dale Earnhardt Jr. shaving kits, some Rusty Wallace shampoos, two Jeremy Mayfield deodorants, and two Kasey Kahne toothpaste kits. After I bought this stuff, and a couple coffees with a picture of someone named Jamie McMurray on the cups, a soap opera magazine for Otto, and an *America Today* newspaper, I handed half of my haul to Otto and led the way back to the shower rooms.

Otto handed back the Jeremy Mayfield deodorant. "For Otto, is not important."

"Oh, very, very important..."

He made a proud and dismissive grin. "Otto smell like man, not *goluboy.*"

"It's not perfume, Otto. It stops you from smelling at all."

"But what is?" A dismissive pout screwed onto his goateed face. "Smell is good. Veemin, they like man smell like man. It make bazooms heavy and the peach ripe, eh?"

"Bazooms? Ripe peaches? Where do you pick up this stuff?" I gave his impish beard a reprimanding tug. "*Man* not like *man* to smell like man. It makes my nose heavy when you smell ripe. C'mon, nincompoop."

"Why say to Otto ninnypoop? Not nice . . . bazooms and peaches very nice."

We paid a fee to an attendant, were handed a key for a locker and some white towels with a single blue stripe down the center. Clothes stored in lockers and towels around our waists, we went down the line of partitioned shower stalls looking for two empty ones.

I'm happy, even a little bit proud, to say I don't spend a lot of time in locker rooms and public showers. But when I find myself in those environs, I'm always a little taken aback by how hairy most men are. Sure, I have my share of body hair, but compared to most, I'm the dunes next to the rain forest. Locker rooms are always a potent reminder that men are primates in the most primal, fur-bearing sense. It was like walking into a Dian Fossey research facility, shaggy truckers trundling to and from their lockers like simians in their day to day.

There's something about a shower that makes me contemplative, and as I lathered up, I began to wonder where Nicholas was. Had he gone back to New York? Probably not. He didn't know whether I had been abducted by ne'er-do-wells and was probably doggedly trying to figure out what happened to me. At least I hoped he cared enough to do so. Then again, he had his future bride to think about back home, who was probably anxious to have him back. I wondered idly if Nicholas had come out to Omaha because he had cold feet. Were my troubles a convenient reason to postpone the nuptials? And was what Fowler said true, that Nicholas was his son? If I ever made it to that wedding maybe I'd find out. And Vargas: would he have gone back home to the pie stand and Amber the nymphomaniac by now? The FBI would definitely still be on the case. Did they have any idea who had abducted me? Would they be waiting in New Mexico? Should I be wearing a disguise?

Even as I succumbed to musing as I bathed, Otto succumbed to his lyrical impulses and launched into song. At first I thought it was one of his soaring Soviet anthems, but suddenly recognized it by the tune as a popular trucking song. As usual, he made a complete hash of the English lyrics:

> *East bound is down, boarded up, and stuck in!*
> *Wagon donut they say can't be gone*
> *We get along, way to go, and quarter of nine is*
>   *better*
> *I am easy hound, just wash up panda fun*
> *Keep full heart, hound, never metal*
> *Sun never shines in flakes*
> *Letting hands on deck, a causeway fun to make*

The buoys are first of Atlantic
And fear of the sharks banana
We fling them back does not matter the flakes

The other higher primates in the room took notice, and one in a cowboy hat and his birthday suit approached Otto's stall. He had a prodigious belly and looked unhappy.

"Garv, eetz fat cowboy!" Otto pointed gleefully, and the trucker looked even less happy than before.

"Uh, don't mind him..." I began.

Bloodshot eyes beheld me from under the brim of the well-loved cowboy hat.

"This little feller makes a lot of noise. He makin' some kinda joke?"

Another trucker stepped next to him, a soggy Sasquatch buttoning his shirt, but no less friendly than the nekked cowboy.

I hurriedly rinsed the soap from my body, talking almost as quickly. "Honest, guys, he's just a crazy Russian, doesn't know the language. He's harmless. A child, really. Not quite right in the head. Tortured by the KGB. So, you know, if you could just cut him some slack..."

"Russian?" Nekked Cowboy rumbled.

"Garv, Otto to get cowboy hat, yes? Like our friend."

"See? He's like a child."

The two truckers looked from one to the other, then slowly turned back to their lockers.

That's when Otto broke back into a new song:

"*Like a rimjob cowboy* . . ."

"Otto, shut the hell up!" I grabbed my towel. "Please?"

Nekked Cowboy was back. "Whaddid he say?"

"I apologize, really, he doesn't know what he's saying, he gets all his lyrics wrong. You should hear him sing Meatloaf. He-he-he. Otto—come on, let's be going."

"*Sing* Meatloaf?"

"Yeah, you know, 'By the Dashboard Light' . . ."

Cowboy just knit his brow at Otto as the latter smiled up at him and made his way to the lockers. There was a moment there when I thought Nekked Cowboy would grab Otto and bounce him around like a tire. But he let him pass.

"Otto, no more singing!" I hissed.

"But why, Garv? Otto to sing all time when tub to soap."

"Just get dressed, quickly." I looked back apologetically at Nekked Cowboy.

A long string of quiet, but no less frantic, prayers streamed through my brain as I stabbed my foot into my trouser leg.

Nekked Cowboy tapped Otto on the shoulder.

"You some kind of comedian?"

Sasquatch appeared beside him. "C'mon, Carl, the guy's nuts. His partner here said he was sorry."

"He called me a '*rimjob cowboy*,' Roy. You heard it. An' after I warned him."

My guess was that Carl had been on the road way past his bedtime, strung out on bennies or Vivarin, and was preternaturally irascible as a result.

My fingers began to misalign the buttons on my shirt.

"Honest, fellahs, he doesn't know what he's saying. He's a simpleton."

"I don't care if he's a Baptist!" Nekked Cowboy started to flush, and I knew then that the confrontation meter was tipping into the red. "Nobody comes in here and makes fun of Calgary Carl Jones."

Another trucker stepped forward, this one fully dressed in jeans, plaid shirt, vest, and the gentle bearded countenance of Mitch Miller. "C'mon, Carl. Get some shut-eye. Don't mess with that runt, not worth your time."

Otto was humming to himself, and finally turned from his locker to behold the menace standing behind him. "Ah, my friend!"

"Otto..." I implored. "Please, Otto..."

"You see, Garv?" Otto took an index finger and began bouncing it off Cowboy's belly button. "Very nice fat man."

Calgary Carl lurched forward at Otto, who seemed suddenly to vanish. Carl crashed headfirst into the open locker, and Otto was suddenly behind him giving him a shove.

"*Byk bychara!*" Otto whispered in surprise—

labeling his attacker a redneck. "Garv, cowboy not nice!"

As Carl lumbered to his feet, several of the other truckers gathered around.

"Whoa! Hey, guys, let's simmer down, just some miscommunication here…" Garth, the sensitivity trainer.

I didn't hold it against the truckers assembled. One of their own was, by all appearances, under duress and possibly attack. A couple of them came forward to restrain Carl. The others closed in on Otto and me.

"What's goin' on here?" A tall, angular trucker with a long white scar down his face came forward.

"These two were razzin' Carl," one of the crowd accused.

Scarface turned to me. "Who are you two?"

"Just passing through. He's Russian, doesn't speak English well, insulted Carl by accident…" I tried to explain.

"He called Carl 'fat,' right to his face…" Sasquatch pointed.

"An' he sang 'Eastbound and Down' as somethin' about sailors fuckin' dogs," someone else said. Interesting interpretation.

Otto looked dismayed. "Yes, Otto say to cowboy 'Very nice fat man.'"

"He doesn't know what he's saying," I insisted, my eyes scanning the direction of the exit. "To him, 'fat' isn't bad. He's translating it in his head from Russian as something like 'jolly,' or 'happy.'"

Scarface eyed me shrewdly, and I continued.

"You think a runt like Otto would intentionally come in here and start a fight with you guys?"

Otto didn't understand a lot of what was being said, but enough. He stepped up to Scarface, grabbing him by the forearms in what he felt was a friendly gesture. Otto never picked up on the notion that Americans aren't quite as touchy-feely as his comrades back on the Ural steppes. It was plain to see that Scarface didn't like being touched by a stranger.

"Please, Otto very ashamed to tell cowboy any bad. War in bathtub, eetz not lookink." Then he looked at Scarface's elaborate belt buckle, which was about the size of a steak platter. On it was the silhouette of a reclining and buxom stripper, the same symbol emblazoned on truckers' mudflaps from Portland to Portland, except this one had red rhinestones for nipples. Below it said KEEP ON FUCKIN'.

Otto is, among other things, a silversmith and engraver, and is never shy about showing admiration for the craft at large. Or admiration for the nude female form. Or in this case, both.

"Oh, my Got!" Otto enthused, staring at the belt buckle and then pointing. "Eetz big and very nice!"

Then he reached to touch the overly elaborate belt buckle.

I can't say for sure what happened next, except that there was a sudden tumult behind me as I made for the fire exit. I slammed through the door and an alarm sounded, matching the alarm bells going off in my head.

Believe me, if there were any chance I could have helped Otto physically—and let's face it, I did my level best to help him verbally—I would have. But that Slavic dumbbell just kept making one gaffe after another. If only he'd just shut up.

I was racing across the parking lot, jacket and shoes cradled in my arms, dodging cars at the pumps, leaping over fuel hoses, headed for where I last saw the Pixie dry-cleaning van, my bare feet slapping the macadam. In my half-dressed state, I must have looked like a boudoir interloper on the skedaddle. The jingle of the fire bell faded with distance, and I didn't know if the truckers were after me or not. But zippy, unhalting, and furious flight has been the hallmark of a number of my narrow escapes. My fighting abilities are largely untested. I have the lack of permanent and disfiguring injuries to prove it.

I scrambled under an eighteen-wheeler or two, crab-like, and came to where the van had been.

Had been.

OK, the Tupelca trio obviously hadn't abandoned me here. They needed my vuka. Angie wouldn't leave me there. So they must have pulled around to get gas or go to the store. But I hadn't seen them. Not surprising, as I was pretty focused on a set course for the moon when I launched out of that locker room. But I didn't dare head back into the fray, and at the moment was safely sheltered from view of the truck stop by a maze of Macs, Peterbilts, and Kenworths. I put my hands on my knees, leaned over, and tried to get my breath back.

Otto suddenly rounded the corner of a tractor trailer.

"*Poluchit' pizdy!*" The sleeve of his jacket was torn, and there was the beginning of a shiner around one eye. "Garv, my friend, I very glad you go quick. Why fat man to be angry? And man with very nice..." He gestured at his belt.

"Buckle. You OK? They coming?" I scanned the sky, which had been sunny but was now turning dark with clouds.

"Yes, of course." He gestured to where the van had been. "But tell to me: where to Angie and Tulips, eh? Not lookink. I thinkink maybe we must *pizdyets*, yes?"

"Yes, we should *pizdyets*," I panted. *Pizdyets* was his Russian word for everything from "it's over" to "let's go." What it actually means, well, is not for polite company. Like many of his Slavic mutterings. "You didn't see the van?"

"Otto not see."

"Come on." We darted around to the end of a truck and caught a view back toward the gas pumps, where a group of agitated truckers were checking all the nearby hiding places, much to the bewilderment of onlookers. No Pixie van in sight.

I leaned against the truck, thinking. Couldn't I

have one day's peace? Is this what it was going to be like all the way to New Mexico? Farmers with pitchforks, Wal-Mart greeters amok with shopping carts, Navajo trinket salesmen with turquoise and silver nunchakus?

"Otto to say something bad to fat cowboy?"

"We'll talk about it later." I didn't want to get into it, not then. "Not good to call a man fat, not good to touch strangers with big nasty scars on their face."

"I dunno." Otto stroked his beard. "But we must make to go, *s'ebat'sya*, yes? Ah, look..."

He bent down to pick up a twisted piece of wire from the ground, admiring it. There was no piece of junk too small for him to see as possibly useful.

"Otto, stop picking up trash and concentrate. The van has to be here somewhere!" I yanked my running shoes on and donned my jacket.

I peered around the corner again in vain hope—and was rewarded. The van was slowly turning the far corner of the truck stop diner. I could see Norman searching for us from the driver's seat, Angie in the passenger seat. I could also see some truckers headed our way.

I put a foot on the truck cab's running board. "Up here."

A few footholds afforded us access to the cab's roof, and then we scuttled onto the top of the trailer itself, lying flat. *The tiger never looks up.*

Atop the trailer I could feel a cold wind start to kick up, and noted clouds roiling in from the north, not too unlike those I'd seen over Omaha. We could hear the truckers filing along between the trucks, and I slithered close to the edge to take a look. Angie and the three Tupelca were now standing beside the Pixie van, scratching their heads.

I waved to Otto. "Now or never—let's go!"

We shimmied down the far side of the truck.

"Garth!" Angie waved. "Over here!"

Otto and I broke into a run.

"Start the van!" I shouted.

"What?"

"Start the goddamn van now!"

The four of them stared dumbly for a millisecond before seeing our pursuers and scrambling hurriedly into the van. I glanced behind me and saw the pack of truckers had rounded the corner out of the truck maze as fast as their Timberlands could carry them.

By the time Otto and I reached the van it was already moving, away from us, back doors open. Timmy had his hand extended. "What the heck is going on? Get in!"

With the help of a quick tailwind from the approaching storm, Otto bounded past me, latched onto Timmy's hand, and was yanked into the van with such force that he tumbled head over heels.

"Slow down!" I shouted.

"Hey, slow down!" Timmy shouted into the van.

That's when I tripped—one of my laces had come undone. Stormy sky, a white, streamer-like shoelace, and asphalt kaleidoscoped as I tumbled, and the next thing I knew five angry truckers had their hands on me and were holding me up like they'd just pulled a rabbit out of a hat. I thrashed for all I was worth, but they had me firmly in their grasp. I was going to take a beating, I had no doubt of that, so I focused on trying to cover my face, my eyes, and my crotch all at once.

If I had an ancient alien vuka spirit inside me, maybe they would knock it out so I wouldn't have to go to New Mexico. That mildly amusing notion was fleeting, and the sound of thunder made it even more so.

"Let's drag him on the interstate!" someone hollered.

"Put him in the Dumpster and ram it with the semis!" hooted another.

"Make a bug shield outta the cuss, strap him to the front of my rig!"

From behind my forearms I could see Carl the Fat Cowboy approaching at a trot. His fist was balled, and it was plain he meant to find purchase with it on my body. I curled up tight and tensed.

A ferocious wind hit me, and I thought it was just the result of being punched by Carl, like the moment of panic just before the pain hits. Then I was spinning, sand and gravel stinging my face—I thought maybe I was on the ground being kicked. When I peeked, I found I was indeed back on the ground, but I could see a black snake writhing in the sky. Was I already unconscious, awakening in the hospital, and this was the doctor's stethoscope reaching toward me?

I shielded my eyes again with one hand, but now through the torrent, I could see the black snake tossing the truckers aside like Neptune flicking sailors off the deck of the *Argo*. The snake lurched toward me, but never struck me, swerving instead to one side and taking out another trucker. It was no wider than five feet across, spinning impossibly fast. *It couldn't really be a tornado, could it?*

Curled into a ball that would be the envy of any armadillo, I lay there and awaited the snake's wrath. But the dervish's torrent suddenly subsided, and I peeked just quickly enough to witness the black snake dissolve back up into the sky. The world suddenly seemed impossibly quiet.

"Garth!" Angie was kneeling over me, gasping with fright. "Holy buckets! Did you see that? Are you all right?"

The Tupelca were suddenly there with the van, hoisting me into the back. Before the doors closed, I saw the truckers hiding under one of their rigs, staring after me like the Argonauts before the Colossus of Rhodes.

chapter 20

There are plenty of times in life when one feels one's been somewhere before, a sense of déjà vu. In most cases, it's a dumb situation, like cutting a bagel toward your hand. Or leaving a frying pan handle pointed out from the stove where you bump into it. Or like setting your car keys in the car trunk *just for a second*. Wisdom is often nothing more than weaving a path through the minefield of your past mistakes.

Unfortunately, my sense of having been "there" before was being in a situation where something completely unworldly occurs, and in such a way as I've had the inkling I made it happen. Perhaps it's not a very common phenomenon for anyone else, but it was beginning to seem a perennial occurrence for Garth Carson. And we're not talking about a phenomenon like smacking the photocopier and suddenly having it work.

I was currently faced with being possessed by an ancient spirit that needed to be exorcised. And this had indirectly pitted me against an angry mob of truck drivers who were, improbably, chased away by a tornado.

At a certain point, one has to consider whether a string of similar events such as this is more than coincidence. And at a certain point, one just gets plain freaked out.

We were hurtling along the interstate through Fort Morgan, hell-bent for Denver and a turn south toward New Mexico. Angie and I were in back, my darling engrossed in a Sudoku puzzle book, her brain clicking away. Across from us, sitting on the floor, were Timmy and Brutus, both reading sports magazines. Norman was up front at the wheel, Otto riding shotgun and humming tunelessly as he surveyed the passing terrain.

Wilco was feigning sleep at my feet. Every once in a while I'd see his eye tweak open and that little evil smile cross his lips. I wasn't convinced he still yearned for an excuse to sink his teeth in me so much as to somehow tell Angie about that episode with Amber.

And just where was Wilco when the tornado hit? His saving grace was supposed to be that he howled when a tornado was about to strike. Ha! He most certainly did not—I'd asked the crew in the van.

Unlike the other humans, I couldn't concentrate on reading. I found myself unable to do anything but ruminate. And idly hope I could get rid of Wilco somewhere.

What if the weird stuff that's happened to me over the years has been caused by this vuka in me? What if I am cursed, or the walking damned, or telekinetic? Did I smite my enemies with a tornado? Could I really be living out some sort of bizarre, protracted quest of the Greek tradition? I only hoped Hera or some other god was looking out for me.

I'd never been able to read anybody's mind that I knew of. I'd be a phenomenal taxidermy dealer if I knew how much loot someone wanted for their used wildebeest before I made an offer. This was the first time in my life I felt I needed some spiritual guidance, when enough bizarre things had happened that I didn't know how to make sense of them all or to know if they meant anything. And I wasn't going to find the answers with my traveling companions. Gabby and Stuart hadn't raised me and Nicholas in a religious household, so I didn't have any particular affiliation, any rabbi, reverend, or Parsi priest, to whom I could turn.

And here I was all the way out west, virtually in Denver. The only person I knew in Colorado was a guy to whom I'd once sold a bird of prey, a Native American named Two Shirts.

Wait a sec.

Birds of prey are protected species, and one of the only legitimate methods of selling them is to Native Americans who want to use them for religious rites.

The U.S. government even has an eagle repository where birds found electrocuted by high-voltage power lines, as roadkill, or seized contraband are portioned off to the Native American shamans upon application. Two Shirts was a middleman, and the only reason I could sell to him was because he was a shaman.

But what could he tell me? What did I want him to tell me?

All I knew was that I needed a second opinion.

I went forward and tapped Norman on the shoulder.

"I need to make a detour."

"Bathroom break?"

I shook my head. "Need to see my witch doctor."

OK, so Two Shirts isn't a witch doctor. I should show proper respect. Especially in as much as I was putting no little faith in his abilities to give me spiritual advice. Sometimes you grab at straws because that's all there is to grab.

The van gang was none too pleased with this detour, but I put it to them this way:

"The vuka and I need to see this person before we go on. If we don't, we may not get him into his jar. It won't take long, I promise."

Angie was supportive but wary. I could tell by the way she kept feeling my forehead to see if I was running a temperature.

I guess I expected Two Shirts to live on some dust-bowl reservation with skinny dogs wandering around and lots of ragamuffin kids playing in the dirt. What do I know? That's the way reservations tend to be depicted on TV and in the movies.

What I found instead on Zuni Lane was a row of ranch homes right out of a Steven Spielberg film, each different but also much the same. Driveways. Lawns. Basketball hoops. Sprinklers. Shutters. Addresses painted on the curb. I expected to see a uniformed milkman and his bow tie making deliveries.

I'd tried calling ahead through information, but there was no answer.

As we approached the address, I could see there was someone mowing the lawn in pale blue shorts, a black Ramones T-shirt, white socks, and white sneakers turned green from the grass cuttings. No ponytail, but his black hair was down to his shoulders.

"Two Shirts?" I had to yell over the Briggs and Stratton powering his mower.

He stopped mowing and turned. He looked at me, and then past me at the rest of the crew piling out of the van, stretching their backs. Wilco took the opportunity to piss on Two Shirts's mailbox.

"I'm Garth Carson."

The look on his face was one Jehovah's Witnesses must see constantly.

"I'm from New York. I sold you some birds."

He put one hand on his hip and used the other to wipe his brow with the front of his T-shirt.

"About two years ago I shipped you a vintage golden eagle mount, for the feathers."

A smile flickered on his face, though it didn't quite light up.

"OK, I remember now." He pointed at my motley crew. "What's all this?"

"Hard to explain. That is, it'll take some time."

"Whose time?"

"Can you spare some?"

"It's nice to meet you and all, Carl, but..."

"Garth."

"Sorry." He looked me in the eye, less perfunctory and more searching. "What is it you want?"

"I know I don't know you except for the thing with the bird and all, and that we spoke on the phone a long time ago..." I felt like a complete ass. How could I have thought to impose on somebody I didn't know?

"Uh huh." He pushed a lever on the mower handle and the motors puttered to a stop. "Something freaky going on?"

"Freaky? Well..."

"If it wasn't freaky you'd have gone to a minister or a psychiatrist or something. White people only come to me when it's something freaky."

"I'm not religious, so even if..."

"That big dude looks like he could mow my lawn in about ten minutes. My back is killing me. Think he'd mind? Then we could talk."

Timmy was soon at the mower, and Two Shirts

and I were under a tree in his backyard, sitting on the newly mown lawn, inhaling the heady bouquet of decapitated grass.

"Look, Two Shirts, maybe I was wrong to impose upon you, but..."

"I'm a shaman." He shrugged. "That's what shamans do, get imposed upon. We like hearing about other people's freaky problems, makes our lives seem simple by comparison. So tell me what's bugging you that you happen to be driving around out West and pop by. You want some sunflower seeds?"

He held up a plastic snack package.

"No, thanks. I feel like an idiot telling you this stuff, but I think there's something wrong with me. Spiritually."

"Let's have it."

"See, there have been some very odd things going on in my life for the past five years. I've been drawn into situations, to objects, that have supernatural powers. Well, hypernatural, actually. Things like bear gall bladders, which have—"

"Yup, special medicine there."

"And a hydrogen sphere that can mass-hypnotize people."

"Read about that in *Weekly World News*. Don't tell me it's true?"

"And then the horn of a mythical bovine from Asia that imparts telekinetic powers. I was almost killed by a mind-reading freak. And pygmies."

"Pygmies?" He spit some shells into his hand.

"This isn't a dream or anything that you had? 'Cause I'm no shrink."

"Scout's honor." I held up three fingers. "And now, it seems I have an ancient spirit inside of me that needs to be exorcised or I'll be murdered by a serial killer convinced he'll become immortal and return to his home planet if he takes it from me. I was just at a truck plaza, and a gang of truckers attacked me, and just when they were about to beat the living crap out of me, a tornado came down out of the sky and kicked them around like bowling pins, but left me alone. Oh—and I've had run-ins with a man who thinks he's a werewolf."

"No shit?" Two Shirts's eyes widened briefly, and he spit more sunflower shells into his hand. "That's fucked up, all right. What do you want me to do about it?"

I threw up my hands and let them drop in a show of complete helplessness.

"I get the feeling that maybe I'm cursed or something. Why did all this suddenly start happening to me?"

"What do you think?" He held up the plastic package. "Sure you don't want some sunflower seeds?"

I waved off the seeds. "I don't know what to think anymore. Is it all some whopping coincidence, or is there some kind of fate at work? I want to know what you think."

Two Shirts sighed and scanned his lawn, his jaw

taut, and he seemed not so much to be searching for an answer as for a way of expressing his thoughts.

"You probably have seen enough movies to know that my people are animists. We believe everything has a spirit—rocks, trees, lawn mowers, everything. Those objects that got you in trouble? Well, some people, maybe scientists, might say that they had powers because various atoms that were part of complex compounds in these objects had free electrons that reacted with other atoms nearby, causing the release of energy at certain wavelengths and frequencies that created an unusual effect. But any hep physicist will tell you that there are four basic forces that make matter do what it does: weak forces, strong forces, electromagnetism, and gravity. Even they will tell you that these four forces remain a mystery, but they suspect all four are governed by a single force that they can't quite see with their electron microscopes and particle accelerators. And yet whatever that force is, it makes things do what they do."

"Wow, you seem to have done your homework."

"You hafta look at all sides." He smiled briefly to himself. "So fundamentally, animists and quantum physicists agree. Every object contains and manifests forces we don't really understand. It comes down to semantics—they call them forces, we call them spirits. A physicist will see a rock and say the forces manifest themselves by making the rock very stable, dense, and hard. To me, the physicist's observation is superficial. As a shaman, I look deeper, at the spirit itself, not just its shell. If I asked you, Carl—" He stood.

"Garth."

"Sorry, Garth—if you believe in levitation, what would you say?"

"You mean aside from a Vegas magic act? Generally, no."

"I'll be right back." He ducked into his aluminum garden shed and came back out holding a dark gray block a little larger than a pack of cigarettes. It had an eye hook on the back, with an attached string. From his other hand he tossed some nails on the ground in front of me. He dangled the gray block over the nails, and they jumped into the air and attached to the magnet.

He shrugged. "You can call that electromagnetism, but it is also levitation. Now watch."

Squatting, he took a nail and rubbed it vigorously on the base of the magnet. He then took another nail and set it on the ground. He touched the first nail to the second and lifted it off the ground.

"See, the force from the magnet went into the nail. Or, you could say the spirit of the magnet went into the nail. And the nail is now a magnet and attracted to other magnets, other nails."

"So you're saying that forces and spirits can move from one object to the next. Like the nail, I might have picked up a spirit which attracts other spirits."

"Could be." He sat back on the ground next to the

magnet and nails, the package of seeds reappearing in his hand. "What kind of spirit did you say is in you?"

"My grandfather picked it up and it was passed to me. It was one of five that were buried in a hill in New Mexico, in jars. The guys over there are Tupelca, you know, the fraternal order, and they told me this whole story. There's a guy out there trying to kill the five people who carry the spirits, to collect them all like trading cards and tap into their collective power. The four other grandsons have already been ritualistically killed, their corpses left with a white gecko—"

"White gecko?" Two Shirts's eyes darkened. "Man, that stuff is bad medicine, my friend. You say those guys are Tupelca?"

"You know about—"

"Five white geckos is the sign of the ancients among the tribes south of here, like a curse on a mummy's tomb. The original Tupelca were bad dudes, prided themselves on being so good at hunting that they were almost supernatural. Used to hunt my people."

"Hunt your people? You mean..."

"Yeah, you know..." He held his arms apart and mimed shooting an arrow from a bow. "Tracked them down and killed them. They were cannibals, kept the skin of my ancestors as trophies, like the Jivaros kept shrunken heads of their enemies. They possessed special powers, *nanucanaxle*—"

"*Nanoo...?*"

"—that allowed them to become one with animals, some even to *become* animals in order to take trophies."

"Please don't tell me: werewolves?"

Two Shirts answered with a shrug. "Anyway, all the Southwestern tribes got together and finally wiped the bastards out, so the story goes. If there's some spirit of a Tupelca still around—or in you—that could be your problem right there. Where are you going to get rid of this evil spirit?"

"Those guys know, somewhere near the Mexican border."

"You know them?"

"Not really, but they saved me from some other people, the FBI…"

"FBI? You some kind of fugitive, Garth?"

"As far as I know I'm just a person of interest, one who currently would rather not be questioned again."

"That's a drag. Best thing you can do is get rid of this…"

"Vuka. The spirit is called a vuka."

"You sure these Tupelca know how to get rid of it?"

"They say they do. Why else would they be going to all this trouble? Why, could you get rid of it?"

"Me?" He shook his head. "This is stuff from the ancients, not my people. Only ancients or somebody who knows that shit can deal with it."

"OK, here's another whacked-out question."

"Have at it."

"Someone suggested that the ancient Tupelca were aliens."

He chuckled humorlessly. "People love aliens from outer space, the fallback explanation of the conspiracy-prone. Buncha crap, you ask me. Aliens to this continent, maybe. It has been suggested that the Tupelca were not native to North America, that they came from elsewhere, maybe even Peru or Ecuador where they shrunk heads to capture and retain people's spirits to make a person powerful. Here, hold out your hand."

He spilled the spent sunflower shells from his palm into mine.

"Close the hand, make a fist."

I did so, and he clasped my outstretched fist.

"Now repeat after me: *Mecca Lecca Hi*..."

"Mecca Lecca Hi..."

"Mecca Highnie Ho."

"Wait a minute. That incantation is from that old *Pee-wee Herman Show*."

Two Shirts smirked and let go of my hand.

I opened my hand and the seeds were gone.

Staring at my empty palm, I finally said: "So what does that mean?"

"It means you can fool some of the people all of the time and all of the people some of the time." He opened his hand and showed me the empty seeds. "That was a stupid magic trick I learned in college. Did it in the bars to impress the girls."

I loosed an exasperated sigh. "And the reason you did that was . . . ?"

"Look, I can't help you, Garth. I wish I could. You have a really interesting problem. The only advice I can give is to make sure what you see isn't necessarily what you believe. Be careful, and watch out for the con. You may have this spirit and you may not. Think about it as you go on your way. And your string of trouble with powerful objects may have some other source. A rite of discovery may be the only way to find out what that is."

"You mean something like Jason and the Argonauts?"

"Watch out for Medusa." He chuckled softly. "She's one wicked bitch."

chapter 21

On our way back to the highway, I finally found a box store and purchased some cheap new clothes: chinos, white oxford shirts, underwear, socks. The usual. They didn't have an approximation of my standard tan blazer, so I had to settle for a tan zip-up Windbreaker with a fleece liner. I also bought some toiletries to replace the race-fan brands I left at the truck plaza. A couple of four-dollar pillows and a cotton blanket rounded out my purchases.

Back in the van, we ate pizza, and then I bedded down. I had only dozed the night before. With Angie curled in my arms, my leg had fallen asleep, but not me. Now, though, even the rumble and sway of the van didn't hinder a quick slide into deep slumber.

I awoke to Angie's voice.

"Garth? Wake up, sweetie. We're stopping for dinner."

"Dinner? We just ate." I could make out Angie sitting next to me cross-legged on the floor of the van, Wilco in her arms.

"That was six hours ago. We're in New Mexico, only hours away from our destination."

"We're not keeping Wilco."

"Who?"

"Vargas's dog."

"I named him Poochie."

"If he were our dog, you could name him Poochie. However, he belongs to Vargas, and he named him Wilco."

"Why don't you like him? I think he's sweet. Otto likes him."

"It's him who doesn't like me." Wilco gave me a sidelong look and nuzzled Angie's bosom. "He tried to bite me."

"What did you do to him?"

"I violently and without provocation tried to pet him. Look, if you want a dog, we can get a dog. A nice, sweet-tempered rottweiler or pit bull—I'm easy. But not Wilco."

"Garth, I want you to want a dog." Angie raised her chin as Wilco licked it. Little bastard would stop at nothing to make my life miserable.

"Wilco's not making it any easier."

Otto squatted next to Angie and petted Wilco.

"Doggie very nice, eh?"

Norman stuck his head around from the cockpit.

"Let's go."

Timmy and Brutus opened the back doors and everybody piled out. Except me.

"Go ahead." I held up my box store bag. "I'm going to change."

Norman looked worried. "Why not change when you get back?"

"Why not change now?"

He fidgeted a moment before he turned and followed the others toward some chain restaurant at the end of a shopping mall parking lot. The festive red sign on the roof said CHIPPIES, what appeared to be yet another insipid and unctuously upbeat chain restaurant.

I closed the back doors and put my shopping bag on top of one of the cardboard storage boxes. Snapping off tags, I quickly donned the new duds, put on my Windbreaker, and started stuffing my laundry into the shopping bag.

"Garth?" It was Norman at the back doors, knocking. "Coming?"

"Yup." I gave him a weary smile.

"What can I say?" Norman's eyes glowed softly in the late afternoon sun. "I feel I can't let you out of my sight. Things have a way of happening to you. We've already had to save you twice."

As we walked across the parking lot, my eye was drawn to giant banners strung across the adjacent main street of the town:

ALIEN DAYS, JUNE 21–23

On lampposts were hung vertical banners with

what has become the standard alien depiction—some pale, google-eyed, doughy-looking figure holding one creepy hand up in a gesture of greeting. You'd think interplanetary visitors would be a hardy lot. These always looked like emaciated Pillsbury Doughmen to me.

We took a large round table in the corner amid Chippies' traffic signs, sports memorabilia, vintage posters, and other contrived decor. I think the menus were even more heavily laminated than those at the Pickle Barrel where I ate with Gabby. Menu planks.

"So, Norman, what's the drill?" I'd had little chance to ask him about what was entailed in the final leg of our journey, of the actual place we were going.

The three Tupelca exchanged glances, communicating something mysterious almost like ants touching antennae. When I first met them, they'd seemed exceedingly normal and drab. Brutus and Timmy had said very little on the whole trip. Norman only a few sentences more. They reminded me somehow of those Bible-thumpers who come to your door— clearly they were possessed of their creed and their mission, in a way it was difficult to penetrate. I didn't much doubt that they were fanatics.

"Our destination is a few hours south yet. And access to it is restricted, so we have to go in by a back way and drive a dirt road with the lights off, then climb the hill."

"Restricted?"

"It's on federal lands. Fenced, but we know a way in."

"How will we be sure nobody else is there?" Angie said. "I mean, what if the FBI or the Coyotes know we're going there and are waiting?"

"We won't be positive. But the sooner we make it there, the less chance there is that someone will have figured it out. I'm hoping that the Coyotes don't know for sure that the Javelinas are the ones who grabbed you. And even so, they may not think that our aim is to try to put the vuka back in the jar, but simply to protect you."

The waitress showed up, a bouncy broad in an ill-fitting wig and a name tag that said MEIGHAN. "Y'all here for Alien Days?"

"I hope not." I smiled, but only outwardly.

"Just what are Alien Days, Meighan?" Angie asked. She's always the one to ask strangers questions and get them talking. Me? I'm too afraid people won't shut up if you get them talking. And you'll never catch me calling a waitress or waiter by their name. It sounds too much like I'm ordering a friend around. *Bob, get me some ketchup, willya? Excuse me, Bob, I ordered the onion rings.*

"Gracious," the waitress exclaimed with a roll of her eyes. "Well, it's just about the biggest huge thing for five hundred miles around. All them peoplefolk who believe in UFOs come here for a festival party 'cause it's near all sorts of site places like Area 51, Roswell, Aztec . . . you know, where the zip flyin' discs smash crashed and such. Alien Days is a lot of hoot fun. Got a parade show and everything. Y'all want something t'drank?"

Hoot fun? Peoplefolk? I had been dimly aware of the Western fondness for redundancy, but Meighan's vernacular was a stellar example.

When she'd gone with our grub order, I said to Norman:

"Lemme ask you something. How and when did you find out about all this? I mean, what makes you think it's true, enough so that you leave your families, assault an FBI agent, and kidnap me for a little sojourn to New Mexico?"

"A Coyote defector to our dwelling revealed the story, with copies of the original Order of the White Geckos charter. In it were the details of the dreams the founding members had, about the appearance of the white geckos and that the spirits of the founders would be passed on until the next appearance of the white gecko, when the spirits could be freed through ritual sacrifice by *El Viajero*."

"Can you clear that part up a little for me? Why do the Coyotes need these five spirits? What will they do with them?" If nothing else I wanted to make sure they had their story straight.

The gold flecks in Norman's eyes fairly glowed. "They can contact their planet and send for help."

He looked proud when he said that. Timmy and Brutus stared at the table in front of them, heads bowed in what looked like reverence.

"OK, so now the Coyotes have obtained four vukas into this guy called *El Viajero*." Angie folded her arms in thought. "Do you know who this *El Viajero* is? How to recognize him?"

"No." Norman shook his head. "And he could be very difficult to identify. It could be anybody."

Brutus spoke up, more animated than I'd seen Droopy since we met. "The more vukas *El Viajero* gets, the more powerful he becomes. That's how his followers believe, they see his power."

"By now he can assume any identity," Timmy added almost boastfully. "That's why you can't trust the FBI."

"You've got to be kidding," Angie protested. "You mean, like a shape-shifter kind of thing?"

I reflected on what Two Shirts had told me about *nanucanaxle*.

"He can now assume any identity," Norman assured us. "You saw what Garth did back there. With just one vuka he created a tornado—imagine having four times that power."

"Any identity?" I cleared my throat. "Even one of you?"

They exchanged glances, and Norman answered. "Why would we be taking you to return the vuka if one or all of us were Coyotes?"

I almost asked the werewolf question, but held my tongue—partially because it sounded idiotic.

Angie and I exchanged a glance. She squirmed slightly in her seat, a bit of body language I knew meant that she would let the matter drop for the present but that she wanted to discuss it with me privately later. Just as if we were faced with a plumber telling us our entire junction transfer drain is shot and will cost ten thousand dollars to replace.

Two Shirts's admonition came back to me: *look out for the con.*

If these Javelinas were lying to us, it was because they thought we wouldn't like what they had to say, which might result in a lack of cooperation. Should there be some ulterior motive for this adventure that would cause me to bail out, I would rather Angie, Otto, and I had the opportunity to ditch them on the sly. Best not to tip my mitt, to play along until I had some idea which way to turn. If we did part ways with them, we'd need some form of transportation, which didn't as yet present itself. My nascent plan was that if it came to that, we'd have to lure the Tupelca away from the van, then drive off and strand them somewhere so they couldn't follow.

I was mindful of a certain mechanic of football offense: keep running and passing to the right, and when you've suckered your opponent to shifting his defense almost entirely to that side, go left. I was a running back without blockers, without a hole to run through.

Otto, sitting across from me in his boxy suit, had been gulping his milk like a ten-year-old. He wiped away his white liquid mustache. In his hand was some flat piece of metal he'd been admiring, probably picked it up in the parking lot. "Please, gentlemen, I thinkin' that maybe be very careful. Dogs like wolf, waiting for us come to them. I dunno. We careful to toe tip, making eyes seeing, yes? Not lookink. Garv, is possible *El Viajero* is *vurdalak* like Oz?"

He can't pronounce Angie's or my name correctly, but he was dead-on with *El Viajero*. Maybe you could chalk it up to the commies in Cuba. Go figure.

Norman looked to me for a translation.

"He says we should approach this hill very carefully to make sure the Coyotes aren't there waiting for us. He thinks they'll be there waiting for us."

I left off answering Otto's question. He may seem like an idiot sometimes, but he understands more than he lets on. *Vurdalak* is Russian for "werewolf." The only reason I knew that word was because he used to be hooked on *Buffy* reruns and would always loudly applaud the wolfteen character named Oz. "Vurdalak *much to love Willow, yes? But Willow to love Tara. Not lookink.*"

Our food arrived, and I took the opportunity to go wash my hands. And make a quick call.

"Nicholas?"

He cleared his throat. "Oh, hi, Mel, what's up?"

"It's not Mel. It's me, Garth."

"What now, honey? I'm kind of in the middle of something." Then I heard him say to someone else: "I have to take this, it's the bride-to-be, excuse me." I could hear some scuffing for a few moments before he came back on the line. "Make it quick. Where are you?"

"Better not say, but I'm with those three Tupelcas we saw at the arena, and I'm with Angie and Otto, too."

"So it was *those* clowns who grabbed you. No more Fowler sightings?"

"Nope."

"Angie and that Russian runt are there, too?" he whispered hoarsely.

"Yeah, and the dog."

"What dog?"

"Vargas's mutt. Look, I'm not sure of anything, and this whole adventure is giving me the creeps. We're on the road, headed for a certain place. I may decide to make a break for it with Angie and Otto. Keep your cell on, I may need help in a hurry. Plane tickets or something."

"Can you give me your current location? Frick Frack me."

I had to think a moment.

"*Fracka fricka, spatta fooza thatta gabbaspye*... umm...*mickavulo jutala yaka spamulatosadim*. That's it. Oh, and *ipso croon*, of course. Got it?"

"I've got company a lot of the time. Bricazzi and Stucco. But I'll keep it on, see what I can do. Did you say Wilco is with you?"

I heard footsteps coming down the hall and hung up. I started walking back to the table and sure enough, Norman turned the corner. We just smiled at each other in passing.

Back at the table, Otto was showing our waitress one of his tricks where he can make a spoon dance across a lattice of string between his two hands. What parking lot or trash can the string came from was open to conjecture, but as I noted, his pockets were full of little odds and ends.

I sat back down next to Angie—Norman's seat to my right was vacant. Brutus and Timmy were eating, watching Otto's lame attempt at wooing our waitress, Meighan. I was taking in all these details as my mind started the process of considering escape, toward following my own agenda. My brain hadn't passed a verdict on the plan of action, but my unconscious mind was making its case before the court of my conscious mind. The judge was grumpy: just a lot of loose circumstantial evidence.

Angie squeezed my hand under the table and we locked eyes for a few beats.

I didn't need a vuka to know what she was thinking.

She was thinking what I was thinking.

ack on the road, we continued south, the dark silhouette of the mountains to the west crowned with a halo of a ruby sun. The east was purple melting to black on the horizon. We were now really leaving the plains and getting into desert terrain. Tumbleweeds, adobe, cactus—the whole nine yards, just like on a tortilla package. I'd never really been to the desert before. Had always wanted to go. Just not that night.

I made a point of sitting in the back of the van with Angie and Otto. Norman was driving, Timmy riding shotgun with Wilco in his lap. The only Javelina with us was Brutus, and he'd drifted off to sleep on his side facing the wall on the floor, opposite us.

Angie was back working on her Sudoku puzzles. Otto was sewing a sleeve of his Soviet suit jacket. Torn during the truck plaza fiasco. Otto always had things like needle and thread on him. Forever Ensign Fixit.

I'd finally managed to read the *America Today* newspaper, which on page four had a lengthy article about the big game hunters' deaths. The papers had grasped the serial killing angle, and my name wasn't even mentioned. When I finished the article, I put the paper aside, and my brow furrowed. "Uh-oh."

"Garth, what are you thinking?" Angie whispered, her lips brushing my ear.

"Why didn't I think of this before?" I held out my hand and ticked off my musings finger by finger. "Titan was killed by a ram's head. Sprunty? A black bear. Bronte? Elk. Draco? Mule deer. I know personally, from my appraisals, that the ram, bear, and elk were all old mounts."

"Old?"

"Uh huh. Like from the first decades of the century. And those animals are all indigenous to the Southwest."

"You mean..."

"New Mexico."

"Well, we know that as part of the ritual to release the vuka, the victim has to be killed with the same piece of taxidermy that—"

"The pronghorn."

She just cocked her head in confusion.

"My pronghorn. The one I rented to these guys. It's from my grandfather's collection."

"Oh my gosh! But, Garth, it's not here."

She followed my gaze and put a hand over her mouth to stifle a gasp. I was looking at the dry-cleaning boxes.

"*Psst!*" I crooked a beckoning finger at Otto.

He crept over on all fours, and then we all looked at Brutus, who was still asleep and facing the wall.

"What is in the box?" I whispered to Otto, pointing at the dry-cleaning boxes.

"Box?" He looked at it. "Mebe Otto to examine, eh?"

I gave him a thumbs-up, and he responded with an oversized wink.

"Garv, Otto thinkink, mebe our clients, they not lookink, yes?"

"Maybe, Otto."

His head drooped, and he gnashed his teeth with self-reproach.

"I very sorry, Garv. I not make good to brink clients, eh? In future I must better to beezness think."

"It's OK, Otto, you couldn't know. You did what you thought would help."

"Yes, but clients my responsibility."

"Not now, Otto. Back in New York when you're renting taxidermy..."

"But you tell to me, Otto, I very much need a help at you, to take beezness, make clients, yes?"

"OK, I did say something like that."

He looked offended. "You not mean?"

I rolled my eyes. "Yes, I meant that you should take care of the clients, of course, but—"

"But what? My responsibility, I take. Eh? But maybe Otto make caution." Otto tiptoed forward to the open cab door. Delving deep into a pocket he came up with some rusty wire. Gently, he wound one end around a bolt on the divider, close to the floor. He stretched the wire tight across the door and fastened it to a bolt there.

After giving us another exaggerated wink, he crept over to the dry-cleaning box I'd pointed out.

I kept one eye on the front where Norman and Timmy were, the other on Otto as he drove his whole arm into the first waist-high box. I could see he had hold of something, and as he lifted it, foam peanuts clung to his arm. Angie crept over and brushed them back into the box. A growing mound of white peanuts rose with whatever he had hold of, and the two of them shoveled the packing material back down as the object rose. I couldn't stand the suspense, and went over to help. In the dim light of the panel truck, I could see that Otto had hold of a horn. An antelope horn.

We exchanged glances of fear.

I looked deeper into the gloomy box and saw an eye.

"Goodness gracious!" Angie gasped.

"*Mat boga!*"

My vision swam, my heart seemed to have stopped. The van swayed and my balance failed me. I staggered and thumped against the wall.

My bump was felt up front, and Timmy's face appeared in the cab doorway. His eyes went wide when he saw Angie and Otto standing over the box holding my pronghorn. Then his eyes met mine—it was clear we both knew the pretense was up. "Brutus!"

As the van swerved to the side of the road, Brutus awoke and rolled toward us.

Arms outstretched, Otto flew through the air at Brutus. I grabbed Angie and turned toward the back doors. The main thing was to get the hell out of there, to put as much distance between me and that pronghorn as possible.

Timmy heaved himself through the cab doorway and promptly tripped on Otto's wire, falling hard to the floor.

I shoved open the back doors just as the van jolted to a stop. Angie and I stumbled out into the chasm of dark desert night.

"Otto, run!" I shouted. I saw him struggling with Brutus, whose outstretched arm held a small revolver.

"To run, Garv! Otto take care of clients!"

Then I saw Timmy's bulk stumble forward and bury Otto. Wilco was barking, from somewhere.

I stopped, panting, looking at the little numbskull's arms and legs wriggling around under Timmy like a monkey under a hippo.

I'd left Otto once before, at the truck plaza, largely because he hadn't listened to me and had brought all that mayhem upon us himself. But this was different. This was another in a series of fearless acts to protect me and Angie.

"To run, Garv!" came his muffled voice, as if calling from the bathroom. "Otto to take care of clients, come to you soon."

I wasn't convinced. But at the same time, I felt Angie hanging on my sleeve. Sorry, Otto, she was my priority. And there was no sense in all of us getting nabbed. I grabbed Angie's hand, turned from the van, and ran into the dark desert.

I couldn't see a thing, could only feel Angie's fingers in mine and the pavement under my feet as we raced down the highway away from the van.

Oddly, the thing suddenly on my mind was snakes. One always hears about snakes at night on roads in the desert. Supposedly they seek out the warmth of the macadam, but I wasn't enough of a herpatologist to know how true that was. My guess at that time was that if the scaly beasts were about, they'd be as likely to be on the warm macadam as anywhere else, so I veered off the pavement into the scrub. I could see the silhouette of the mountains against the sky, so we headed in that direction, the smell of sagebrush filling my sinuses as low shrubs scraped my pant legs.

I glanced back toward the van on the road, hearing shouts. The barking had stopped. I ran faster and could feel Angie struggling to keep up. Running is my best defensive move—it has saved my bacon a couple times—and I flew like the wind.

The shrubs gave way to a clear stretch, and I could just make out a path or road angling off toward the right. This wasn't the highway, but another road, the pavement broken and crumbling under my sneakers. I searched in vain to see if this led to a house, but there were no lights ahead. There was something else, though, and it turned out to be a chain-link fence and gate across the road.

"Garth, what about Otto?"

We came to a stop at the gate. It had a heavy chain and rusty padlock securing it.

"He can take care of himself," I gasped, hoping that was true this time. I squinted at a sign on the gate: NO TRESPASSING. PRIVATE PROPERTY. "Besides, it's me they want to kill, not him."

I pulled on the gate and it gave enough for us to slide through.

"C'mon."

I slipped through and then helped Angie. That's when Wilco trotted through with us.

"Good dog." Angie patted him on the head.

"Just what we needed." I sighed. "If there's a gate, it must mean there's something down this road."

"What about snakes?"

"They'll have to get out of our way." By now, the van was just a dot of light back by the highway. I clasped Angie's hand, and we jogged down the road. I'm a sprinter, and not accustomed to marathon flights for my life. I was getting pretty winded, and Angie more so.

The shape of a small dark building crouched ahead, and we stopped again when we reached it.

"Looks...like a tollbooth." Angie leaned against it. "What...what would a tollbooth be doing here?"

I pointed to a sign next to the gate. "Parking, four dollars."

"Parking?" She looked from the sign to me. I looked at Wilco, who wagged his tail lazily. I think he thought this was fun.

"Looks like more buildings up ahead. Whatever this is, it's abandoned."

Walking at a good clip across the weed-sprouted parking lot, we approached an archway, beyond which were some unusual curved, tall, and angular shapes that didn't make sense to me.

"What is this place?"

"Garth, look." Angie pointed up at the arch. Across the top were letters that looked like they were supposed to be carved from stone.

"Disneyland?"

"Dinoland," she corrected. "It looks like a theme park."

I shuddered. Last time I was at an amusement park my life had been in danger. A terrible sense of déjà vu gripped me yet again.

"Let's go somewhere else." I grimaced, searching the darkness in the opposite direction.

"There is no other way except back to the highway. Besides, I need to rest. We need to hide."

Wilco trotted ahead past the ticket booths and we

followed. This time, Angie had me by the hand, leading me.

"I don't like the looks of this, Angie."

"Holy moly! Dinosaurs."

"My love, could you just once just say something like 'holy shit'? If you've ever considered crude expletives, this would be the time. I promise not to be shocked."

She sniffed, ignoring my comment and gazing up and around at the looming shadows of things from the distant past.

We stood in a plaza, a dry fountain in the center, surrounded by life-sized statues of the Mesozoic classics. My nerves were not settled by being among replica monsters. A thirty-foot-tall brachiosaurus was dead ahead, big as a construction site crane. A triceratops to the left was facing a tyrannosaurus, ready for battle. There were parasaurolophuses clustered together to the right, flanked by the ever-popular stegosaurus. Other prehistoric leviathans, both four-footed and bipedal, were beyond, but my fourth-grade fascination with dinosaurs was sufficiently distant that I couldn't tell you what animals they were. It was like we'd stumbled into *The Valley of Gwangi*, only at night—I guessed I could pass for James Franciscus in the dark.

Under and surrounding these monuments to extinction were little concession stands, no doubt once rife with T-shirts, corn dogs, and Orange Whip.

There were no rides, praise be, in this defunct

theme park. This had the look of a tourist trap just for those who wanted to drop in and have their picture taken with their favorite thyroidal lizard, spring for a fossilized trilobite or two, pile back into the Vista Cruiser, and blast off to El Paso or Tucson.

Hot on the heels of our revelation about my pronghorn, it was extremely eerie standing among these freeze-frame terrors in an abandoned tourist attraction. There was something portentous about it all, like this place was trying to tell me something, to direct me. Dinosaurs: ancient monsters fossilized in the earth. Like the vuka? Like the Tupelca, extinct? And yet here they were, but only in representational form. Like those three mild-mannered killers in the van? At the same time I kept drawing parallels to things I remembered from back when I studied the classics in college. I was on a voyage, more or less finding myself shipwrecked in odd places. Situations from which I had to escape. All this gave me a sense that the ancients were right there, watching, possibly manipulating the situation.

Of course it was possible that the only thing watching me was Wilco, who currently sat in the dirt giving me sidelong glances.

"Angie, I know I'm supposed to be your protector..."

"You keep assuming that role, Garth." She clasped onto my upper arm. "I'm pretty good at taking care of myself, and you at times."

"I know you are. Which is why I feel I can tell you

that I am scared. Really scared. I'm beginning to believe this stuff. I feel like there is something inside me, and it's been causing all these things to happen."

Angie gripped me harder. "I can't say I know how you feel, being a target, people trying to kill you and all these wild stories..."

"That's just it. I'm wondering if this vuka thing has been what's caused everything." I sat on the edge of the fountain. "Pipsqueak, the white crow...this thing inside me has made me psychic or something, given me a connection with objects and people containing hypernatural powers."

"I'm scared, too, Garth." She sat next to me. "But you know what? When we're together, even though I'm scared, I find myself being able to do things, survive things, that I never thought possible. I get strength from you."

"Well, I guess that's what it's all about. Being partners." I put my arm around her. "We work as a team, draw strength from each other. At the same time, I keep putting you in danger. I don't know what I'd do if you got killed. Lord knows I've very nearly gotten Otto killed, I don't know how many times. I feel bad for leaving him behind again—hope he's OK."

"He's pretty resourceful."

"And let's not forget how these little episodes keep throwing a wrench in your career."

"Pshaw. Garth, there are things more important than all that."

"You should be in Chicago right now, making a name for yourself."

Angie and I sat in silence for a little while as the night got darker.

"Let's make a deal." Angie put out her hand. "I promise not to get killed if you promise not to get killed."

We shook on it, then kissed on it, huddling close. It was getting cold out in the desert.

"Did I ever tell you about Arnold?"

I felt her nod. "The possum, the one your mother had put down."

"Of all the things that have happened over the last few years, that still is one of the worst days of my life."

She gave my arm a squeeze. "Is that why you don't want a dog? Because of Arnold the possum?"

I shook my head. "No, I don't think so."

That's when we saw headlights approaching the parking lot.

"Security guard?" I looked at Angie.

"Out here?" She shook her head. "I doubt it."

From reflected headlamp glow we could see the impish figure of the pixie on the side of the dry-cleaning van. The vehicle slowed, then nudged its bumper against the chain link and began to press.

"Uh-oh." I stood. "Come on."

As we ran toward the parasaurolophuses, I heard the gate give way and the van roar into the parking lot.

We reached a plywood concession stand and hid behind it. I searched the ground for anything that might be useful as a weapon: a two-by-four, a brick, a bottle, anything. The only thing on the ground were broken tumbleweeds, small stones, and dirt. The door to the concession stand was just plywood, with a simple hasp and padlock, so I kicked it in. Flicking the light switch to the left of the door didn't accomplish anything.

"Here," Angie said, her house keys tinkling. Her keychain had a miniature flashlight on it, and since we'd been in darkness for a while, the tiny bulb seemed to light up the shack like it was a tanning booth.

The concession stand was largely empty. There was a back counter and a front counter where the stand opened up. Under the front counter were two wide, empty shelves containing a few stacks of dusty sweatshirts with the Dinoland logo. We didn't have to say anything, we knew what to do—put on a couple of the sweatshirts to help stay warm. I put on four, all extra large.

A beam of light shot through a seam at the edge of the shuttered front counter. We put our eyes up to a crack and saw the van slowly drive through the tollbooths and squeak to a stop in front of the fountain, right where we'd been sitting. The headlights blinded us, so we couldn't see anyone inside the van. But I could see the pixie cartoon on the side, grinning. Wilco trotted into the light, wagging his tail.

"Angie, I think we're both going to need to be extra brave. I think the only thing to do is split up. I'll draw them away so you can escape back to the road at sunup. Here, take my jacket. You hide here—with all the sweatshirts you should be able to stay warm enough overnight. It's going to get cold out here in the desert."

"No, Garth. I'm not staying here alone."

I held her face in my hands and kissed her, felt her start to breathe heavily as she prepared to cry.

"Yes, you will. It may be our only chance to get out of this. That way you can get the local police or somebody out here to stop all this. I'm not just being manly and protective here—this is for both of us."

"No!"

"Look, we're together even when we're not physically together, am I right?"

I took her silence to mean agreement, however reluctant.

"Draw strength from me. Then I'll be here with you, and you'll be with me as I lure them away. I'll be careful. Remember, I was a Boy Scout, I can handle it."

"That was more than thirty years ago." She loosed one short sob, but then I heard her gulp, sniff, and suppress her fear. "You weren't even an Eagle Scout."

I rolled my eyes. "Let me tell you, Eagle Scouts aren't all they're cracked up to be, believe me. And just because I only reached the rank of Star doesn't mean I didn't learn a thing or two. I'll be OK, I promise."

"Remember our deal?" Her eyes searched mine. "No getting killed."

"It's a deal." I shook her hand, kissed her forehead, then slid out the door. I kept the concession stand between me and the van as I dashed between the legs of an allosaurus. When I reached a perimeter fence, I found a portion that had been downed by soil erosion undermining some posts.

Now it was time to draw them in my direction. I shouted.

"Wilco!"

Damned if the dog wasn't already at my side, his dog tag winking starlight at me.

We scampered up and over a hill. On the night breeze I thought I heard my name being called. I stopped and listened, heard it again. It wasn't Angie. I shouted the dog's name again to keep them following me, and when I reached high ground and had a view of Dinoland, I could see the van driving off through the broken gate toward the main road.

Be strong, Angie, I'm with you.

chapter 23

The dog trotted ahead of me with a distinct sense of purpose. I wished he'd stayed with Angie to keep her warm. Of course, I'd called his name, but I couldn't think of anything else to shout to draw the three Tupelca away that wouldn't sound like I was trying to draw them away.

So why follow Wilco? I figured the snakes would get him first that way, and if nothing else, maybe he somehow knew where he was going. You hear those stories about Eastern families vacationing out West, losing their dog, and the dog somehow finds his way from Golden Gate Park to Darien, Connecticut. As much as I didn't like or trust Wilco, I had to assume he was still a dog at heart, complete with the full package of canine instincts and wiles.

And so we crossed the scrubby terrain dotted with yuccas. The desert night was spectacular—a pellucid sky like the calm surface of a lake through which you could see bright pearls on the dark bottom. Being a city slicker, it had been a long time since I'd seen the stars and constellations so clearly, the coruscant smear of the Milky Way shimmering diagonally across the sky.

I wasn't what you'd call a model Boy Scout as a lad. I reached the rank of Star and rested on my laurels, much to the displeasure of the troop leaders. One is supposed to be always advancing, earning more merit badges, striving to be an Eagle Scout. That irked me—attaining the rank of Eagle Scout was touted as a veritable transcendence into a wholly superior being, as though any scout who didn't attain that rank would have their outdoor skills shrivel up like a dead spider once they moved on from the scouts.

Even though I hadn't attained the godly rank of Eagle Scout, I had retained a few outdoor skills. Granted, after thirty-some odd years, they were a little rusty. Navigation without maps can be complex and disastrous, but I'd been taught that a few basic skills can serve one well. Compared to the star of Bethlehem, the North Star is disappointingly ignominious. But using the Big Dipper, it's a snap to locate the North Star and thus it is easy to get one's bearings. The main thing when lost—as I effectively was—was to move in a straight line and not go in circles. So I kept the star over my right shoulder.

I also knew to keep moving during the cool of

night, and try not to perspire all my water away in an hour of blazing sun. But how to find water?

Wilco was following a slight trail that I figured must be a pronghorn antelope or deer trail. I seemed to recall that many game trails eventually led to water. And as it happened, the winding trail led more or less true to the southwest.

You might think I'd be tired after a couple hours' hike. I wasn't. I'd venture to guess New Yorkers walk four or five times as far while commuting and foraging as most suburbanites do in a week of walking only to the driveway or parking lot. So we may not always be the most genial pedestrians you'd ever want to meet, but New Yorkers can walk and then some. I was also keyed up about my predicament. For once I wasn't too worried about Angie. The talk we'd had about being together and yet apart made me feel better. I felt she was safe and tried not to imagine otherwise. She was a heck of a lot safer back there near the road than out in the middle of the desert, I can tell you that.

My mental acuity was further sharpened by what I guess you'd have to call survival overdrive. I had to figure my way out of this. At three miles an hour walking speed, that meant I was approaching ten to twelve miles from Dinoland due southwest. I had not reviewed a map of this area, but I knew southwestern New Mexico to be a sparsely populated region—it stood to reason since they used to detonate atomic bombs down this-away. The last town we'd driven through was an hour north, so sixty-some-odd miles, which put me seventy-two or so miles south, southwest of that town. Granted, that didn't tell me much, but having at least some idea of where I was could be crucial.

And at least I was warm enough. What with all the exercise, I had actually removed two of my Dinoland T-shirts and tied them around my waist.

Wilco led me over a rise. Below was a long flat valley. Unlike the rest of the terrain we'd seen, this was scattered with something that looked ominously man-made. As we approached, the shapes became familiar. Trucks. There was a still-life parade of military trucks and craters stretched toward the horizon. As we approached, I realized we were seeing *what was left* of trucks, personnel carriers, and all manner of military issue vehicles that had been blown up and made into Swiss cheese by machine gun fire. Some of these machines I'd never seen before—wide and stout, sort of like Hummers, but with open backs like a pickup truck, or with a machine gun turret, or with what looked like a tow truck hitch in back. I knew a little about military aircraft and nothing about tanks and trucks and such. But none of that knowledge was required to deduce that we were on a military testing range of some sort. Either planes came in from above, bombing and strafing these targets, or artillery set up on the hills and practiced their mortar fire, or tanks and such flanked the imaginary enemy. Maybe all of the above. Either way, this was a shooting gallery and I was standing right among the ducks. Everything seemed quiet enough now, but what with night-vision technology, I imagined that soldiers might come out here to plink any old time.

Between the shattered vehicles were blackened craters. I climbed aboard a truck hood and scanned the distance by starlight. The junkyard procession stretched for some distance, maybe ten or fifteen blocks—over a half mile. The junk was arranged in a column leading toward the other end of the valley.

For whatever danger this place presented, it was also someplace that had been driven to, meaning that there must be some rudimentary road out of the valley leading to a depot where the trucks came from.

"Now we're getting somewhere."

Wilco gave me a sardonic look, as if to say "We've been out here a few hours and you're already talking to yourself?"

The dog was four steps ahead of me, trotting down the line of trucks toward the horizon. He looked back at me nervously from time to time and seemed uncertain of this new route we were taking.

Some of the trucks we passed were burned-out shells, but others were only partially damaged or flipped over. I imagined each of these vehicles had a story, had people and lives attached to them. These relics were totems to a past of drama, of life and death and heroism. To me they were also a testament to man's legacy of war, of grave miscalculations on a global scale. A legacy of fear, of imagined solutions through death that we have all inherited. Hey, I'm not a simpleton, I don't pretend to have the answers. Our planet is an immensely complex orb. But standing in the desert at night among these vehicular tombstones, the world suddenly looked like a sad place where we're all haunted by our legacy of war, where many of the events of our personal history are unduly influenced by forces outside ourselves.

Not too unlike me, cursed by the legacy of my grandfather.

"'My name is Ozymandias, king of kings!'" I shouted theatrically, gesticulating toward the great accumulation of wrecks. My bold dictum echoed faintly across the desert. "'Look on my works, ye mighty, and despair!'" Then there's the legacy of an English major—literary and remarkably apropos witticisms on demand.

My audience had taken that opportunity to lick his balls. I guess it was a bit much to expect Wilco to be a Shelley groupie.

Walking alongside the trucks meant climbing in and out of craters, so I elected to cut through the wrecking yard and get onto even ground on the other side. That's when I noticed a half-track with a faded white star on its flank. Sort of like the ones the Germans had on *Rat Patrol*.

"Wow!" I had to go up and touch it. To the uninitiated, a half-track is more or less like a large pickup .truck in front but has treads like a tank in the back.

The front bumper looks something like a cow catcher on an old locomotive, but with what seems like a massive steel rolling pin horizontally across it. I imagined this was designed for smashing into and rolling over obstructions. I put my hands on the rear treads and was surprised that they were not giant links of steel like on a tank but more like a large corrugated fan belt. It felt like a tire, but in a strip with crosswise treads that went around all the rollers and sprockets.

A machine gun was mounted over the passenger side of the cab, and there was an open back for troops. There was no roof at all, and no divider between the back and the cab. Aside from a few bullet holes, it appeared untouched. I climbed up into the back. How could I resist playing with the machine gun?

The gun was mounted on a circular ring of iron sort of like an open turret. Rollers on the gun mount allowed the gunner to swing the gun a full 360 degrees around the metal ring. Pushing aside a few heavy metal containers, I ducked under the ring, stepped onto the passenger seat, and into the center of the turret. I grasped the worn handles on either side of the gun and tried to roll it sideways. It wouldn't budge, but I was able to pivot the heavy gun up and down. The breech atop the gun was closed, but after fiddling with it, I managed to flip it open. I then had the fun of slamming it shut—ah, the sweet sound of war machinery! How often I had seen movies and TV shows where soldiers opened the breech, slapped in a belt of ammo, and slammed the thing closed again, ready to mow down the enemy. I wondered if the half-track had ever seen action, whether the gun had ever been fired against an enemy.

I know, it was kind of pathetic, but I couldn't help having a romantic notion of war. That's how it was sold to me as a kid. Gritty men in desperate circumstances, sticking it out, pushing themselves to the limits of their physical and mental abilities. Heroics. I also believed that somehow men's fascination with war was genetic. Little wonder if it was. How else to explain how men are so reliably duped into thinking that purposely subjecting themselves to mortal danger—to dying a slow miserable death on a battlefield, their guts hanging out—could be fun?

I looked around like someone might catch me climbing down into the driver's seat. The weathered seat cushion crunched under me as I assumed command.

"Cool." There were two large dials to my right, centered on the dashboard, and a smaller dial on the left and a huge steel steering wheel in front of me. On the right was a large angled floor shifter, with another one in front of that. Farther right on the dash was a glove compartment, hanging open. How odd, I thought. On a hook on the dash between me and the glove compartment hung goggles.

Just after passing through the McEscargot in Reims, France, September 1944:

"*Aw, Sarge! They forgot to give us ketchup. How am I supposed to eat my snails without ketchup?*"

"*Calm down, Dooley. Check the glove compartment. I think there are some ketchup packs in there under the maps and wet wipes.*"

I glanced to my left and saw Wilco staring up at me from the ground, clearly impatient with my dawdling. But how often do you find yourself able to play with military ordnance?

I noticed there was no place for a key. Well, I guess that would be kind of stupid.

"*Dooley, you have the keys?*"

"*I thought you had them, Sarge.*"

"*Darn it, Dooley—they're on the seat. We're locked out. Go to that farmhouse and see if you can find a coat hanger.*"

But there was a black button on the dash between the two big dials, a switch below that, and below that a series of plungers—one would be the choke. I flipped the switch, depressed the black starter button and there was a loud grinding sound under the hood.

"Whoa!" The half-track had obviously been put out there relatively recently, as it hadn't been blown up, and someone had to start it to get it there. Nobody around to steal the battery. And I couldn't imagine a soldier charged with driving the half-track out there wouldn't fill the tank. Why chance running out of gas along the way? Uncle Sam paid for the gas. So maybe there was enough fuel to go somewhere if I could start her—much less drive her.

I pulled out the plungers and cranked it again. This time the starter caught the flywheel, and instead of a grinding sound the half-track went:

Wuh-wuh-wuh-wuh . . .

It was turning over sluggishly. A loud backfire sent Wilco running. Then there was a belch of smoke and the half-track rumbled to life, pretty as you please.

I cackled with glee.

"So *cool!*" Women have their foibles and men have theirs—namely that there's a ten-year-old inside who still commands the ship at a moment's notice. The engine jounced and vibrated the whole truck, the rattle of metal all around me.

Could I figure out how to get the thing in gear? I mean, I knew how to drive a shift, but I knew nothing about driving a truck, much less one that was part tank. Terms like "double-clutching" left me wondering if there shouldn't be an extra pedal somewhere.

There were four levers to my right. One was labeled TRANSFER CASE, which I surmised was for the cable winch I spied under the front rolling pit. The other was labeled TRANSMISSION, and another to engage the front-wheel drive. There was also a large hand brake.

I depressed the clutch, wobbled the transmission gearshift, and felt around the shift plate for the H pattern. Well, it was more like an H with an N to one side where reverse was. I tried front left, let the clutch out slowly, and the machine lurched forward so violently that it stalled. Trial and error followed, but the end result was that I got the thing moving and out to the side of the junkyard. I'd figured out what double-clutching was: you had to depress the clutch to go into neutral, let it out, and then push it in again to put it into gear. Double-clutch: *duh*! I also wondered again about how much gas it had—I peered closely at the dials and none of the three seemed to be working.

Only the small left headlight worked, and not very brightly. But the starlight did a fair job of lighting up the pale desert, and I saw Wilco trot up next to the driver's side, tail wagging. I opened my door. He leapt into my lap and clambered into the passenger seat.

The noise from the truck was even more horrendous when it moved. The engine valves rattled furiously, and it handled like a mobile bottling plant with four flat tires. First gear was extremely sluggish, and it wasn't until I ground it into third gear that I felt I wasn't driving through mud. The vibration from the treads in the rear resonated through all the armor plating so fiercely that Wilco kept skittering down onto the floor no matter how hard he tried to brace himself against the seat. From the way the gas and clutch pedal lurched around, I guessed a lot of the extraneous vibration was due to shot engine mounts. My hands were going numb from the rattle transmitted up into the steering wheel. But all this was a good thing. Anybody within a couple mile radius would definitely hear me coming, which I hoped would obviate anybody shooting at me by accident.

And let's face it—come sunup, without water, I'd be in deep trouble out there. I was already thirsty, and if making tracks with this rattletrap could help find civilization or just shelter before sunup, I was ahead of the game.

The line of junked vehicles ended abruptly as I shifted into fourth gear. The valley was splayed wide before me with the track curving gently to the right toward a gap between two buttes. I stuck my head out the window and tried to look back at the shooting gallery, but all I could see was my contrail of dust. Yup, anybody watching from the air or high ground would easily spot me.

There was no windshield and the cold air nipped at my eyeballs. I grabbed the swaying goggles from the hook on the dashboard and had a heck of a time putting them on and steering straight.

Wilco finally found a position from which he couldn't be vibrated, his front paws on the dashboard and his rear wedged into the corner of the seat. I was secretly pleased, of course, with his discomfort, and that his usual sly glances my way were now replaced by a general look of alarm.

The sky to the east was brightening ever so slightly as we reached the buttes, and the track passed between them in a slow descent through a narrowing canyon. Larger rocks from the canyon walls lay in my way, and at first I tried to avoid them, but then I tried hitting a few just to see what the old warhorse could handle. The intermittent crash of boulders into the rolling bottling plant had the added benefit of jolting Wilco from his new stance and onto the floor again. He'd probably bite my fingers off for this, but I was holding out hope that having the upper hand for a while might instill some parity between us.

Around a curve, the canyon walls plummeted and another valley opened below us—we were spilling from one valley down into another. I killed the headlight, depressed the clutch, and we stopped with a screech of brakes sharp enough to split a coconut. In the combined glow of the moon and the eastern sky, I could make out the pale track winding through the shrubs. But I could also make out something else below, a pattern on a knoll to one side of the track. Another shooting gallery of some sort? A target? There were a series of straight lines on the ground, in what seemed a random geometric pattern.

I searched the sky for aircraft. Nothing. I would have killed the engine and taken a better look and listen, but I didn't want to risk the half-track not starting again.

I was about to proceed but something was bothering me. A sense of foreboding. Like I'd been there before, and something bad had happened. So I did kill the truck's engine.

Surprisingly, I got what looked like a sigh of impatience from Wilco.

I opened the truck door and hopped down onto the ground. The desert seemed impossibly quiet without the rumble of the half-track, and behind the gentle whistle of the breeze through the sage I could still hear the bottling plant echo in my head. I climbed into the back of the truck, shooed Wilco from the passenger seat, and ducked into the machine gun turret. I wanted the higher vantage to study what lay ahead, so I put an ammo box onto the seat to stand on. What was it about this place that was so familiar? This had the feel of a recurring dream, one in which you knew a monster was beyond a door. But in the dream you never opened the door.

Nothing moved below that I could see, but I felt vulnerable. The machine gun was cold, and as I tried to move it again to one side, I got to wondering whether it worked. A fifty-caliber machine gun would go a long way toward making me feel less vulnerable. Of course, I'd never fired any gun larger than a twenty-two as a kid. Then again, I'd never driven a half-track before.

I stepped down off the ammo box and unbuckled the lid. Empty. I popped a couple of others strewn around the back of the truck before hitting pay dirt: an ancient chain of fifty-caliber shells. I always thought they came in cloth belts, but this one was held together, shell to shell, by metal clips.

All over America people toss their fridges curbside, making sure to remove the doors so some kid might not climb in and suffocate—but out here they leave whole boxes of fifty-caliber shells right next to a machine gun. Well, I guess they didn't exactly expect Spanky and the gang to traipse by way out here.

The ten-year-old boy inside welled up again, the tingle of Christmas morning buzzing my brain. *Cool.*

There was a bracket attached to the left side of the gun that was clearly intended to hold the ammo box—same size. So I lifted a spring-loaded tensioner of some sort and slid the ammo box into the bracket, letting the tensioner rest back onto the shells. The tensioner seemed designed to keep the chain of shells from leaping wholesale from the box when the gun yanked on them.

I laid the end of the belt into the breach with one shell aligned with the barrel, then I closed the breech.

There was a short handle and trigger at the rear of the gun that seemed ridiculously small in proportion to the rest of the thing.

I'd be lucky if the thing fired at all. In fact I'd be lucky if the barrel wasn't rusted and the thing didn't blow up in my face. Mindful that the gun might explode when I pulled the trigger, I hunkered down before giving the trigger a squeeze.

Nothing.

I opened the breech again, and it all looked right as far as I could tell. But what did I know? And what were the chances the thing would work, anyway? I was lucky that the vehicle even started. And that I figured out how to double-clutch.

Having given up on the gun, I took to scanning the knoll below again.

Nothing stirred. My sense of foreboding was

telling me to try to determine who it was before approaching. There was no way of determining that without sunlight. No way was I sneaking all the way down there in the dark on foot for a look-see.

And I was both thirsty and tired. So I climbed down and got back into the truck cab. Stretching out onto the seat for a little shut-eye seemed a capital idea if I could manage it. I was still wired, but knew I needed rest. I'd try to snooze until dawn, when I could see what was ahead a little clearer. I had no reason to think I was being pursued, and hopefully Wilco would give some kind of indication that someone was approaching.

But I felt a little vulnerable with no roof and the windows all open around me. A closer examination of the window areas revealed flip-up armor plates with small portals in them. Made sense. In battle without them, anybody sitting in the half-track would be Swiss cheese when the bullets started to fly. So I heaved the hinged steel plates into place and bolted them there. The interior seemed a lot more secure with the window armor in place.

"Bark if you hear anything, OK?"

Wilco shot me a glance that was all expletives—I don't think he'd forgiven me for the bumpy ride. He was curled on the floor on the passenger side—I think he was enjoying residual heat from the truck engine. I put on another Dinoland sweatshirt, reserving the other space for a pillow.

I stared up at the stars, thinking to myself that I'd

probably not be able to fall asleep, but that just resting my eyes and body would be of some value. I guess I underestimated how tired I was because next thing I knew I was out.

And dreaming.

chapter 24

I awoke huffing and puffing, as though I'd been running, the images from my sleep stark, sharp, and terrifying. The meaning of my dream was unclear but unsettling. People and places were out of context. As was I. Where in the hell was this place? I sat up in the truck cab, squinting into the dawn-lit blue distance through the small gun portal in the windshield armor. The sky was bright but my perch and the valley below were still in deep shadow.

It came back to me: Dinoland, wrecking yard, half-track. My guess was I'd slept for about two hours. Even though my chest was warm from wearing three sweatshirts, my feet were freezing.

I climbed down out of the cab, unsteady, stamping my feet to warm them. I swung my arms, which were cramped from being folded under my head. With nothing to drink since the day before, the arid mountain air had rendered me parched, and my tongue was like sandpaper. Physically, I felt alien to myself, like some kind of robot that had rusted overnight.

And on top of it all, I was still gripped by the murky panic that woke me. What was it I'd been dreaming? There were lots of fractured pieces, dark images, angst.

There was a huge temple of some kind, ancient, but it was near Angie's and my apartment in Manhattan's west teens. There was an earthquake, and we'd looked out at the temple from the backyard to see an erupting volcano. People on the street were running, and there was fire in the sky. It was night, and we couldn't see in the subway because the power was out, but there were a lot of people. I held Angie's hand, we had to keep moving, to be safe, to get away, I wasn't sure. But the subway gave way to a cave, one that had subway ads on walls lit by torchlight. Then not ads, but posters.

Posters of five white geckos, in a circle, nose to tail, like those on Draco's cape and Fowler's medallion.

"Garth, you're freaking yourself out!" I croaked aloud as I paced between the half-track and a nearby cliff face. My throat was so dry I sounded like an old man.

No, we weren't trying to escape. The crowd in the subway was moving toward some place. To find someone. To find something, some people, to catch some people.

God, I was thirsty. Like a TV jumping back and

forth between two channels, my mind flicked from dream to reality to dream...which was which?

To kill them. We had hatchets of a kind I'd never seen before. They looked ancient, made crudely of stone and leather and wood. I said to Angie:

"Are we going to kill them?"

But the hand in mine was no longer Angie's, but Gabby's.

I wondered if there was any water in the valley down below.

I don't remember what she said, but it was in her eyes. The killing glee was in my mother's eyes.

I said, "Mom, I don't want to kill them."

I had to have water soon.

I could see Gabby's visage by the torchlight, the wrinkles and creases of her face stark, wriggling, and sinister. Swarming all around us were featureless throngs of people—no, they'd morphed into coyote people, with muzzles and panting tongues—moving around us in the same direction. Gabby was standing before me in the torchlight, and I could see my possum Arnold in her arms, looking up at me with those innocent, shiny black eyes.

Gabby said: "In doing so, you killed him."

I stopped pacing in front of a cliff. The dark miasma of my dream dissolved and the rock face before me came into focus.

Sun clipping the top of a far mountain set the stone before me ablaze in a fiery mantle.

Stained onto the glowing rock, faintly, was the

shape of five white geckos. Nose to tail. In a circle. Same as on Draco's cape. Same as on Fowler's medallion.

Vatic as any oracle, the five geckos on the rock face were as formidable as the heads of Cerberus snarling at Hades's gate.

This was where my grandfather Julius Kit Carson came with the other four.

This was where the vuka spirits moved into them and began this legacy.

This was where the Tupelca and *El Viajero* meant to extract the spirit.

This was where I would die.

And I'd helped them bring me here—I'd gone along with Norman and his pals, and then I'd traveled across the desert to place my own neck on the chopping block.

I was utterly alone, terror-stricken.

Escape. Run.

I found myself in the half-track barreling down the hill, my eyes blurred with tears of abject panic as I stared through the gun portal, my brain addled by a lack of moisture, my ears filled with the cacophony of the half-track's cold, clunky mechanization. I glanced at the passenger seat. Even Wilco had gone.

My hysteria wasn't helped by the tableau ahead— it was the mound, all right. The one I'd seen from above with the geometric shapes was now plainly a disused archeology dig. Fowler's archeological dig from years back. There were wooden surveyor's stakes, with broken strings tangled in the tumble-weeds and surrounding sage. Gashed sifting screens rusted off to one side next to some sawhorses, and a heavy wooden table was flipped over, various rusted spades and shovels almost covered by the blowing sands. And in the middle of this detritus were half-filled trenches, long and rectangular.

Maybe there would be a puddle of water some-where?

I veered the half-track to one side of the mound and down a gully.

And slammed into the back of a parked car.

chapter 25

Into a parked car? The sky reared up before me: I drove over it.

Thrown from my seat, I heard the treads thrumming on the car's roof. The half-track almost flipped over on its side as I lost control.

But the truck slammed to the ground upright and I bounced back into my seat.

Through the portal I saw someone standing about fifty feet ahead.

White hair. Pale palm held up to stop me. It was a woman in what looked like a monk's cassock.

It was Gabby.

I ratcheted back the hand brake. The truck fishtailed in the soft sand. The engine bucked, the rear treads faltered, the engine quit. Stalled.

Gabby? Reality or dream?

Stopped, I found myself in a cloud of dust, unable to see anything, coughing from inhaling sand into my already dry lungs. I tried to restart the truck, but the engine wouldn't kick over.

Blue dawn fought its way through the sandstorm, and a portal of gloom opened before the windshield.

Gabby was still there. And she was walking toward the half-track. I was terrified of my own mother, if the spectre even was her.

"Garth!"

That was Nicholas's voice. I was afraid of the image of my mother, but the sound of my brother's voice was like the clouds parting after a hurricane.

"Nicholas!" I wheezed. I clawed at the door, trying to find the handle and a way out, and in the process released the window armor, which hinged open and slammed the side of the truck.

Nicholas's faced appeared in the window next to me. As usual, he was wearing a tweed suit and thin tie, even out here in the desert.

"For Christ sake, you idiot! Look what you did to the rental car! What am I going to tell Avis? Garth? Ack!"

I threw my arms around his neck, sobbing for dear life.

"Garth, it's OK, stop it, you're hurting me... you're worse than Otto, now stop it."

"Nicholas!" That was Vargas's voice. "Is he OK?"

"I don't know...I think he's having a panic attack," Nicholas said as I choked him in my half nelson of panic. "Help me get him out of this goddamn thing. What is this?"

"A half-track, I believe," Vargas intoned.

Those were the last words I heard until I came to, minutes later, on the ground, Gabby, Nicholas, and Vargas kneeling over me.

The sky behind them was the solid royal blue of early morning, and they were almost in silhouette.

"He's dehydrated, you can see that, can't you?" Gabby said this to Nicholas, then noticed my eyes open. "Vargas, hand me the water."

Gabby poured some bottled water into my parched lips and I could literally hear the membranes sucking up the moisture. I grabbed the bottle from her and sucked the contents down in two long gulps, collapsing the plastic bottle.

"More," I gasped.

"If you drink too fast, you'll get terrible cramps." Gabby wagged a finger at me. "Where's Wilco?"

"Gabby," Nicholas began with a sigh, "let's not get into that. Garth, you didn't really have Wilco with you, did you? Like you said on the phone?"

"We're at the mound, where the dreams happen, the five white geckos, we have to get away." I could barely get the words out fast enough—I was afraid the ancient spirits would reach up through the ground like zombies and pull me under.

"Calm down. The state police caught those three Tupelca bozos walking along the road. Otto got the van away from them and came to help you guys but you ran off into the desert, so he and Angie got to the cops."

"You are safe now, Garth." Vargas's dramatic Latin inflection came with a squint of wisdom that would have made Ricardo Montalban proud. "They caught the three killers, the crazy Tupelca who kidnapped you. You are safe now, with us. Would you like a cheese curd?"

He held out a package of the white waxy squiggles, Milwaukee ambrosia. I mechanically took one, and it squeaked like a balloon animal as I chewed. Even though I was still thirsty, I realized I needed the salt, too. I took another. It was then that I managed to focus on Vargas's attire. He was again in his scoutmaster shorts, and a bright orange gym T-shirt.

I took in the sight of the three of them: Yoda, Simon Templar, and Montezuma's answer to the Eagle Scout.

"He needs herbal tea, not cheese!" Gabby looked exasperated. "Yes, Garth, you're safe now with us."

Nicholas grimaced, mumbling: "Be a lot safer if our rental wasn't totaled."

"Gabby, what are you doing here?" I was deeply puzzled.

"I contacted Nicholas about Fowler. Once you told me he was involved...well, I began to worry. Someone had to deal with him, and since I cast the spell on him I have the ability to control him. I called Nicholas and he had a private jet..."

"Private jet?" I cocked an eye at Nicholas.

He gave a dismissive wave. "Somebody owed me a favor."

"What about Wilco?" Gabby insisted.

"Gabby, would you stop..." Nicholas moaned. "Poor kid has been through enough. Garth, where'd you get this half-track, anyway?"

I sat up, taking another cheese curd, and checking my surroundings. We were about twenty feet from the half-track. I glanced back.

"That?" I tilted my head in the direction of the vehicle in question. "Found it. So the police caught them? Norman, Brutus, and Timmy?"

Nicholas and Vargas spoke at once: "Yes."

I turned and looked back up the gully. Nicholas's little compact rental car had been flattened by the giant steel rolling pin on the front of the half-track, the ground littered with the sparkle of safety glass. You could still hear the wreck pop, click, and crack. Just on the other side of the car was a steep slope up to the top of the mound. "*El Viajero*. Their leader, the one with the four vukas in him. The police don't have him, do they?"

Vargas stroked his chin. "The Traveler? Hmm."

"Who is *El Viajero*?" Nicholas looked at me, then at Gabby.

Gabby seemed to ignore the question. "Angie told us these was a dog with you. Did he come with you here?"

"Wilco was with me until I came down off the ridge. He vanished while I was asleep."

"Well, a dog may have been with you, but not Wilco." Nicholas chuckled.

Vargas looked at me askance. "My dog was found by security at the Qwest Arena, and has been with me since. He is back at the motel with Angie and Otto."

"No, it was Wilco. He had the big dog tag and everything."

Gabby made a ring with her thumb and forefinger. "About this big, bronze, like the amulet Fowler had around his neck?"

I shivered and looked uncertainly at Vargas.

"Garth, pay no attention to..."

"Nicky!" Gabby glared at Nicholas—he fairly shrank, like a mouse into a teacup. It's astounding how a mother retains the power over her adult children to instantly rein them in with a single word. Humbling indeed for the recipient. But likewise satisfying for the sibling witness. Ah, family life.

My gloat was slight and fleeting. I looked at Gabby. "What are you trying to say?"

The desert wind hissed through the sage and scrub around us. I could feel the dirt drying on my tearstained face, the sweat rolling down my neck and into the small of my back. The ground began to vibrate, to hum, like someone had flicked on a compressor in the ground.

Nicholas jumped to his feet. "What the hell is that?"

"Earthquake?" Vargas slowly rose.

"What the hell is that sound?" Nicholas demanded of Gabby, like she should know.

"*El Viajero.*" She smiled knowingly, as a mother

does in front of a naive child. "He's here. It is the four vuka, the Tupelca, awakening, looking for the fifth spirit."

From atop the mound came a howl.

We spun around to see Fowler standing above us on the mound, like some Aztec priest atop Templo Mayor. He was naked, silhouetted against the sun-streaked sky. Dangling from his outstretched hand was the medallion.

"*Infexa calupa testa noosi kledpti!*" His shout echoed across the valley.

"Not that kook," Nicholas moaned.

Gabby shot him a withering glance. "Fine way to talk about your father."

icholas looked like he'd taken a sucker punch to the gut.

"Yes, you were adopted." Gabby said this like she was passing along the time—classic Mom. "Now, let me take care of *El Viajero*."

She turned back to Fowler, stepped forward, and spread her arms. *"Jeppa flezzi rota yetfehdop!"*

"What are they saying?" Vargas pleaded to no one in particular.

"It's glossolalia," I said. Mom used to get into some of that during the Saturnalia back during the *Addams Family* days. I rose to my feet, steadying myself on Nicholas's shoulder. "They're speaking in tongues."

"Garth, come on, this can't be true." Nicholas gripped my arm. "OK, so I knew I was adopted— didn't take too much research to find that out. I wanted Gabby at the wedding so she'd 'fess up. If I'm going to be a father I need to know who my father is. At least I thought so. But if he is my father . . . I was better off not knowing."

The ground jolted under our feet, and we all went to steady ourselves.

"Something moved in the ground!" Vargas bawled.

Gabby moved closer to the base of the mound, confronting Fowler. He stood over her like some chieftain about to make a human sacrifice.

"*Tetta rickto lest nova peti vum!*" she yelled, undoing her robe and letting it fall to the ground.

"Eww," Nicholas whined, turning away. "Why does she have to take off her clothes? She never did that back in Skunkville."

"*Revva sopa wotto! Revva sopa wotto! Revva sopa wotto!*" I didn't need a translation—Fowler was clearly invoking the spirits to rise up as he stood in the cold shadow of the surrounding hills.

Whatever was in the ground, it shifted again—you could feel that it was large. Huge. Powerful. It felt like the ground was about to open up under our feet.

I took a few strides and clambered into the back of the half-track, scrambling up next to the machine gun turret where there was something to hold on to. If the Tupelca ancients were going to take me, they were going to take me with nine tons of rusty armor plating. Nicholas and Vargas were suddenly next to me—if nothing else it was a good vantage from which to watch the unfolding clash between Fowler and Mom. Like two sorcerers crossing wands.

There was a loud yawning sound like that of a waking giant; dust clouds exploded behind Fowler, along with a burst of light that framed him in an immense and ominous shroud. Could he really be summoning up spirits? Was he causing this the way I caused the twister at the truck stop?

What I'd thought was just a crazy, skinny old man was now the silhouette of Mephistopheles on steroids. Fowler broke into one of his howls.

And then from the growing sandstorm on the mound behind him emerged a flash of silver. It started as a black horizontal curve and steadily grew into a glittering hump like the rising crest of a wave. The ends of it stretched out farther and farther to either side as it rose. It was a very smooth, long curve, but to the right I noted what looked like a fin. There were lines along it that looked structural, almost like long, thin panels. When it was as wide as a crosstown block, it began to taper back in as the belly emerged. I realized then that it sort of looked like the giant blue whale model at the Museum of Natural History, except clad in chrome and six times as large.

There were no propellers, there were no rotors, there were no jet engines; aside from the storm of sand and earthy thunder pounding out from the hillside and beneath our feet, the colossal chrome whale rose silently behind Fowler. Light shone from beneath, reflecting brightly—but this was eclipsed by a sudden fountain of what looked like lasers. The lights formed a grid pattern on the bottom of the whale, but the beams ricocheted in our direction so intently that we had to shield our eyes.

"*Fracka fricka moota itta ipsa croon!*" Nicholas gasped.

"*Fracka fricka toto dip ipsa croon,*" I agreed.

"Don't you guys start!" Vargas scolded. "This weapon, does it work? It looks loaded." He pointed at the machine gun. Before I could shrug—I was too busy gaping at the floating chrome whale—Vargas pounced on the gun, opening the breech, checking the ammo box.

The lustrous leviathan cleared the top of the mound. It could have been a disc—from our vantage it was hard to tell. But my sense was that it was oblong, flat but cigar-shaped. How could something so huge, so massive, rise up so effortlessly? The technology, I marveled, must be so incredibly advanced.

In her long white braids and eighty-year-old birthday suit, Gabby was undaunted, shouting her incantations and throwing sand in the air. Another old animist practice.

Well, I never believed in UFOs, but seeing is believing. What else could this thing be? Unless there had been some quantum advance in science, this thing wasn't from the third planet. And this saucer had been buried in the mound, which meant that it was all true. The Tupelca were aliens, and this was their craft from all those eons ago. Maybe Fowler's medallion was being used to channel the spirits from him into the ground, like a transmitter. Or like a remote car starter or garage door opener. Or some whacked-out UFO bullshit like that.

I reflected on Two Shirts and his demonstration with the magnets, how the power of one went into another.

But I took a moment to do a vuka check. I didn't sense anything coming out of me. My pronghorn wasn't anywhere around, and I was still alive, so that meant my vuka hadn't been released. I didn't feel any evil, cannibal, werewolf Tupelca spirit clamoring out of my soul to join the other four white geckos in their interplanetary spacecraft.

The quake from Thor pounding his anvil shook the earth ever harder. As the shimmering colossus rose, it became impossible to look directly at it because of all the light refracting off the bottom. Through the cracks between my fingers I could make out Gabby's tiny bent form immersed in the quills of light, like she was walking into the kingdom of the divine.

I heard a mechanical ratchet in front of me, from Vargas's direction. Then another. A very distinct sound familiar to war buffs and *Rat Patrol* aficionados alike. It was the sharp *clack-chuck* of a machine gun being cocked.

When I tried to fire the gun, I hadn't cocked it.

Battle ready, the scoutmaster and Chicken of Death bellowed: "*¡Reloj, bastardos ajenos!*"

Nicholas and I harmonized: "What'd he say?"

Vargas swung the gun toward the source of the light, to the right and over Gabby's head. Like a zoom lens, my eyes focused on his meaty brown finger curled over the ridiculously small trigger.

"He'll hit Gabby!" Nicholas ducked under the gun mounting ring and grabbed Vargas's arm.

The gun spat daggers of fire with the unforgiving chop of a jackhammer shattering concrete. Tracer bullets, the kind that glow, spat in a stream up toward the ascending craft. Hot empty shells clattered to the floor, and the spent metal clips that linked the shells were jumping around all over the place. There were loud sparks and pings on the craft, and I heard a few ricochets.

Thor's pounding and the fifty caliber's blasts combined in a cacophony that made me cover my ears instead of my eyes.

Nicholas grabbed Vargas by the shoulders and pulled him from the gun, and as he did so the gun's barrel tipped down and pointed at Fowler. I was still averting my eyes from the stinging rays of light, but stole a glance up at Fowler.

Atop the mound in his glory, arms raised with the medallion dangling, I could swear I saw the daggers of flame, the tracer bullets, pass right through him.

The steady rise of the chrome whale slowed slightly, but it kept rising.

I detected a line hanging from the side. A rope? On a UFO?

I saw Fowler's silhouette turn, grab the line, and wrap it around his arm.

"What the hell are you doing?" Nicholas yelled to Vargas over the storm.

Vargas was indignant. "If I am the first to capture a UFO, I will be quite rich and famous, no?"

Nicholas gave him a derisive shove. "You could have killed Gabby." But his concern gave way to curiosity as we watched the craft rise. The laser lights tracking it flicked off. Thor rumbled to a sudden stop.

Without the fanfare of the light show, Gabby looked a lot less bold. Naked and shivering in the cold gully, she stood uncertainly before the mound.

"Gabby, for Christ sake, put on your robe and get away from there!" Nicholas shouted.

She shrugged in agreement and tiptoed back to where her robe lay in a heap in the sand. She donned her cassock and trotted over to the half-track.

The dust storm from the craft's ascent simmered to an end. The relative quiet of the desert wind hissing through the sage and scrub filled our ears.

But in the distance, behind us, bouncing off the hillsides, thumped chopper blades.

Someone was coming to join the party.

From below, we could now see that the titanic craft was square in back with fins on either side of the bottom. In front it was rounded to a small point. In the center of the underside was some sort of rectangular attachment the size of a car. This attachment was obviously mechanical, fitted with both black and reflective surfaces in irregular shapes.

Sunlight hit the hump of the gleaming whale as it cleared the hilltops, light mirroring back down onto the far hillsides in a shimmering white line. Emerging fully from the purple gloom of the valley, it glimmered like a rising celestial body, with a small, demented wolfman dangling from a rope underneath.

The thump of the chopper blades wavered, getting louder. I couldn't tell where it was coming from. Suddenly from behind us, a blue USAF helicopter blasted overhead. It arced out over the mound, slowed at the apogee of its turn, and shot back toward us.

We covered our faces with our forearms to block the effects of the rotor-induced sandstorm as the helicopter settled deftly in the gully downhill from the half-track.

Two goons in black jumpsuits and black-visored helmets appeared and trotted toward us holding automatic pistols. Right behind them was Colonel Lanston.

"Stand away from the gun!" Lanston pointed her pistol at Vargas, and the streusel man slowly raised his hands and ducked out from the gun pulpit.

"Out of the truck. Now!"

We obeyed her, and were soon arrayed—covered in dirt from our struggles—on one side of the half-track. Gabby in her druid's robe. Nicholas in a dusty brown tweed suit. Vargas in a mud-smeared "Gold's

Gym" T-shirt and Boy Scout shorts. Me in four Dinoland sweatshirts. This motley bunch wasn't so much *Rat Patrol* as some ludicrous reality program: *Survivor: Alien Days.*

The two helmeted goons kept their guns trained on us as Lanston craned to look up at the ascending craft. When she turned back to us she was livid.

"You idiots," she spat.

"Look, Colonel, it's not our fault that Fowler—" Nicholas began.

"Fowler! He's the biggest pain in the fucking ass of all of you. Do you have any idea how many years we've had to put up with him? Do you know how many times I put in a termination order on him only to have it rejected?"

"Excuse me." I cleared my throat. "Did you happen to notice the UFO over there? It just came out of the mound right here in front of us."

She glanced up at the craft, squinting this time.

"Is that Fowler up there?"

We nodded.

"Shit." She stared at the ground, a look of regret chiseled into her brow. "We couldn't saturate this place with troops. It would have drawn too much attention. But we don't and now look what happens. The bozos are all here."

I cleared my throat. "Uh, now that the cat is out of the bag, do you mind telling us what it is?" I jabbed a finger skyward.

"Yes, I do mind." She squinted bitterly. "It's my

job to keep assholes like you people from places like this. We spend millions upon millions to keep that waste dump Area 51 in the news, Roswell and the Aztec site, too, so all the conspiracy freaks will leave this place alone. We arrange for little sightings of strange lights to keep the simpletons fixated, we donate money to UFO festivals and wacko research projects, TV shows, and movies. We practically created the whole goddamn conspiracy theory to mask sightings of our projects so there won't be any serious compromise of our national security interests. Anybody takes a photo, it's just some kook and another hoax. Which brings us to today—we plan the launch of one of our most important projects for the one day when every UFO nut is at the Alien Days festival way north of here, staring in the wrong direction."

"But for all our efforts, there was just one person, one nut job—Fowler—who latched onto this and wouldn't leave it alone. Literally! Look at him. Damn it to hell. I should have just drilled him myself years ago."

"Is it from outer space?" Gabby's gray eyes widened expectantly.

"You know what I am, honey? I'm a psychologist." Lanston looked more like an angry beast. "My job is to try to make you and all the other dipshits believe this alien nonsense, so that all the sensible people dismiss it. The power of selective reasoning always wins out. We wanted people to believe in little green men to draw their attention away from what we're doing."

"I always thought they looked like emaciated Pillsbury Doughmen."

Lanston just shot me a hard look and continued.

"Fowler is psychotic. He thinks he's a werewolf, for Christ sake. Or as we say in psychoanalytic circles, he's a clinical lycanthrope. He thought he was becoming that animal, just like a Tupelca, to steal the souls of his victims so he could come here and reunite with ancient spirits. We knew this white gecko thing was coming, and that the white geckos meant Fowler was headed here. He recruited those fez-wearing sad sacks by showing them the ravings from your grandfather's fraternal charter and got them to drag you all the way out here in that dry-cleaning truck. All so they could go to another fucking planet and be immortal. And now Fowler has you all believing in this Tupelca fantasy, too. We hoped to head him off, not have it come to all this."

"No." Gabby shook her head. "It was us. My husband and I turned Fowler into a werewolf many years ago."

"Is she your mother?" Lanston looked exasperated and waved the gun at me. "Must be, because she says things almost as stupid as you do."

"So if that's not a UFO, then what is it?" Vargas waved his hands in the direction of the saucer. "It is huge, and it lifted off without any means of propulsion that I could see. It was like . . . antigravity."

"And we have Einstein over here." Lanston

sneered at Vargas. "When you four were young, at your birthday parties, did you all get UFOs?"

Her audience shared a puzzled reverie.

"Did you get antigravity orbs?"

She still had us stumped.

"Maybe you got balloons?"

"You expect me to believe that's a balloon?" Gabby complained.

"We told the public it was balloons a long time ago, but nobody believed it. It's a high-altitude airship. It's part of a missile defense system, the Aerospace Relay Mirror technology to direct lasers to shoot down missiles. So there isn't any antigravity involved, just helium, nitwits. Same extraterrestrial technology that made your birthday balloons float in midair. We've been using a lot of metallic balloons, ever since the fifties. This one is extra reflective to deflect any errant laser pulses."

Put a stick up my rear and wrap me in cellophane—I felt like an A1 all-day sucker. I had stared at the rising airship and made the brilliant deduction that it was a UFO, because what else but a UFO could rise so effortlessly? Deductive reasoning? I believe they call that *inductive* reasoning. Seeing what you expect to see, making what you experience fit a template. It's the fuel that fires the imaginative engines and propels conspiracy theories.

Watch out for the con.

I looked over at Nicholas, who had been uncharacteristically quiet during this harangue. A first glance would tell you he was just hanging back, but I could see him calculating. His eyes were darting from the guns to the half-track to the nearby rock . . . he was thinking one move ahead.

"Señorita Lanston? Are we under arrest?" Vargas had his hand half raised. "Because I have to go to the bathroom."

She ignored him. "All this Tupelca nonsense came to people in dreams, passed one generation to the next. There is no empirical evidence for any of this story, and there are no five vuka pots buried in the ground here that had the spirits of five geckos in them. There's an airship hangar in the ground here. Fowler's story is bullshit, *do you all understand that?*"

Like a troop of truants, the four of us looked at each other and mumbled in the affirmative.

"Are you sure you understand? There is nothing here other than a top-secret weapons launching facility. Fowler set up his archeological dig here on the far end of our bombing range and we kicked his ass out of here to build an installation, not hide a UFO. You: are there any Pillsbury Doughmen here?" She pressed her gun to my chest.

"No! No..."

"You? Do you see any UFOs?"

Vargas stared down at the gun on his chest. "No. I implore you, I really have to pee, please..."

"And you two..." She waved the gun at Nicholas and Gabby, like she couldn't decide which to press the gun against. "You see any Tupelca, vukas, or spirits around here?"

They shook their heads.

"What was that?"

"No!" they said in unison.

"Good! Very good." She looked genuinely relieved, then turned to go back to the helicopter. But the goons stayed where they were.

Retreating, she said to them over her shoulder:

"Kill them."

chapter 27

Kill them.

You never quite get used to hearing those words, no matter how often you hear them. You do, however, get better at reacting to them. For instance, my reaction used to be to try to laugh it off. *Surely this must be a jest of some kind.*

That didn't work so well.

My reaction had improved, though it's tactically so subtle that most people fail to appreciate its cunning: I freeze up like Moosehead Lake in February. You could have knocked me over with a dandelion when she said those words—just by blowing the seeds in my direction. Hey, at least I've learned not to speed things up by making snide remarks. And I wasn't making any sudden moves that could get me in Dutch, either.

Fortunately, others—like Otto—had more proactive reflexes. But he was no doubt somewhere hitting on trailer park girls by the limpid blue waters of the Desert Winds Motel swimming pool. I hear they now have color TVs, too.

Kill them. Why? Not because we had discovered some secret government liaison with aliens, but because we had discovered that there was no secret liaison with the government. It was worth killing us to insure the UFO theories lived on to protect their secret projects.

The goons took a few steps back and raised their pistols. Lanston was all the way down at the chopper, climbing in.

A second black helicopter shot out over the mesa behind us and swooped low over our heads. Nobody heard this one coming. In fact, we still only heard a whirr, like the sound of a grouse taking flight. This helicopter was flat black, long, thin, and angular, sort of like a giant dragonfly.

Alarmed, the goons ducked and swung their weapons toward it.

And away from us.

Vargas fairly took flight, I don't know how, but only as a *luchadore* can. The dreaded Chicken of Death was executing his very own Mexican kung fu. His Oaxaca karate. His Chihuahua jujitsu. *El Gallo de Muerte* was deploying his signature Tijuana takedown, none other than *El Huevo Podrido*. Vargas's legs forked one goon's middle, and his arms came up to his opponent's neck. So linked, the force of the impact sent them end over end like a wheel across the desert scrub.

Like a billy goat, Gabby head butted the other goon in the back just as Nicholas lunged and grabbed for the gun. A shot fired into the air, and the gun fell to the ground.

"Garth!" Nicholas scooped up the gun and tossed it to me.

I caught the gun, and saw Lanston jogging back up the gully. I looked down the sights of the pistol at her. "Stop!"

She stopped all right, and trained her gun on me.

"Drop it!" she shouted.

I fired.

Don't ask me exactly how or why—I just did. Maybe I was just getting a little tired of being pushed around, maybe it was the dehydration and lack of sleep. Don't mess with Garth when he's cranky.

Then again, maybe I could blame my sage friend Dudley, who had a somewhat shady past but had reformed and occupied himself stuffing songbirds. After a few bourbons, he'd reflect obtusely on the old days. Out of nowhere, he'd muster up his most rumbling Southern accent and advise something like: "If anybody ever points a pistola at you while you are pointing a pistola at them, never hesitate. Empty your weapon, sir." I'd never given it much thought. But as soon as I was there, in that moment, that sage advice clicked. Instantly.

I've also heard that you can tell when someone is

about to try to kill you the second before it happens. Not just because they are pointing a gun at you, or say something dramatic like "It's curtains for you, bub." Supposedly the better Western gunslingers had developed this sense, when their opponents hadn't even drawn their guns, or even said anything at all. Now, I've been subjected to murderous intent before, but haven't exactly made a study of it. Perhaps I was learning something inadvertently, because when she said "drop it," I knew—*knew*—she was about to blow me away. And probably the rest of my cohorts, too.

If I knew anything at all about guns other than pulling the trigger, or to stiff arm the pistol at arm's length like they do on cop shows, I could also tell you how many shells that gun held. I would maybe even be able to tell you what make of gun it was and what caliber shells it employed. Then there might be a chance I would also be able to tell you after the fact exactly how many I fired. Because assuming it was completely loaded, the pistol had stopped going *BLAM BLAM BLAM* and started going *click click click* by the time I realized Lanston had crumpled to the ground.

Not bad shooting for a mere Star-level Boy Scout, if I do say so.

"Garth!" That was my mom's astonished voice. I looked, and her face was contorted. She grabbed me, raised her hand, and for some reason I thought she was going to hit me. Generally, it's safe to assume your mom'll be PO'd if she sees you shoot someone or do anything that might result in a poked-out eye.

But the hand grasped my cheek and a big toothy grin blossomed on her wizened face. "Good shooting, boy!"

Garth and Vargas had the two subdued soldiers sitting sheepishly in the dirt, hands behind their heads.

I heard a groan and squinted in Lanston's direction. She lay on her side between two sage bushes, one foot up on a rock, moving slightly. I looked at the gun trembling in my hand.

"I had to...I mean, I had to, didn't I? Is it murder?"

"Garth, you did the right thing!" Nicholas panted from his tussle. "If you'd dropped that gun we'd all be dead now. Self-defense."

"But is she...should we..."

The second helicopter zipped back overhead and then descended directly down a little behind the other helicopter.

Post a sign: VALET PARKING. The gully was getting crowded.

"Hold it!" came over a loudspeaker.

Now who?

Through the latest rotor-induced dust storm we could see the figure of a tall, slim woman flanked by two beefy men in suits. All sported more guns.

I looked at Nicholas, and our eyes met. Do we shoot it out? Hell, I was out of bullets. Or do they call them shells? I kept finding myself regretting I knew so little about guns.

Nicholas smiled and whispered: "It's only Stella." His gun hit the sand.

I looked up, and sure enough I could see her glowing skin contrasting against some light green pantsuit. And the two guys in ties? Brickface and Stucco.

I tossed my gun aside. Hey, what were the chances someone would say "kill them" twice in one day?

s the newest arrivals to the gully drew near, I was poised to ask a slew of questions when Stella looked at Brickface, then Stucco, and murmured:

"Kill them."

This time there was no moment to react before the shooting started.

But it was brief.

Brickface put a bullet into the chest of one goon, and Stucco dispatched the other. The men in black jumpsuits slumped over, twitching, impossibly dark blood rapidly pooling around them. I turned away, and almost tossed my cheese curds.

I suddenly felt extremely weary. Not physically tired, just emotionally and morally exhausted. How a person can so casually end someone else's life, I don't know. Maybe it's just me, but nothing makes humankind seem a more worthless enterprise than an insouciant rubout.

Vargas was comforting Gabby—she'd burst into tears.

Stella glanced in Lanston's direction. "Who shot her?"

I raised my hand, averting my eyes from the two dying men.

"You must be joking."

Nicholas stepped up to Stella, his face red with fury. "Was that really necessary?"

Stella, still with a gun held loosely in her hands, stepped around him and leaned casually on the half-track, a smirk on her face. "Just obeying orders."

Brickface and Stucco had holstered their guns and busied themselves taking pictures of the balloon with little digital zoom cameras. Oddly, the balloon had ceased to rise. Like a silver hummingbird in the sky, it just hovered over the nearest hillside, a couple thousand feet up, Fowler an itsy-bitsy spider dangling on a thread below in the light of the rising desert sun.

Nicholas's eye twitched, the way it used to when we were kids just before the bully he confronted beat the crap out of him.

"Whose orders? Since when did Wilberforce/ Peete begin putting out contracts on military personnel and telling the FBI what to do?"

Stella was taking her time lighting a slim brown cigarette, her gun pointing lazily at Nicholas. She took a deep drag, and smiled. "First of all, let's not forget these two dead men were intent on killing all of you a few minutes ago. They themselves are government murderers and had it coming. Secondly, you should know things aren't quite so simple, Nicky. Alliances are sometimes both ways. In this case"—she gestured with her gun at Brickface and Stucco—"the FBI and Wilberforce/Peete have mutual interests here. We didn't want this Air Force project to succeed. That is, nobody wanted them to kill Fowler and you four, which we knew they would if you reached this..."

"Hold it," I interjected. "What possible interest could—"

"Insurance, Garth." Stella didn't let me finish. "This balloon project was developed by Gibraltar Aerospace under contract to the Air Force. There is a similar project in direct competition to this one being developed by American International Systems under contract to the Missile Defense Agency and under-written by Wilberforce/Peete. Get it now?"

I nodded and said, "No. Who or what is the Missile Defense Agency?"

"I get it." Nicholas sighed. "The MDA is a branch of the Pentagon developing laser weapons, and they are in a race with the Air Force to come up with some-thing first to keep their funding. If the Air Force proj-ect is a success, and American International doesn't get a contract to develop their system, Wilberforce/Peete has to pony up considerable cash. They insured American International Systems against not getting the development deal." He shot a look at Stella. "Have I got it right?"

"You have." She tipped her ash at him and grimaced at the brightening sky. "Curiously well."

I scratched my head. "So the Air Force and the MDA—both part of the Pentagon—are competing against each other for aerospace balloon supremacy."

"It's all about lasers," Nicholas said dryly. "These balloons aren't flimsy but are made of dense, light-weight composites so they don't look much like a balloon. They go way up, and have mirrors to reflect land-based beams at targets in the stratosphere."

"Our tax dollars at work. But what's the FBI got invested in the failure of the Air Force's balloon project?"

"We've been trying to find this secret location for a while," Brickface chimed in. "Who do you think has to put up with all the UFO conspiracy fallout that the Air Force invents? The FBI does. So we'd like to see this alien saucer stuff come to an end. Wilberforce/Peete, acting more or less as American International's agent, clued us in on how the murders were tied to Fowler and why the Air Force had taken such a keen interest in a serial killer."

Stucco put in his two cents. "How we gonna get him down from there?"

"Just what are *you* doing here, Nicky?" Stella asked pointedly. "How did you know where to come?"

"I'm here to help Garth, that's what I'm doing here."

"You're not, by any chance, here on behalf of Gibraltar Aerospace, are you?"

He ignored her. "Look, if you killed these two it must mean you're dispatching witnesses to the MDA, FBI, and Wilberforce/Peete's involvement. Are you going to shoot us? If you are, let's get this over with. We've had about enough of this nonsense."

"I haven't," Vargas protested, speaking rapidly. "Shoot him if you want. I didn't see anything. I'm no witness. I didn't see anything."

"Um, I'm with Vargas." I patted the air toward Nicholas. "Let's not rush this."

I caught movement out of the corner of my eye, in the direction of Lanston. I ducked. Maybe I was getting flinchy, could have been a small bird. Or maybe my reactions were improving.

There was a gunshot and I knew my reactions weren't half bad. I scrambled to the far side of the half-track, behind the rear treads. I found Vargas and Gabby there—they'd been closer to the rear of the vehicle when hell broke loose. Gabby looked pale, wan—not well. Was she just tired or suffering some sort of serious ailment? Nicholas came ducking around the front of the truck and hid behind the huge front wheel.

Gunshots continued, some pinging off the opposite side of the half-track.

I looked at Nicholas, and shouted over the gun battle: "I guess Lanston isn't quite dead."

"Sorry, killer." He shrugged. "She must have been wearing a vest. Kevlar. You just knocked her out."

I scanned the half-track, and then gestured to Vargas and Gabby. "Vargas, help her into the back, and sit with her. Nicholas—you're with me, in the cab. Let's blow this pop stand."

"Pop stand?" He winced. "In this piece of junk?"

"*Armor-plated* junk. Let's get Mom out of here, how's that?"

"She's not my..."

"She is your mom more than anybody else. And I'm your brother no matter who your genetic father is."

He looked a little surprised, and betrayed a grin.

"OK, brother. Let's blow this pop stand."

chapter 29

I was hunkered down in the driver's seat, Nicholas was crouched in the passenger seat. My thumb hovered over the black starter button on the dash, my foot pumping the accelerator, and periodic bullets plinking the truck's armor.

How many times had someone else been in this position? Your car stalls on the railroad tracks and here comes the Chicago Limited.

Start, car, start!

Wuh, wuh, wuh, wuh...

You're in the approach to the Holland Tunnel on a blazing summer Sunday afternoon, ten thousand irritable motorists behind you in a traffic jam when your engine stalls.

Start, car, start!

Wuh, wuh, wuh, wuh...

You're parking at Muldoon Point with your

girlfriend, watching the submarine races, when The Blob oozes into view.

Start, car, start!

Wuh, wuh, wuh, wuh...

Remind me to send a letter of commendation to the White Motor Company, if it even still exists. Had Bobby and Peggy Sue been necking in an M3 half-track instead of a '57 Chevy, maybe The Blob never would have devoured them.

The half-track roared to life, exhaust billowing in a blue-black cloud around us.

Hunched over the steering wheel to keep a low profile, I shifted the truck into gear and we lurched forward. Through the little gun portal I couldn't detect the whereabouts of Stella, Brickface, and Stucco, but I assumed they'd taken up position behind rocks to my left. Lanston was last seen somewhere to my right. We were probably headed directly between them, into the fray.

"Where'd you learn to drive this thing?" Nicholas shouted.

"*Rat Patrol!*" I wound the truck up and ground it into third.

We rumbled down the gully, and I realized the helicopters were in the way. Now I could have sneaked around them, if I were careful. But then I thought, *Why be careful?*

I ground the tranny into fourth, bullets plinking off the sides of the armor plating.

Titan's rolling pin on the front of the half-track

smashed into the Air Force helicopter and bashed it into the FBI helicopter. We pushed them for about twenty feet before the sky heaved into view—up we went over both of them. Rotor blades whirled and splintered before us, bashing into the metal armor of the half-track. Fiberglass shattered and flew in all directions. Metal crumpled and tore, rivets popping. The truck's rear treads shuddered as they ground over one of the chopper's engines and we slammed back down on terra firma.

Nicholas roared with laughter. "Perfect!"

"So, you are here for Gibraltar Aerospace, aren't you?" I shouted back. "That's what I overheard Lanston talking about. Gibraltar was sending someone."

"I'm here for you, first and foremost."

His equivocation was palpable, even over the clank, rattle, and drum of the vehicle, shards of fiberglass still clicking free of the undercarriage.

"By way of Gibraltar? All makes perfect sense. You were darn quick to stop Vargas from shooting that balloon. Gabby wasn't anywhere near his line of fire. And I'd be willing to bet a hundred dollars you don't have a subscription to *Popular Mechanics*—how'd you happen to know all that stuff about laser balloons?"

Nicholas shot me a look from where he had braced himself between the door and the dash. I detected a brief calculation, then an internal shrug as he looked me in the eye. "Technically, it was Gibraltar's insurer, Global Underwriters, that hired me. When I started looking into this, about the Air Force kicking Fowler outta here, you telling me the Air Force was involved, things started to fit together. So I made a few calls and then went to Global to sniff them out—I knew they were involved in underwriting things like this for aerospace contractors. They wanted me to find Fowler, and I knew the best way to do that was to stick close to you. I had to make sure Fowler didn't interfere with the liftoff, to back up Lanston. I didn't count on Lanston getting smart and trying to kill us all. And I didn't figure on Stella showing up."

"Well, well, well. My brother using me as bait to catch Fowler." I snorted. "Doesn't this all just figure?"

"Garth, I would have come out here anyway, you know. No reason not to come and get paid for it on top of helping you out. Hey, I never would have gotten to you at Vargas's so quick without Gibraltar's private jet. And they flew Gabby here, too."

Damn him. Risk management espionage? Couldn't he ever do something out of brotherly or filial obligation? There always had to be an angle with Nicholas.

"So let me guess. You're getting married as some sort of arrangement with Mutual of Omaha? Because it damn well couldn't be for love."

His face reddened, and the skin around his eyes got dusky as he tried to contain his anger.

"You've been needling me about this marriage, trying to get a rise out of me, and now you finally have. Happy? And what is it you want from me? Some sort of admission that I have weaknesses, that I need love? Well, I do, everybody does, I just don't think I have to wear it on my sleeve all the time the way you do. You and Angie fairly taunt me with your family bullshit, thinking you can change me by making me feel inadequate. Did it ever occur to you two that I don't need to be changed, that I can change on my own? That I needed to find the right person for me and work it out? And you, Garth, act so friggin' high and mighty. You have your girl and your love and your little taxidermy paradise, but isn't it funny, the one thing that's missing?"

I'm not sure if I asked him about what was missing or not, but he answered anyway.

"*A dog*. Garth is afraid of getting a dog and I'm afraid of getting married. What do these things have in common, brother dear?"

The barrage of emotion from him was almost unprecedented, and I admit that I was fairly stunned.

"Well, I'll tell you what the common element is, Garth. It came to me a few weeks ago. I visited Skunk Junction, where the house used to be. All wiped clean. Except for one thing. There are some rotten boards still in that tree out back. The one where the tree fort was. The one where you kept that possum, Arnold."

There were a bunch of biting, hurtful things I could have said. But I decided to save it, to think on it a bit more. Besides, we still weren't out of the woods. Or the desert, as the case may be.

The gully spilled out onto a desert floor and the half-track crossed the shadow line from the hills into searing sunshine. The track ahead was clearly defined for a vehicle, but not for where Nicholas was going with this rampage.

"You still don't get it, do you? OK, I'll spell it out for you. I loved Dad, and through my scheming, I ruined his finances and he died trying to recover the money. In effect, I killed Dad. And you loved that *puppy*, you handed him over to Gabby, and she took him to the vet and had him put to sleep. You killed Arnold. Face it—we both have what people like to call *issues*. Different kinds of love are at issue, but we're both afraid of being hurt, of reliving—"

"Did you think this all up? Yourself?"

"—a past that Gabby wiped clean when she took down the house. *Yes*. I thought of it all myself." The way he said that made me wonder if the woman in his life hadn't pitched in.

"I mean, it's pretty obvious, isn't it?" He turned and squinted into the distance, and I watched as he took a deep breath of desert air to try to compose himself. "And let's face it. Gabby hasn't made any of this any easier. We were brought up in pretty unsentimental circumstances, insular with no extended family. Then she wiped out the house, the only anchor to our family's past, and lit out. It's like you and I just came out of nowhere. Well, I did anyway. I was left on the doorstep. All makes sense now, doesn't it? Yes, I'm scared shitless of getting married."

I stared ahead at the flat expanse toward the shimmering horizon. Nicholas was certainly a changed man to some extent, more so than I had imagined, despite his dual purposes. For one thing, he was right for a change. I was just plain scared about the dog, because of Arnold, because that possum also represented a bunch of things about our childhood that were disturbing and alienating. I couldn't put my finger on it exactly, and I'm no good at psychoanalyzing, especially myself. But I had the feel for what had been haunting me, and in the end the heart is often a better doctor for the head than the brain.

And perhaps, somehow, all this vuka nonsense, all this sense of being cursed, was a manifestation or extension of having Kit Carson and my past thrust upon me.

The rattle and clank of the truck seemed even louder as it filled the conversation void. I felt I should say something, but I wasn't sure what to say or how to react to what he'd just said.

Occasionally I follow my own advice, and this was one of those times. *If you don't know what to say, don't.*

After ten minutes, I could discern a dark line in the distance. Then telephone poles. And traffic. And the perimeter fence.

From the back, Vargas's head appeared between me and Nicholas.

"Garth. Nicholas. Your mother, she is not breathing well. We need to get her to a hospital."

I pushed the accelerator to the floor.

The half-track made quick work of the fence.

chapter 30

The hospital PA system came alive with a peevish, pissy male voice.

"Attention: whoever has the large military vehicle parked in the hospital's front driveway, please move it at once or it will be towed. This is the final announcement."

For once I didn't care if my car got towed. Besides, there was a lot of other stuff going on that was more important. Nicholas, Vargas, and I were seated in the hospital waiting room. Angie and Otto arrived, tethered up Wilco outside, and joined our vigil. On pins and needles, we waited for word of Gabby's condition from the doctors.

Otto, the picture of solemnity, approached Angie and me. Standing before us, his eyes were downcast, his suit jacket and tie were folded neatly in his arms. He held them out to me.

"Garv, Otto to make very big wrong, to bring KGB as client to you. I disgrace Garv Carson Critters, and make danger, so it is that I must resignate my command."

I pushed his *beezness* uniform back toward him.

"Otto, you brought Angie to me, which was good. You could not have known those three were KGB."

"But what does matter? All same to danger."

"Otto, I should apologize to you. It is me that keeps getting you into trouble. It is only when I am in trouble that you get in trouble, yes?"

"Mebe, but ..."

"And who always comes to my rescue? You. You come when Garth needs help. You are a very special friend, and I need you to stay and run the Carson's Critters."

"Otto," Angie began, "you are not only our friend but family. You stay with us. And in our hearts."

He'd transformed from abject humility into a monument of nobility, chin high.

"My friends, Otto, he to make like brother to both you, father to dog, and Stalin for boss of beezness."

"Holy ..." Nicholas began, pointing the remote at the TV and upping the volume. "Get a load of this."

We all turned to see a CCN news segment with a red banner at the top reading: LIVE—BREAKING NEWS.

On the screen was a live helicopter shot over a small-town main street, where a huge crowd assembled. The announcer was quite excited:

"At 10:10 this morning, in the middle of the Alien Days parade here in Flats Junction, New Mexico, a spectacle appeared in the sky. A silver, disc-like object came over a nearby rise and settled on Main Street to much commotion. Local police restored order and cleared the area. Authorities at nearby Kirtland Air Force Base and the Department of Homeland Security were notified."

Angie gasped. "You're telling me that is the laser balloon you saw this morning? It doesn't look much like a balloon."

"And if Vargas hadn't shot it full of holes..." Nicholas groaned.

"Hey..." Vargas folded his arms defiantly. "If it had been an alien ship, and those little bastards came at us with those probes, you and your rectum would be thanking me right now."

Otto had recovered from his resignation and was winking at a nurse, but paused a moment and focused on the TV. "Of course, balloon very nice, yes? KGB has many balloon to come from outer space. Garv, why balloon on tele-vee?"

I'd long ago given up trying to get him to say "tee-vee" as opposed to "tele-vee."

"It's a secret balloon that landed by accident in a town, and they think it's a spaceship from outer space."

Otto stroked his beard, in deep contemplation. "Thinkink maybe balloon not so secret, eh?"

The announcer continued:

"*The police are now approaching the craft, to a side of it where there appears to be a tether of some kind...*"

"That's the rope where Fowler was hanging." I pointed.

We were all leaning forward, riveted to the image on the screen. You could see two police officers looking under the slightly raised craft. They jumped back and drew their guns.

"*...there appears to be...*" The announcer was at a loss for words.

The crowd behind the barricades surged forward, police running at them with hands raised, urging them to keep back. The helicopter camera zoomed in on the two officers pointing their guns under the balloon.

The cops leaned forward, looking more closely... and a dog raced out from under the craft, vanishing into the crowd.

I looked at Nicholas.

He looked at me.

We both looked to Vargas, who said: "This is not possible."

"Mr. Carson?" There was a guy in a colorful smock standing behind us, a stethoscope around his neck.

"That's me," Nicholas and I said in unison.

"Your mother is fine. She just caught a bit of a chill, I think—she has a slight fever, nothing to worry about."

Angie jumped up and gave me a big hug of relief.

"Whew." I beamed at Nicholas. "Nothing to worry about."

He looked sidelong at the tele-vee.

"Except maybe the dog."

chapter 31

It was a few days later, in New York, and I was wearing my grandfather's tux, one of those I narrowly and dramatically saved from Goodwill agents when I was but a lad. Garth in his tux could mean only two things. New Year's Eve or a wedding. It was the fourth week of June.

Nicholas had finally been hooked, not that a total of fourteen other women didn't show up to witness the phenomenon. Or maybe it was to throw the rice? I think it was his fellow snoop and ex-cop Maureen who organized the rice throwing. All fourteen of the women didn't open the little sacks of rice. They kept the little rice sacks intact, and like a phalanx of baseball pitchers, the gang of ex-girlfriends wound up and threw them at Nicholas. A couple rice balls beaned Nicholas right in the head, and he shot them a dirty look as the bride dragged him into the limo for the ride to the reception.

Which was upstairs on the roof at Gravy's Tavern, of course, over on Irving Place. The weather cooperated, which in June these days is a minor miracle. Nice spread, too, plenty of champagne, oysters, cracked crab, steak tartar, and expensive scotch. And beer, just for me, I think. The only thing missing were cheese curds.

The crowd wasn't huge, but it made up for volume in eccentricity. There were a number of lawyers, cops, PIs, insurance investigators, and any number of shifty-looking types who I imagined were reformed art thieves and cat burglars. A little combo thrummed out some jazz in the corner. It could have been a wedding reception for Peter Gunn.

Angie was absolutely glowing, as if she were the bride herself. And not just in the way that certain women do when they become enthralled with the ceremony of matrimonial union. We'd found out the day before that her art jewelry had gotten honorable mention in the *Couture Magazine* show, which meant that it would be pictured in the magazine's next issue. Which, aside from my pride in her as an artisan and artist, was a great relief to me in as much as my most recent escapade—having kept her from attending the show—hadn't thrown a wrench in the works.

Otto was tossing back the Stoli like there was no tomorrow, and chasing it with milk. He was incapable of having a cocktail—hard liquor is only consumed rapidly, no tinkling ice cubes and nuanced tippling. He rarely drinks, but when he does, he removes the bottle cap and throws it away in a ritualistic flourish. And yet he was astoundingly sober for having made his way through two-thirds of a fifth. Nicholas had tried to have me tell Otto he couldn't come, but I said he'd have to try to explain it to him. So Otto came, and was enthusiastically—albeit none too expertly—dancing with every woman he could get his hands on.

Including Gabby. She'd suffered no long-term ill effects from our adventure, and seemed to have chosen to completely ignore any debunking of her supernatural bent during the ordeal. Like many older people, her convictions were unshakable even in the face of contrary indicators.

As best man, I'd already made my toast, the crumpled speech on the table next to me. Sure, I could have written it myself, but why not bring in the best ringer there is? I'd read Shakespeare's "Sonnet 116":

> *Love alters not with his brief hours and weeks,*
> *But bears it out even to the edge of doom.*
> *If this be error and upon me proved,*
> *I never writ, nor no man ever loved.*

When I got to the last lines, Angie burst into tears and threw her arms around me. I think Angie's exuberance was somewhat champagne enhanced. Which illustrates an essential piece of knowledge I would impart to a young male to enhance his understanding of women: they like to cry. Why else do women rent films designed to make them cry?

Anyway, most of the big wedding moments had passed. The city was darkening, candles on the tables were lit, a turquoise glow was framing the western skyline. Little white Christmas lights strung overhead had just popped on, and I was at a table by myself in a corner. A contemplative mood had descended upon me, and I watched Angie and Otto and Gabby and Nicholas and his beaming bride move about the room as though in slow motion. I was conscious that this was one of those occasions that the mind's eye records to be shown again and again. Weddings and funerals usually make the top ten list at the brain's retrospective cinema.

And of course the whole event was made more poignant by the previous week's to-do—which for all intents and purposes had been put to bed. We never did hear what happened to Lanston, but I received a short message from Stella comprised solely of my back wages and my pink slip. I'd decided against lodging a complaint with the Air Force about them trying to kill me. They'd never admit to it anyway, and frankly I didn't want to remind them of my existence. Besides, their beef was with the Missile Defense Agency now.

Fowler had vanished. Either that or he was in the New Mexico ASPCA. CCN reported that the dog that ran out from under the balloon on TV was captured shortly thereafter and sent to the dog pound.

Of course, different dogs can look alike, can't they? Needless to say, everybody at the Alien Days festival figured out it was a balloon, though I didn't doubt there would be some skeptics in any event.

All that business about Fowler being a werewolf, about the dog in the half-track not being Wilco...I couldn't accept it and therefore just didn't. I have a certain understanding of how the world works, and I rank the power of coincidence and happenstance way over the numinous realm. I stood at the mound that morning staring at a flying saucer, certain of what I was seeing, and yet I couldn't have been more wrong. It was just a newfangled balloon.

I remember when a pal and I used to frequent a saloon where the bartender could make a cigarette go through a quarter. We'd each watch one of the bartender's hands to make sure he didn't substitute a quarter with a hole in it. And yet, each and every time the bartender did switch quarters, somehow.

Vargas was back in Vargo with Wilco and Amber and all the streusel you could shake a stick at. Everything was put to bed as far as I was concerned.

Almost. I sat there in the corner of the family gala wondering:

How did Fowler become so obsessed with his father's legacy as to start a killing spree?

An old leather document folder landed on the table in front of me, the kind that folds in thirds. The cowhide was dry and cracked.

"It's all in there, Garth," Gabby said, sitting down next to me.

I glanced at the cracked leather trifold, then back at her.

"What you wouldn't tell me at the Pickle Barrel?"

She nodded. "It was your father's dying wish not to tell you, not to perpetuate this legacy. How could I break that promise?"

"So why now?"

"Because you already know most of it, and the danger has passed."

I picked up the folder, undid the buckle, and looked inside. It was dated 1948 and began "My Son." I flipped ahead, spotting words like "vuka" and "evil" and "Tupelca." It was signed in a great flourish, "Julius Fowler Carson."

"Fowler?"

"Yes, J. C. Fowler was your uncle, from Julius's second marriage. 'J.C.' stands for Julius Carson, of course. His mother changed her last name to Fowler, your grandfather's middle name, to keep all this from catching up with them and avoid any connection to the madman who had been her husband. Your uncle J. C. Fowler was married briefly but the woman abandoned him with Nicholas, your cousin. Stuart and I raised him as your brother. All this that just happened, with the vuka and the Tupelca, was your grandfather's obsession. What you have there is the letter he addressed to his son Stuart, your father, asking him to kill you and the five other grandsons at the time of the next white gecko."

"Kill me? His grandson?" I tried to scan the letter quickly to get to that part but the light was bad and the handwriting worse.

"He wanted the Tupelca to go home to their planet, and wanted one of his sons to fulfill the prophecy at the next coming of the white geckos."

"Kit Carson put a hit on me, through my father?" I just stared at her.

"Your grandfather passionately believed that whole vuka and Tupelca story. It came to him in a dream on the mound in New Mexico—he felt he'd been charged with finding the next *El Viajero*, the one to collect the vuka and return home. And he left one of these documents for each of his sons. Well, you can imagine... Stuart cut all ties with his family and wanted nothing more to do with them. And wanted it kept that way."

"But not Fowler. He decided to become *El Viajero*. So if he thinks he has the other four vuka, won't he still come for me?"

She closed her eyes and shook her head. "The time of the white gecko preceding the summer solstice has passed. Fowler would have to wait another hundred years. If he's still alive."

"And..." I hesitated, then looked up from the tablecloth into her eyes. "What about my vuka?"

She smiled and patted my hand. "Did it bother you when you didn't know you had it?"

I considered answering that but changed subjects. "Does Nicholas know?" I tilted my head at the tri-fold.

"Not all of it. I'll tell him before I fly out tomorrow. I didn't want this to overshadow the hand-fasting."

"What's going on here? Why are you sitting in the dark?" A little girl with dark eyes and dark bangs stood before us. Mel's precocious daughter, Dottie.

I held out my fist and bumped hers.

"Mai Tai!" we said in unison. That was how Nicholas greeted her, and by association Dottie had started doing the same with me.

Gabby leaned toward her. "We were just talking, mother to son."

"But Garth is too old to have a mom!" Dottie protested. "Gabby, you must be his grandmom."

Judy the bartender approached, her long yellow French braid swaying. "As bridesmaid, part of my duties are to keep the party going. Garth, it's your turn to dance with the bride. By order of the groom."

I stood, the ancient leather folder in my hand.

"So what am I supposed to do with this, Gabby?"

"Do you want it?"

The trifold's crumbling leather felt like the rancorous, toxic handshake of a mummy, his curse palpable and fairly tingling in my grasp.

"No." I dropped it on the table. "I want to dance with the bride."

Melanie met me halfway across the dance floor.

She was sparkling white and beautiful in the way only brides can be. She had her wedding gown held up in both hands and I could see by the bare feet poking out from under it that she'd kicked off her shoes.

"Sure this is a good idea? I'm liable to step on your toes."

Mel just smiled and put herself in my hands. I gave her a lively spin while flashbulbs popped, and the heady scent of summer trees and greenery filled me.

"Garv!" Otto grabbed my arm and yanked me away from the bride. "To come!"

I heard someone hitting a glass with silverware, and Angie was suddenly on my other arm.

"Nicholas wants to make a presentation," she said, and I detected a bit of an impish twinkle to her eye.

The crowd parted as we approached a table next to the bar where Nicholas was standing. A cardboard box was at his feet, and Dottie stood next to it, fidgeting excitedly.

Nicholas raised a glass, and those assembled who weren't holding me in place (or was I holding them up?) raised their glasses.

"To my brother, Garth, my best man today and every day, and to my growing family…"

Maybe it was the scotch he'd been drinking, but for once he looked sincere. Mel trotted up next to him, kneeling down to the box.

"…a family which is about to get just a little bigger."

I saw Melanie take something nondescript from the box and put it in her daughter's arms.

Dottie enveloped it, being careful not to let it go, and approached me.

I knelt down, and Dottie opened her arms.

The sight of it gave me a start—I thought it was a puppet or something, and I have mixed feelings about puppets. My reaction prompted Dottie to squeal:

"It's a puppy!"

"Awww..." Angie sighed, beginning to emotionally liquefy at my side.

"Eetz very much lookink...Nice doggie, eh?" Otto began to sing:

"What is price this doggie from shop window? (arf! arf!)"

As I gazed down at the squirming ball of black and white fuzz in her arms, with its button eyes, pink tongue, and round belly, I was taken with the fullness of the moment, of being presented with something newly alive, innocent, and full of potential. This animal had no past, only a future.

"Such doggie it is swims with tail."

The night was filled with warmth, with laughter. The twinkling lights seemed like stars of promise, of all the good stuff there is in life. Family, friends, love. And a drunk little Russian barking like a Pekinese.

"What is price this doggie from shop window? (arf! arf!)"

Like my father, I wanted no part in a haunted past of spirits and death—look what that did to my grandfather and uncle. And to those three idiots in the

Pixie dry-cleaning van. I knew then that there was no vuka in me, that such hokum was the only thing that had ever possessed me. That and a fear of my own past.

"*Tell to me shopkeeper—is dog on sale?*"

I never did read that stupid document.

And the wedding was the last time I saw Gabby.

About the Author

Brian M. Wiprud is a New York City author and outdoor writer for fly-fishing magazines. He won the 2002 Lefty Award for Most Humorous Crime Novel, was a 2003 Barry Award Nominee for Best Paperback Original, had a 2004 Independent Mystery Booksellers Association bestseller and a 2005 *Seattle Times* bestseller. Information on his tours and appearances can be found at his website www.wiprud.com.